ANARCHISTA

Volume Two of *The Continental Divide*

Alanson Rand

Acknowledgments

Special thanks to Joey Clark, Debbie Witt, and Cathy Rathbun for pointing out when I was making no sense.

Copyright 2016, 2021 Alanson Rand
Cover art and design copyright 2016 Timothy Stead
Editor: Timothy Stead

ISBN (print edition): 978-1-946843-03-6

Also by Alanson Rand:

KEY FIGURES IN THE REVOLUTION OF 2043

Victoria Lang MD, a former director of Chalys Pharmaceuticals
Ada Lang, her daughter
Mae Esteban, MD, Surgeon General of the United States

Krista Warner, author of *The Rake*
Arista Molle, a television journalist
Jackson Falling Knife Ripley, a former stained-glass artist
Elise Ripley, his wife

Lt. Commander Tala Ripley, Strategic Warfare Officer, USS *Patrick Henry*

William Gibbon, President of the United States
Gabriel Cheyn, Vice President of the United States
Marcus Grimes, Gabriel Cheyn's Chief of Staff
Noah Hayborn, Speaker of the House

National Security Forces
Bob Downs, Watcher
Raphael Vinola, Deputy Watcher
Philip Cochon, Day Chief – Intelligence
Ari Stein, Night Chief – Intelligence
Hideki Buta, Day Chief – Acquisition
Ryan Beckmann, Night Chief – Acquisition
Sara Hogue, Day Chief – Tactical Operations
Tom Riddick, Night Chief – Tactical Operations
Peter Mochyn, Day Chief – Cybermeasures
Anton Kopelli – Audio specialist contracted by the NSF
Milosz Mihalic – Assistant to Kopelli

FROM THE FRYING PAN

Day 32
Saturday morning, September 19, 2043
Brasser's Low-Tel Motel, Thornacre, Ohio

Krista tried to roll out of bed, but her skull felt like her brain had been removed overnight, and the hole pumped to capacity with liquid pain. She let her head drop back to the pillow, but then her bladder started to throb.

As she stumbled to the bathroom, she stubbed her toe on a bottle, and memories of the previous night's bacchanal returned. "So this is what a bloody hangover feels like," she whispered. "Like I've been licking a feckin hamster all night."

With her eyes closed and hands in front of her, she found the shower and turned it on. Every drop of water pummeled her tender skull, and the showerhead thundered like Niagara Falls, but she soldiered through the torment and cleaned the bits she could reach without bending over. After drying off, her fingers traced a rough line of stitches behind her leg, and she recalled some weird surgery the night before.

Light streamed through the open curtains, and with her eyes still closed, she groped for the rod. The curtains closed with a swish, and she opened her eyes to the darkened room. She swept her clothes up and sank onto the side of the bed, and she'd just finished putting her socks on when she realized something was missing.

"Ada?" she called out in a husky whisper. She cleared her throat and tried again louder, but the room felt empty. The bedside clock said 11:43 AM, though, so she was probably out getting breakfast. Her stomach rumbled at the prospect of a meal, but she had no desire to eat.

To find food, or Ada, she'd have to leave the room, so she searched for her shoes. Her foot found them near the bed, but as she reached for them, she lost her balance and tumbled off the bed, planting her face into the grungy carpet. Grunting and swearing, she sat up and slid on the sneakers. However, her fingers felt as nimble as overstuffed sausages, so she gave up trying to tie the laces and sat glaring at the room's door. Outside it were Ada, food, and her car, and she'd have to get up and go out eventually, but the light leaking around the edges of the door was so bright that she decided to sit in the darkness for a while longer, perhaps until sunset.

Her chest suddenly felt hollow. She reached for the cigarettes on the night table, but they slid off and thudded on the carpet. When she found her lighter and managed to get her numbed fingers to flick it, the flame flared like a handheld sun and roared like a wildfire. She crossed her legs and cupped her chin in her hand, and just as she started to feel relief from the pounding headache, the door opened wide. Light and noise streamed through it, along with Ada.

"Morning, sunshine!" she called out, and Krista hissed and cringed. Ada dropped a paper bag on the desk and flung the curtains open. "Why are these closed? It's like a cave in here!"

"Be quiet, wouldja?" Krista whispered. "And why would you be so damn chipper?"

"I slept like a rock. I always do after a spiritual lituation." She reached into the bag. "Hey, I got something for you."

"Earplugs?"

Ada placed a cardboard crown on Krista's head. "I name you Queen of the Rebels! Ta-da!"

Krista winced. "Take it off. It hurts."

"Well, somebody got stung by a grumblebee this morning!" Ada switched on a desk lamp and shined it in Krista's face. "Wow, you look like crap."

Krista glared at her through bloodshot eyes. "Die."

"Now that was rude!"

"*Please* die. Would that be better?"

"You're just hungover. After you've binged four or five times, your liver will harden off, and you won't feel it so bad. But it'll suck for the next two hours." She rummaged inside the bag and pulled out a paper cup. "Here, I bought you some coffee."

Krista's eyes brightened a little. "Coffee good. Coffee heal. Coffee magic." She grabbed the cup, took a sip, and gagged. "Coffee bad! Where'd you get this pisswater?"

Ada pulled a cup of orange juice from the bag, sat in a chair, and propped her feet up on the bed. "Out on the highway. The restaurant across the street was closed, so I walked around and found a fast-food place. The dining room was closed, but the drive-through lane was open. They just had drinks left. No food."

"That's what happened in Washington – as soon as the virus appeared, the food disappeared. Everyone's hoarding the stuff."

"We need food, or this little road trip's over, Krista."

"I know. Maybe we can hit some stores along the way and do a little of our own hoarding." She took a long draft from her cup. "This coffee might suck, but at least it's got caffeine. My headache's going away."

"No need to thank me."

"Thank you. And thank you for stitching me up last night. I saw your sewing in the mirror, and it looks like a surgeon did it. A really wasted surgeon, but still, it's holding me together."

Ada beamed. "That's the first time I ever sutured a wound."

Krista winced and drained her cup. "And thanks for not telling me that before." She climbed to her feet and braced herself against the desk. "I need a little more time before I can drive. My headache just came back."

"You'll need another two hours at the most. Hangovers don't last long. Look, while we're waiting, would you do me a favor?" Krista grumbled something unintelligible, and Ada drew a deep breath. "Would you authorize me on your tablet? I'd like to surf around and see if I can find out what happened to my mom." She looked into the cup and spoke in a quieter voice. "I'm also worried that I'll find out, but I have to do it or I'll go crazy."

"Well now, I'd bet she's okay. From what you told me last night, it's the Federals that should be worried. But if you want to surf, I'll set you up on my tablet. Only surfing, though. Don't fool around with my files, all right?"

FEW CARS WERE DRIVING ON THEIR SIDE OF THE ROAD, but the traffic heading east was heavy. "I'm glad we're not going in that direction," Ada said.

"Maybe they're all going fishing or something." Krista adjusted her sunglasses, which helped cut down the glare, but the reflections from passing cars still felt like lasers boring into her eyes. "So I'm guessing you didn't find out anything about your mom this morning?"

"No, nothing. Not even on *Midnight Sun*. The newsfeeds are saying everything's bright and shiny, like there's no virus or anything." Ada lit a cigarette and looked through her window. "I read your posts, though. I can see why you were so angry back in Oxford. That pharmacist was a real douchebag."

"That feckin wankstain skeloon. If he was on fire, I'd break out the marshmallows. I see that douche in a Sacramento crosswalk, I'll be steppin on the gas, that I will."

Ada laughed. "Speaking of running folks over, we oughta stop and wash that guy out of your grille."

"Don't be gross."

"Still, he's gonna stink soon, and I don't want to smell him all the way to California."

"All right, we'll stop at the first carwash we see. Keep an eye open for one."

They rode in silence for a few more minutes hoping to find a restaurant or a food store. Only a few buildings dotted the road, though, and most sold farm supplies.

"This is boring. Can I play some music?" Ada asked.

"I'd like a little quiet. I just got rid of that damn headache."

"Okay. I was looking through your music library, and I'm aching to listen to it. It's been two weeks since I heard any tunes except hundred-year-old crooners singing about glow worms or something."

"Hmm. You like my collection, eh?"

"Yeah. Too much Keriana, though." Ada shook her head. "I can't stand that stuff."

"She's my favorite artist!"

"Well, I guessed that. You have everything she ever recorded."

"As I said, she's my favorite." Krista shifted in her seat and tapped her fingers against the steering wheel.

"She sings like a ghost in heat. It's terrible stuff. The only good thing is that you can dance to it."

"That's because Keriana's music was derived from reggae. She loved the rhythms, and she wove them into Celtic folk themes. It was a fantastic fusion. She loved reggae ever since she was a young girl in Dublin and became better than some of the reggae artists."

"Whatever. Her stuff is still boring." Ada flicked her cigarette onto the road. "She was good for personal drama, though. What a messed-up life! Her kid gets snuffed right after the funeral…"

"That wasn't –"

"…and they never found the body. I'll bet she got chopped up into little pieces and buried in a dozen dumpsters by that serial killer who was offing kids back then…"

"Listen –"

"…and how come the Federals didn't catch the bastard? I mean, they even know what cereal I ate for breakfast. I look at somebody funny, and a Man in Black is standing on my doorstep an hour later asking why. How come they couldn't catch some skeevistic stupervo with a little-girl jones?"

"Because –"

"But that was back in '27. The only people who could get a stiffie back then were the outlaws, what with the Arkies running everything. Only good thing to come out of the freakin Twenties was *The Blac Album.*"

Krista glanced sideways to see if Ada would interrupt her again, but she was looking through the window. "So I'm guessing you're a Blac Sacrament fan?" she asked.

Ada broke out her air guitar and bopped in her seat, singing the bass line to their most famous hit, *Iron Pickle.* When she reached the bass solo in the bridge, she tossed her hair from side to side in a perfect imitation of Blind Billy.

"All right, you're a fangirl. Got it. Stop it before you hurt yourself, wouldja?"

She sat back in her seat and sighed. "Gotta get my Blac Sac fix, Krista. I'm getting withdrawal symptoms." She twitched a few times theatrically. "The Pus Puppets or Massiker will do in a pinch, or even the Algorithmics or Smegawatt if I'm ripped, but Blac Sac is a *need.* I go more than four hours without it, my blood pressure drops and my bones get brittle. I need to reanimate myself by tunneling into that deathmetal goldmine you have on your tablet. You even have recordings of their rehearsals and all their session cuts!"

"Anything Blac Sac did in front of a microphone, I've got it. It's all in the car audio system too. You can play it later on if you want to hear it."

"I *have* to hear it." Ada sighed and sat back in her seat. "Blind Billy. The day he died was the worst day of my life."

"He died nineteen years ago. You're fifteen."

"That's why I cried when I was born. I was holding it in for so long."

"I cried too," Krista said, looking through the windshield. "But that's history. Listen, I told you not to poke around in my files, and you still did. The fate of the nation could change because of them. This is serious, Ada."

"I know, but it was only the music files. Do you have Gabriel Cheyn singing a confession to the tune of *The Star-Spangled Banner?* I don't think so."

"Still, you're not using my tablet again."

"What? You can't be serious! I was just looking around!"

Krista shook her head, and Ada collapsed into the seat and crossed her arms. "I don't believe you. I save your life, and this is how you thank me?"

Krista ran her fingers through her hair and sighed. "Okay, if we find a Mal-Mart, I'll buy you a tablet. You can download my music and listen to whatever you want."

"Hellah!" Ada took her hand. "Thanks. I really am going through withdrawal. I keep hearing those crooner songs in my head and they won't go away and it's driving me totally freakin nuts. If I hear that pizza pie song again, I'll explode. You know the one? 'When the moon hits your eye' –"

"Stop it! I don't need any more earworms."

"Fine. I'm gonna blast that sucker out of my head with some slayin Blac Sac. I'm gonna vaporize it."

"Then keep a lookout for a Mal-Mart," Krista said. "Food first, though."

"Food, carwash, Mal-Mart. I'm on it." Ada looked out at the passing buildings. "Nothing yet. Drive a little faster."

"Chill, wouldja?"

They drove for another hour, and more roadside civilization appeared as they neared Columbus. After driving around a curve, Ada spotted a sign on the right. "There's a Vittler's Green! That's an organic food store! There's one by my house. My mom shops there all the time."

Krista pulled into the parking lot and stopped before a trendy stone-and-timber entrance. A hand-printed banner hanging on the wall said PREMIUM PRICING IN AFFECT. She reached into her pocket, pulled out a handful of bills, and handed them to Ada. "I'd better stay here. Get as much as you can. Anything edible will do, but get something with protein. Some water too."

Ada walked into the store while Krista parked beside a row of bushes at the edge of the lot. Almost a half hour later, Ada returned carrying a single plastic bag. "That was hard. There's not much food left, and what they had was expensive."

"Whatcha got?"

Ada reached into the bag. "Some protein bars, about a dozen bottles of protein drink, six bottles of water, and this hunormous bag of trail mix. That's all I could get for sixty bucks."

"Crap. That'll last us a day or two at the most." She grabbed a bottle of the protein drink and downed it in one gulp. "I was thinking we should head south instead of west. The virus hasn't hit the South as bad yet, so maybe they still have food. Once we get into an area where there's something to eat, we can turn west and go to California."

Ada pulled the atlas from a door pocket. "You said to stay off the interstates, so…it looks like we have to make a left in about ten miles at a place called Black Lick. There's a road there that goes south-ish. We can take back roads all the way to Kentucky, Tennessee, and even into Alabama if we need to."

"That's what we'll do. It'll take longer, but at least we can eat." She slipped the car into gear and pulled out of the space. "Let me know where to turn."

They pulled back onto the highway, and Ada saw a sign for a carwash a few minutes later. Krista pulled off the road and up to a building with three long bays, drove into the middle one, and climbed out.

Ada cupped her hands around her mouth. "Echo-o-o!" she yelled, and Krista covered her ears.

"Cut that out and show me how this thing works," Krista asked, looking at the gun-shaped nozzle in her hand.

"Just pull the trigger, dummy." A jet of water spurted from the nozzle and soaked her. "Hey! Aim it at the car!"

"Your hoodie's filthy anyway. Stop whining."

Ada stomped outside the bay, leaned against the outside wall, and wiped off her soaked blouse. She unscrewed the cap from a water bottle and saw the peaked roofs of houses over a tall wooden fence. However, she heard no slamming doors, voices, or music over there, only a deep and sorrowful sound as if a chorus of *basso profundos* was singing with an orchestra of didgeridoos. It was coming from the north and getting louder, and she looked up to find the source.

SPOT FLICKED AN AILERON and made a small course correction. In 11.2317 miles, it was scheduled to make a hard 93-degree bank to the west, travel 2.1243 miles, and then bank again and head north.

Spot's instruments scanned objects in a narrow band two hundred feet high but more than ten thousand feet wide. A clear dome hung from the fuselage in front of its long wings, from which eight anisotropic electro-optical arrays surveyed the world. Although the fug density was light today, the arrays were having difficulty acquiring objects on the ground. Spot had abandoned visible-spectrum acquisition, relying entirely on the infrared receivers in the dome and the low-power scanning radar in the nose to acquire objects. When it found one, it activated its wing-mounted imaging radars and built a detailed three-dimensional model in under a tenth of a second.

Spot's task was to locate two specific targets: an automotive object and a human object. Even though it had been scanning for three hours, it had found only seventeen human objects per minute aloft as opposed to the ninety-four its programming expected.

The infrared receivers indicated a heat source 473 feet ahead, and the scanning radar confirmed it as a human object. Spot painted it with a pulse from its wing radars.

THE DIDGERIDOO SOUND GREW into a loud thrumming, and Ada heard echoes from the buildings along the road. It was in front of her and to the left, and she squinted in that direction but couldn't see anything. Suddenly, her stomach twisted and her scalp tingled as if she were bathing in static electricity.

THE IMAGE BUILT IN .08 SECONDS: The human object was 60.875 inches high with a mass of 106 pounds. The hair color was undetermined, but that was irrelevant; this wasn't the target Spot was tasked to find.

THE THING FLEW DIRECTLY OVER ADA, and she saw a small gray airplane with long wings and a bump under it like the Blackwing drone pictures she'd seen on the SatNet. "Oh, hell!" she said, and she ran into the carwash.

"What was that infernal noise?" Krista yelled over the whoosh of the sprayer.

"It was a drone! A surveillance drone!"

She turned off the sprayer. "Oh, crap. Okay, this'll have to do. We've got to get moving. Come on."

Ada jumped into her seat. "They're really looking hard for you if they put drones up." She buckled her seatbelt and looked through the rear window. "It passed over and went on, so you're clear. But we need to hide. We oughta hole up today and travel at night from now on."

Krista nodded. "They have spy blimps that can count your feckin freckles, so traveling at night is better. Let's find a place to crash after we turn at Black Lip."

"Black Lick."

Krista turned and backed out of the bay. "Whatever." She pulled onto the highway and drove west toward Columbus. After a few minutes, the road descended into a valley and the fug thickened; visibility dropped to thirty or forty feet, and she slowed down. The traffic coming from the city was bumper-to-bumper, and it was aggressive – drivers honked their horns and tried to drive on the shoulders to get ahead.

"Where do I turn?" Krista asked. "Shouldn't it be soon?"

Ada had stuck her nose in the atlas, trying to read the small map. "I don't know exactly where we are. You have the only car on the planet without a satnav system, which would come in handy now."

"Give me directions, not commentary. Where's the turn?"

"Get in the left lane. It should be a mile or two ahead." Ada peered through the window and tried to find a landmark. "I think." A minute later, she spotted a road sign and looked back at the atlas. "Yeah, this is your turn coming up. Make a left at the light."

Krista flicked her turn signal and drifted left until the shape of a large vehicle appeared in the fug ahead. The light at the intersection had turned red, and she coasted to a stop behind a gray truck.

Ada ran her finger across the atlas and tried to find a place to pull over and hide. "We'll go south and get out of the city. There's a big ole town called Lancaster that way, and we can find someplace to hole up there. What do you think?" She ran her finger along a road on the map. "I said, what do you –" She looked at Krista, who was sitting motionless and staring wide-eyed at the car ahead of them.

"What is it?" asked Ada. Krista nodded at something beyond the windshield, and she peered over the top of the atlas to see. A gray Silverback idled in front of them, with white license plates that said U.S. GOVERNMENT VEHICLE – NATIONAL SECURITY FORCES. Several young men sat in it, all looking forward. She ducked behind the atlas and whispered, "Oh shit, oh shit, oh shit..."

"What do we do?" Krista whispered, barely moving her mouth.

Still holding the atlas as a shield, Ada turned and looked through the rear window. "There's a car behind you, so you can't back up. All you can do is serene your scene and hope they don't see you. Put your visor down so they can't see your face."

"Gimme that atlas. They're not looking for you."

"Hell, no! Get your own. Just put the visor down and pretend you're invisible."

Krista lowered it and squeezed the steering wheel with both hands until her fingers were white. "Ada, give it to me now or I'll –"

"He's looking at you! Don't look through the window!"

"What? Who?"

"One of them turned around to look in the trunk and he saw you and now he's real interested in you. He's looking you over like you're familiar...I think he figured out who you are, oh Christ, we're dead meat now...oh, wait. Wait a second, now he looks like someone just shoved a cattle prod up his ass...his mouth is hanging down, like all the way to the floor! What's up with this guy?" She glimpsed movement out of the corner of her eye and saw Krista slowly scratching an imaginary itch on her breast. "What are you doing?"

"He's not looking at my face now, is he?" Krista asked. She wiped a phantom dust mote off her hoodie, and the Silverback bounced on its springs.

"No, now *all* of them are looking at your boobs. Did you think this through?"

A whimper escaped Krista's lips, and she rubbed harder, making the Silverback bounce more. Ada giggled. "The third guy just elbowed the first one in the face and now they're pounding on each other in the backseat. One of the guys from the front came back and he's trying to break up the fight, but he keeps looking at your boob too."

"I don't want a feckin audience," Krista said in a strained voice. "I want this feckin light to change."

"Yeah, but you have to keep that up." Ada winced. "Ouch! I'll bet that hurt! Right in the eye! An uppercut! And he comes back with an elbow to the nose...I'll bet that schnoz is broken...oooh! Right in the gooch! That even hurt *my* balls!"

Krista parted her lips and blew a soft stream of air over her breast as her finger traced a circle around her nipple. The Silverback rocked even more.

"They're hitting each other with nightsticks now. There's blood splatters on the back window. Can you believe this?" Ada sounded dumbstruck. "What a bunch of buffoons! Holy shit...I think that's a...yeah, the guy in the front just drew his pistol!"

"Change, dammit, change..." Krista implored, and in answer to her prayer, the Silverback rolled forward and turned left toward Black Lick. The driver behind Krista honked his horn, and she punched the gas and screeched straight across the intersection.

"We need to go left," Ada said.

"That's the last place I'll go right now. I'm getting far away from those clowns."

"Yeah, okay. Wow, was that ever scary! Hey, were you faking that?"

Krista glared at her. "Of course! Christ on a crutch, do you think I'm such a common slut that I got myself wet at a stoplight?" She drove on for a few minutes. Her hands were shaking too much to steer, though, and she pulled into the parking lot of a deserted church.

She pulled the parking brake, and Ada sat back in her seat and propped her feet on the dashboard. "Good. I need a break. My heart's still pounding from that," she said. "But that was thrillin! I'm blown away, I mean, it's like you hypnotized them or something!"

Krista rubbed the back of her neck. "Well, all the guys say I've got splendid boobs. I don't get why. I'm just a C-cup." She laid her head back against the headrest. "Guys."

"Yeah, guys. What can you say?" Ada picked up the atlas and opened it. "I better get implants, then. It could save my life someday. Okay, if we're not going down to Lancaster, what do we do now?"

"After I have my nervous breakdown, you mean?"

"Yeah, sure, after that," Ada said.

"We turn south the next chance we get, I suppose. When's our next turn?"

Ada squinted at her map and ran her finger across it. "It looks it's another ten miles till the next turn. It's in the center of Columbus."

DISPATCHES

Midnight Sun
News Post of September 19, 2043

CENTRAL OHIO IN GRIP OF NEOVIRUS

Our single remaining Witness in Columbus reports that conditions there have degenerated into chaos and open warfare, and he warns everyone to avoid the city:

"The good news is I didn't get the virus, and I didn't have to blow my brains out. The bad news is that someone else might blow them out for me.

"The virus is rockin this place hard. Practically everyone who gets it dies. I know people who were fine at sunrise and dead at sundown. And everyone who survived just turned into animals. It's like the evolution clock is runnin backwards now, I swear. In only four days, the city practically disintegrated – rioters in the streets, looting, stiffers in the gutters, and nobody picking them up. Gunfire and bombs, I mean, people are settin off fuckin bombs in the city! And we got no cops, no firemen, no doctors. In four days, we been blown back to the Stone Age.

"There's virus victims just walkin down the street, bleedin out all over the sidewalk, walkin till they die cuz no one will help 'em. God, it breaks my heart to see this. It's like none of us are human anymore.

"Four days ago, this was a nice city. Now it's a hellhole filled with the dead and the demons, and I hope I can get out alive. I'll shoot my way out if I have to.

"Stay away from Columbus, whatever you do. Don't try to come in and help cuz this city is dyin and nobody can stop it. You'll die if you try, understand me? Nobody can survive this."

INTO THE FIRE

Day 32
Saturday afternoon, September 19, 2043
Ten miles east of Columbus, Ohio

Krista and Ada strolled around the empty church parking lot before making the trip into Columbus. The air smelled damp and smoky, as if a hickory fire had roared and then been doused.

"You've got to navigate us through Columbus," Krista said. "Just make sure we don't get lost, wouldja? I want to get through quick. There are cameras everywhere in cities, and the longer we're there, the greater the chances of being seen."

"Don't worry. I'm a good navigator and you're a good driver. We make a good team."

"That we do. How could we do this without each other? I'd be lost by now if you weren't here." Krista wrapped her arm around her.

Ada smiled back. "Isn't it weird?" She stopped suddenly and pointed to a small car parked in the fug ahead. "You know what we oughta do? Let's jack that car and leave yours here. Then it wouldn't matter how many cameras they had."

"We'd be stealing." Ada cast her a scornful glance, and Krista looked away. "Okay, that was a stupid thing to say. We've got to do it, but I don't know how to steal a car."

"I do. Do you have any tools in your trunk?"

"You know how to steal a car?"

Ada nodded. "Don't ask. Do you have any tools?"

"Of course. Want me to get them?"

Ada nodded and walked to the driver's side door, which she could open easily with her lock-pick pins. The ignition was keyed too, so she could boost the thing with a pair of pliers and a little time. She'd finished sizing up the job when Krista returned holding a pink-handled screwdriver. "That's it?"

Krista shrugged.

"That's a tool. That's not *tools*. How do you expect me to boost a car with a screwdriver?"

"That's all I've got. I wouldn't know what to do with tools, I mean, that's what mechanics are for."

"Fine, fine." Ada paced and looked at the ground for a moment. "All right, we can steal the license plates, at least. That might help a little." She snatched the screwdriver from Krista's hand and stalked to the rear of the car.

WEARING THE STOLEN PLATES, they drove into Columbus. As they neared the city center, the outbound traffic disappeared. They noticed traffic cameras at the intersections, and even though they were useless to the Federals in dense fog, they decided to take side roads until they needed to turn south. They found a street without cameras that paralleled the main road, but visibility was so poor that they could barely see the small houses beyond the sidewalks.

"We must be driving into a contaminated area. I'm sweltering." Ada turned the temperature control down and wiped a thin sheen of perspiration from her forehead.

Krista grabbed a tissue and dabbed her face too. "I hate driving in this soup. You never have time to react to what's on the road." She leaned forward and viewed the road ahead. "This place is creepy, like a ghost town or empty stage set. Or like one of those fake towns the Air Force built to hide their missiles."

"No cars on the road, no people on the streets." Ada looked through the side window. "The place looks abandoned –" The fog to the west blossomed in orange light, and the ground shook and rattled the car a second later.

"What the hell was that? It sounded like an explosion."

"That was definitely an explosion, but it was north of where we're going."

"I hope nobody was hurt. I wonder what blew up."

"That was just plastic explosive." Ada peered at the atlas again. "Stop at this next intersection. I need to see what cross street we're at."

"How can you say that?"

"Because you don't have a satnav system. I have to find where we are the hard way."

"I mean, how can you say that was plastic explosive? How do you know?"

"Oh. The shock wave hit us in under a second, so it was a high-expansion RDX-variant nitroamine, probably C-4, you can get that anywhere." She squinted at a road sign. "McKinley. Okay, I know where we are now. We can go."

Krista shook her head and pulled back onto the road as Ada checked out the neighborhood. "There's actually a few people around. I can see them wandering around in the fug over there. They're tanked, though. Stumbling all over the place and stuff."

"Must be a real party town." Krista put her hand to her head. "Believe me, I feel their pain."

"There's another one up ahead. Totally sloshed." They drove by slowly, and Ada squinted through the side window. "This definitely has a zombieflick atmo. It's like shufflers stalking us in the fog and all that, just like the opening scene of *We Are the Menu*. I love it!"

Krista grinned. "So I'm guessing you're a zombie fan?"

Ada held her arms out straight and moaned like the undead. "I have every zombie movie ever made on my tablet. At least I did." She looked through the window again. "Y'know, I almost turned a cat into a zombie once."

"You did not."

"I said almost. The potion just made him stupid. He'd stand on the lawn and stare at the house for hours. Mom ran over him a few months later, and the fool didn't even try to get out of the way. But the end was quick. Mom really zooms up our driveway."

"She squashed him?"

Ada looked down at her lap. "He experienced a terminal loss of dimension."

"That means she squashed him!" Krista sniffed and reached for a tissue. "That's so sad. That poor cat."

"She didn't do it on purpose."

"Still…" Krista wiped tears from her cheek.

Ada turned and pointed out Krista's window. "Look! Another one!"

"Another what?"

"Another shuffler coming from your side." Her eyes grew wide. "Oh, shit."

A young man stumbled toward them wearing a shirt covered in bloody chunks. He peered into the car and then banged his hand against Krista's window, mouthing words she couldn't hear. She shrieked and tried to climb onto Ada's lap as the man retched a thick stream of red and yellow vomit down her window, and Ada punched the door lock button a dozen times and pushed her back.

He doubled over to the ground, and then he grabbed the window frame and pulled himself up. He pulled the door handle, but the jammed door refused to budge, and he pounded the glass with his fist. The car shuddered with each blow, and he struck it even harder while yelling at Krista and spitting droplets of blood on the window. She shook her head, and he stumbled to the rear door and pulled up the handle.

The door unlatched and swung open, and the sour reek of human waste and vomit swarmed into the car. Krista stomped the accelerator pedal, and the car jerked forward with a screech; the man pirouetted like a drunken ballerina and tried to regain his balance, but then he slumped to the pavement and lay unmoving.

The car roared into the fug, and both women panted and searched the road for more of the unwanted. After a few moments, Krista pulled over to the curb. "Jaysus, Mary, and all the saints," she muttered, holding a hand over her thudding heart.

Ada chewed on a strand of hair. "I won't be able to crap for a year."

"I'll be having a coronary any second."

"Don't. I can't drive."

"I should've told you the door locks don't work," Krista said in a quavering voice.

Ada shook her head and muttered a soft curse. "That's it for zombies. I am *so* done with them. They're yesterday's diapers."

"The love is gone, huh?"

"Zombies. They're dead to me." They snorted, but then the laughter died and the jitters returned.

"I can't handle this," Krista said as she rubbed her face. "I just can't. This is a nightmare."

"We have to keep moving, though," Ada said, and Krista nodded and rolled the car back onto the road. She reached for her pack with a trembling hand and opened it, and the cigarettes shook out over the floor and the seat. Ada bent forward and picked them up. "Are you sure you can drive like this?"

"I don't have a choice."

"No, I guess not." Ada sniffed the air. "Hey, do you smell pee?"

"I don't."

"Well, I do."

"Shut up, wouldja? You're giving me a headache."

The suburb of small houses gave way to city townhouses as they moved closer to the city center, but although the place should have been teeming with people, not a soul was in sight. Cars sat on lawns or across sidewalks, and several were burned. Most of their windows were broken.

"This keeps getting worse," Ada said.

"Right. This is Black Dog country. The sooner we get out of here, the better. How long till we make our turn?"

Ada looked in the atlas. "Two miles."

THEY CREPT THROUGH THE NEIGHBORHOOD with Ada keeping a lookout. Just as Krista felt steady enough to reach for her pack again, the car rolled over a bump and something scraped the underside. She hit the brakes and peered at the floor of the car as if she could see through it. "What was that?" she asked.

"Uhh…a speed bump? I'm sure it was a speed bump."

"I don't think that was a speed bump," Krista said. "Open the door and look."

"Why do I have to look? It's your car. You look."

"My door is stuck. You look."

Ada crossed her arms. "Nuh-uh. No way."

"If you're so sure it's a speed bump, what are you afraid of?"

"It *is* a speed bump!"

"No, it isn't," Krista said. "That felt a little too soft."

"Well, then it's a speed bump now, isn't it?"

Krista nodded, swearing under her breath.

"We can't just sit here. Just go, would you? Be a grown-up," Ada said.

Krista keened softly and gritted her teeth as she pressed down gently on the accelerator. The tires crackled as if they were rolling over dry sticks, and then they passed over the thing. "Right. That was a speed bump," she said. "Definitely."

"No question about it. Nothing to worry about."

Krista fumbled with her cigarettes again and managed to get one lit. With Ada on the lookout again, they continued into the center of Columbus. The road widened, and they saw small, brick stores with their pull-down grilles laying in tangles on the sidewalks.

They stopped at an intersection so Ada could read the street sign. She rolled down her window to get a clearer view and heard a faraway tapping that sounded like children playing with firecrackers. She turned to Krista with a worried look. "Small-arms fire. Somebody's shooting ahead. Lots of them from the sound of it."

"Are we heading into it?"

"Maybe." Ada leaned out the window and listened for a minute. "I can't tell. The sound's echoing off these buildings, so it could be coming from anywhere ahead. We can't go there, Krista. We need to turn around."

Krista sat back in her seat. "I'm not going back through that horror. I couldn't handle that trip twice in one lifetime."

Ada opened the atlas and puckered her lips. "We can't go forward and we can't go back, so we have to go left or right. That explosion came from ahead on the right, and we should assume that's where the rest of the fireworks are. I vote for left."

Krista turned the wheel and pulled into a narrow side street. "Where do we go after this?"

"We go six blocks, make a right on Harper Avenue, and turn left on Route 33."

They saw even more broken buildings as they drove, and some were burning. Black smoke billowed into the fug, darkening the street even more; no firefighters fought the blazes, and no sirens sounded in the distance. "Ada dear, my bad feeling just got worse. We need to get the hell outta here. This is a war zone, like the Middle East or something. This isn't America."

"Right, we need to be somewhere else fast. Harper's the next turn, and then we're a quarter mile or so from Route 33. Do you want to turn around now? We're really close."

"Turn around? I want to climb into a hole and hide." She rubbed her temples and grumbled incomprehensible oaths, and then she slapped the steering wheel. "What the hell, let's go ahead. It can't get much worse than this."

They turned onto Harper Avenue, which was as wrecked as the others. They'd gone no more than a half block when an alley appeared on the right between two buildings, and Ada spotted figures moving in the mist. "I think we're coming up to more shufflers."

"If we keep moving, we'll be all right," Krista said, but then two men sprung onto the road ahead. One held up his hands palms out, signaling for Krista to stop – and the other pointed a pistol at the windshield.

Krista raised her hands, and after the man waved his weapon at Ada, she did too. Out of the corner of her mouth, Ada said, "Step on it and run them over, these aren't nice people, Krista, you've done it before so just one more time –"

Krista hissed back at her. "He'll shoot before I move an inch!"

The man with the pistol walked sideways around to the driver's door, keeping a bead on Krista while the other stayed in front. When he reached her door, he yanked the door handle, but the door was still stuck. He screamed and a vein pulsed in his forehead, and then he cocked the hammer and aimed the pistol at Krista's head.

His finger tightened on the trigger, and she wondered if she'd see the bullet coming – and then he jerked to the side as if he were the toy of a spastic puppeteer, collapsing to the ground out of her sight. The other man turned and began to run, but then he twitched and fell face-first to the pavement. A huge man wearing tan camouflage gear and a surgical mask ran from behind the car and shot the prone men in the head with a rifle.

Krista rammed the shifter into drive as he ran to the car. It had just begun rolling when he opened the rear door and jumped in. "Move!" he yelled. "Go, go, go!" She floored the accelerator, and the car bumped over a prone body and squealed down the street.

The rear window whined, and the man climbed out and sat on the doorsill. The rapid tapping of gunfire filled the car for a minute, and then he fell back into the seat and slammed a new magazine into the rifle. "Go faster, for chrissakes! There's gotta be a hundred of 'em out there!"

"What?" Krista pressed down on the gas and hunched over the wheel.

"Just fuckin move! We gotta get outta here 'fore they figure this out. Go straight and bear right on LaSalle."

Ada opened the atlas. "That's in four blocks."

"You're on his side now?" Krista asked.

"It's all right, Ginger, I'm a friendly. I just wanna get across the river and outta this fuckin snake pit. Been tryin to get past that gang all damn day." He lowered the right window and peered out. "Blondie, keep an eye peeled for hostiles."

Pieces of televisions and furniture were strewn at random, turning the road into an obstacle course. Krista steered the car and tried to pick up speed, but she kept hitting the junk.

"Turn's coming up," Ada said. Krista slewed the car to the right, and they'd just pulled onto the road when Ada called out, "Ahead on the right! Two more on the –" The car was shaken by three thunks, and the dashboard exploded into a cloud of plastic pieces. Ada swore and doubled over grunting, while in the backseat, the assault rifle chattered a long burst.

"Ada!" Krista screamed, reaching for her. The car swerved and hit something metallic with a crunch and a shower of sparks. She straightened the car out and turned to Ada, but she was still hunched over.

"Drive straight or we'll be dead, woman!" The tap-tapping of gunfire resumed and filled the car with acrid blue smoke.

"Shut the fuck up!" With one hand on the wheel, Krista gave her a shake. "Ada, please, say something, oh god, c'mon…"

"I'm hit," Ada said in a thin voice.

"Get us the hell outta here!" the man yelled.

"Shit, oh shit…" Krista pressed down hard on the accelerator, and the car jumped forward.

Piles of rubble flashed by, and Friendly fired at something in the fug. He climbed in from the window and looked at Ada. "She okay?"

Krista shook her head, still pushing the car at full speed.

"Not much we can do right now. All right, slow down a little. You should see a bridge-out sign in a few seconds…" An orange and white sign appeared in front of the car and then vanished underneath it with a thump. "That's it! Stop! Stop!" he yelled.

Krista stood on the brakes, and the car squealed to a halt inches from a narrow bridge. She turned to Ada. "Where are you hit? Are you okay? Can I do anything? Talk to me!"

Ada sat up with a groan. A large chunk of something bloody protruded from her left thigh above the knee, and she was spattered with blood from her waist to her ankles. "Pieces of the dashboard. All over my leg. Don't touch. It really hurts to touch." She winced and forced a smile. "I'll be okay. Just get me outta here."

Krista wrapped her arm around her shoulder. "I'll take care of you. I'll fix you right up."

He leaned into the front and saw Ada's leg. "Leg shrapnel wounds aren't bleeders, so she's not gonna black out or anything. It can wait till we're safe. Right now, we gotta get over this bridge."

"*This* bridge? Are you gone in the head, boyo? It's a bloody footbridge!"

"Yeah, but you're going on it anyway. No more than ten miles an hour." He looked through the rear window. "Go on now. We don't have much time before that gang catches up to us."

"You must be kidding. There's no way this car will fit on that!"

"It will. Go."

She lined up the car with the walkway and coasted slowly onto the concrete. Friendly was right: It was wide enough, but with barely a few inches clear on either side. After a minute of driving, she discovered that she could keep the car centered by looking at the side rails. As she began to relax, though, the bridge started bouncing up and down. She tapped the brakes.

"Don't stop! No more than ten miles an hour, but you gotta keep moving. Don't worry about the oscillation. It won't do anything."

"Are you sure about this?" Krista asked.

"I detailed the steel for this bridge. I know what it can handle. Just keep moving."

"He sounds like an engineer. You can trust him," Ada said.

"Yeah, four days ago I was an engineer, but then the evolution clock started runnin backwards. Now it's like fuckin Persia all over again." He pulled himself out of the window, sat on the sill, and scanned their surroundings through the sight of his rifle. "We're clear for now," he said, settling into the back seat. He stretched his arms and sniffed the air. "Hey, somebody piss in this car?"

"Shut it," Krista muttered.

He started chuckling. "I get it! Was somebody a *widdle* bit scared back there?" His chuckle turned into a guffaw and Ada snickered.

"Stop it! That's not funny!" Krista yelled, but that made them laugh even harder. "Really mature, guys. Really feckin mature. This is a serious situation," she said under her breath.

A big meaty hand gripped her shoulder. "Don't get embarrassed about it, Ginger. I shit myself, first time anybody shot at me."

"Thanks, Friendly, I feel a lot better now. Just shut up and lemme drive, wouldja?"

She kept a death grip on the steering wheel and focused on moving in a straight line; she would hit the railing by straying only a few inches, and it was too flimsy to keep the car from going off the edge. When they were about a third of the way across, Friendly leaned into the front of the car. "Pretty soon you're gonna feel a bump. You'll be drivin on the metal deck, but that's okay."

Krista nodded, and a minute later, she craned her neck over the steering wheel and looked through the windshield. "Where'd the rails go? I don't see any rails ahead!"

"This is the unfinished section. They don't put 'em in till after the concrete's placed."

"But I don't see any rails! How am I –" The car fell a few inches with a thump. "What was that?"

"You're on the metal deck. It can handle your weight."

The wheels moved across the deck, crumpling it, and then they heard a sharp crack. Krista sat up in her seat and screamed. "They're shooting at us again!"

"No. That was just a deck weld poppin. Keep movin and you'll be fine. Just go straight and don't stop."

"How can I go straight if I can't see the rails? You didn't think this through! There's no rails! There's nothing but air out there and I can't see where I'm going!" She slowed the car and heard more pops under the wheels, and in a panic, she opened the door and started to climb out. "That's it! I'm outta here!"

"Whoa," Friendly said. "It's a hundred feet down to the river. You'd be dead on impact."

Krista was already halfway out of the car when she heard water rushing by far below, and she screamed until Friendly's big hands pulled her into the car. "Go easy, Ginger. Just keep movin," he said in a calm voice. "If you stop, the bridge collapses and we all go swimmin. See how close you are to the edge, that's all. Blondie, you do it too. Let's go, girls."

Krista leaned her head against the headrest and closed her eyes, muttering incoherent oaths.

"All right, guess I can do it too." He opened the door and looked down. "Four inches this side."

Ada said she saw a foot, and he told Krista to turn a little to the right. By comparing measurements, the trio centered the car on the narrow deck. Krista wailed softly with her eyelids squeezed shut as the deck popped and the bridge twisted and bounced. She burped and tasted the chocolate protein drink from a few hours before.

"Okay, we're doing just fine now. Keep on going," Friendly said.

"How much longer?" Krista gripped the wheel as if it were a life ring in a hurricane; her hands were blanched white to her wrists.

"Not long." He peered through the windshield. "I don't see the other side yet, but the unfinished part's only a hundred feet or so long. Should be there soon."

Ada spotted the outline of railings in the mist a minute later. "Almost there!"

A few minutes later, the front wheels hit the edge of the concrete surface with a jolt and Krista opened her eyes again. Using the rails again as a guide, she sped up. When the rails ended and the car was on the shore, Krista stopped the car with a jerk and sagged in her seat, while Friendly pumped his fist in victory and Ada whooped a hallelujah.

She held out a quivering hand to Ada. "Cigarette. Stat!"

Friendly leaned through the window and checked the bridge, but he couldn't hear any feet thumping across the drum of the metal deck. He wriggled back into the car. "You know that shit will kill you?" Friendly asked. "You really wanna die young?"

"I just want to die before I've got to wear adult diapers," Krista muttered. "I'm too damned close already." She finished the cigarette in a few monster puffs and lit another.

He picked up his rifle from the seat. "Okay, we're gonna be here a while. I'll go check our perimeter." He climbed from the backseat and walked to the end of the footpath where it met a two-lane road.

"How are you feeling?" Krista asked.

"Pretty punked, but it doesn't hurt much if I don't move. I need to take care of this soon, but I want to get outta here a lot more."

"I wish I could be as brave as you."

"You were. That was the scariest thing ever, Krista, but you did it, and that's something I could never do. I mean, it was like a tightrope walk with a car. I think I was more scared than you were."

"Really?"

Ada nodded. "Sure. I just didn't go all emotional about it."

Krista leaned back in her seat and gazed at the ceiling. "Sorry to break this to you, kiddo, but fear's an emotion."

"No, it's a handicap." She scowled. "Oh, hell, I'm starting to sound like my mom. Listen, if I ever say I want a buzzcut cuz it'll make my hair quicker to wash, just shoot me on the spot. It means I've gone over to the dark side."

"Hmm." Krista looked through the window; the fug was already growing dark as the sun set, but it pulsed with yellow light as it caught the flickers from the Columbus fires. "That's it. I'm calling it. We're definitely living in a dystopia."

"Like some sci-fi story where we jumped into a bad timeline or something. Thing is, I don't remember jumping any timelines."

"I know how we got to this beshitted place, but it didn't take some phantasmagorical event. All it took was making one stupid mistake after another, each one worse than the last, each one shredding the social fabric a little more, until one day we realized there was nothing left to save but our own skins…" She shook the thought away and sat up in the seat. "And we've got to save our own skins now. While he's gone, maybe we should just take off and leave him here. We're out of the danger zone, I think."

"Do you know for sure?"

"I don't."

"Well, we might still need Shooty McShootstick, so I vote for hanging with him for now. I don't think he'll try to hurt us."

Krista stared through the window at the darkening fug and shook her head. "I don't think so, either. I get the feeling he's one of the good guys and likes to think he's not."

Friendly walked from the tree line and opened the back door. "We need to go north. There's a lot of noise to the south, and it sounds a little quieter the other way. Better cover too." The car rocked as he plopped into the backseat. "Break time's over, girls. Let's hit the road."

Krista thumbed the car on and turned right. The road was a parkway, but she glimpsed the smokestacks of riverfront factories through the trees. She saw no cars on the road, but dozens were scattered across the shoulders and in the grass. "What's the plan?" she asked Friendly.

He pulled a rag from his pocket and wiped down the rifle. "First, get outta this stinkin ville and get somewhere safe. After that, I plan to make my way to Urbana. Got a brother there, and I can hole up with him. If you can get me as far as Dublin, I can walk west from there. And what are two pretty Buffies like you doing here? Where you headed?"

"Anywhere that's not here," Krista said. "We haven't got much of a plan."

He laughed. "It's real good to have one, keeps you out of trouble and all. If I didn't have a go-plan and some firepower, I'd be dead." He stuffed the rag back in his pocket and then leaned forward and peered through the windshield. "Slow down. I see lights ahead that shouldn't be there. This stretch of road oughta be dark about now." He pulled a pair of binoculars from a chest pocket and scoped the way ahead. "Okay, let's go to yellow alert. Sumthin's not right up there. Do what I say and don't wimp out on me, Ginger, got it?"

He climbed out on the windowsill with his binoculars in one hand. They coasted along the road, weaving around wrecked cars, and then climbed over a small rise. A few hundred yards past it, a propane truck burned at a wide spot in the road, and barely seen figures stood around it. "Yeah, we got goons ahead. They're all over the place. Ginger, strap on your battle bra cuz we're gonna be the Two Horsemen of the Apocalypse in a few minutes. Blondie, hit the deck much as you can. This might get a little rough." Ada bent over with a groan and tried to make herself a small target.

"Can't we just turn around?" Krista asked.

"Nope, we gotta go this way. Don't worry. They're not gonna be expectin the punch they're gonna get."

Krista rolled closer to the throng – it was a mob like in Columbus, milling around the flaming ruins of a truck that had flipped on its side. "Crap, what are we going to do? Drive through this crowd?"

"Over 'em. When I tell you to punch it, you give it all the gas you got, hear?"

Krista nodded, and Friendly pulled his rifle off the seat. He settled his bulk on the windowsill and yelled, "Let's go! Punch it now!"

She floored the gas pedal as the rifle chattered and cartridges tinkled on the roof of the car. Some goons fell, and others ran for cover. Just before they reached the bodies lying on the road, he jumped back into the car and yelled, "Hold on!"

The car hit the prone bodies at sixty miles an hour, and the impact flung the car into the air. Krista's head hit the ceiling, but she managed to hold onto the wheel; Ada screamed and clutched the bottom of the seat. The car landed hard and slid onto the slick grass of the roadside.

Something thunked against the back of the car as they skidded past the burning propane truck. Friendly pulled a grenade from a chest pocket, yanked the pin out, and tossed it under the truck's tank.

The car slid sideways and then spun around, coming to a stop facing the truck. It erupted into a blue ball of flame that rattled the car – and then a mob of goons with rifles ran out of the smoke toward them. She punched the gas, fishtailed the car onto the highway, and sped away into the fug.

THEY DROVE AROUND ANOTHER CURVE. The road split into two lanes beyond it, the southbound lane climbing a hill while theirs continued level and straight. It cut through the hillside, with a tall rock wall to the left and a guardrail bordering a steep drop to the right.

Krista had only driven for a few minutes when something large appeared on the road ahead. As she coasted up to it, she saw a vehicle stalled in the fuggy murk. She tapped the brakes and stopped inches from the bumper.

An old pickup truck was turned sideways with its bumper poking through a hole in the guardrail. Honking the horn brought no response from the driver, so Friendly climbed out to investigate. He returned a minute later and opened the back door. "That chick's not movin, that truck's not movin, so everybody out. We hoof it from here."

Ada opened her door but winced when she tried to move her leg. Krista ran around to her side of the car and helped her up; she could stand, but her left leg flared with pain when she tried to walk. She looped her arm under Ada's armpit to take the weight off the injured limb. "She can't hoof it anywhere. She can barely stand."

"Can't stay here and can't go back. The goons will be comin soon." He looked up at the rock wall and frowned. "I can't drag her up that, either. We got a tough choice here."

"You go on."

"No, you come with me. I'll keep you safe. We'll hide her somewhere."

"It's both of us or none. You go on without us, Friendly."

He reached into the backseat for his gear. "You move on and hide, and I'll give you all the cover I can. Slide down that hill and find a tree or a bush to hide under, and I'll come back after I take care of those hostiles." He studied her face for a few moments, and then his eyes widened. "Huh. You're Warner, aincha?"

She stood as tall as she could. "That I am."

"I'll be damned. Woulda been nicer to you if I knew." He ran to the rock face and called over his shoulder, "You keep that tablet of yours safe! We're all countin on you! Hang some Cheyn!"

She watched him climb, and by the time she found her voice again, he'd disappeared into the trees at the top.

"He's right. You oughta go, Krista. Just help me over the guardrail and go with him. Come back for me later. I'll be okay."

"Bullshit. I'm not leaving you here alone. I'll find another way." She helped Ada sit on the hood and then ran to the pickup, where a large woman with half a head lay sprawled against the steering wheel.

Gritting her teeth, she tried to push her away from the wheel but just moved her bulk an inch. She ran around to the passenger side, reached across the cabin, and turned the ignition key. The truck's lights dimmed and the starter clicked, but the truck engine wouldn't turn over.

She walked back to her car. "It won't move. I wish I had a tank so I could just push the feckin thing out of the way."

"Yeah, that would –" Ada stopped and her eyes glittered. "Help me back in."

"What is it?"

"I have an idea. Lemme check something. Help me in and go turn the car on, all right?"

Krista helped her into the seat and ran around the car. She thumbed it on, and Ada tapped the car's computer monitor a few times; strange diagrams Krista had never seen appeared on it. "I can do this, but I'll need a minute. Go to that truck and turn the wheel to the right. Make sure it's in neutral and the parking brake is off."

"Fine. But –"

"Just do it." Ada peered at the monitor. "Yeah, this'll work," she said to herself.

Krista ran back to the pickup and opened the door. She pushed the body once more but didn't move it, so she climbed onto the running board and tried pushing it away with her legs. The body moved more this time but not enough. Again she tried, and this time she rocked the body into the passenger seat. She slid the shifter into neutral and jerked the wheel as far to the right as it would go.

Stepping back from the truck, she saw her bloody hands and gasped. She staggered back to the rock wall, and then long-delayed shock overtook her. Everything she saw slipped out of focus; an odd thrumming, like a huge bass guitar, played in her ears. Then a powerful wave of dizziness struck her, and she sagged down the wall.

Young men shouted in the distance. Figment spoke in her mind, *This is the wrong time to flake out, Miss Kellen. This is the wrong time to die.*

She shook her head and forced her legs to take a step. Oddly, the deep thrumming sound grew even louder, and she realized it was in her ears and not her head. She looked up to find the source – and then her scalp tingled and her stomach twisted into a knot. The sensations were so overwhelming that she fell hard to the ground on one knee.

SPOT'S COURSE PARALLELED A ROAD following the river. On this leg, it had found 63 human objects per minute aloft, but none were a match. Eleven seconds later, the infrared acquired another object, and Spot pulsed its wing radars again. The image built itself in .09 seconds: an automotive object that was a 100 percent match for the target vehicle.

A human object stood beside it: female, height 70.375 inches, mass 150 pounds. It was a 91 percent match. Spot reported it to the base.

BOB DOWNS LOOKED UP AT THE CLOCK; it was just after 1900 hours and his feet were already numb. He raised himself on his toes and scanned the Wall for anything new, but the dissidents and pre-emergent terrorists were under control this evening.

All except for Warner. Yesterday, it seemed like she was in the net and ready to be reeled in, but the net came in empty. He knew she wasn't within ten miles of Oxford anymore because each road, motel, and restaurant had been checked and rechecked. Beyond that, he knew nothing.

His thoughts turned to Kopelli and his box of wonders. His approach was strange, but at least it was an active step; standing around and waiting for passive surveillance to bear fruit was frustrating. He was built to be an Executive, to be out in the field getting things done, not standing still and waiting to react.

Buta interrupted his thoughts with a shout. "Acquisition! Warner, 91 percent confidence, sir!" Downs spun on the ball of his foot and looked at the Wall above Buta, but it was blank.

"What? Where?"

"Drone ASD-2, west of Columbus, four minutes ago. Location coming up, sir."

"Turn it around and orbit that location. Hogue, move them in, everything we have. Give me ETA's."

"When I have them, sir." She tapped away at her monitors and spoke at the same time into her headset.

He turned to Cochon. "Why don't I see a map?" Before he finished the sentence, a map appeared on the Wall, and a red dot blinked on a parkway northwest of Columbus. "Hogue, move a unit down that road from the north. Get another –"

"Request permission to do my job, sir," she snapped.

Downs was quiet for a moment, and then he said through gritted teeth, "Yes. Very well."

He turned to Buta, who had displayed a black-and-white image on the Wall. "There it is, sir. Five minutes ago." The image showed Warner's car and a pickup truck slewed across a single-lane road. Beyond it, Warner looked directly at the drone.

"That's her. Call it a hundred percent confidence. When that drone gets into range, pulse her as much as you can. If we can't kill her, we'll cook her." He looked closer at the pickup truck. "She had a traffic accident, so she might be immobile. Hogue, launch the Talons from Dayton. If she stays put, we might get her from the air."

"Yes, sir." She paused a moment as she tapped away. "Wheels up in three minutes."

Cochon turned in his chair. "Sir, you might want to see this." Downs looked at a radar image on Cochon's screen. "It's likely she's immobile. Look here on the trunk. Those eight dots are small-caliber impact sites. Here on the door are three large-caliber impacts. It looks like she drove the vehicle through a war zone."

"And yet she lived."

"But it wasn't easy. Look at her hands, sir." Cochon zoomed in and the image grew fuzzy.

"I don't see anything, Cochon. Just give me your interpretation."

"She has blood on her hands, sir. She might be wounded." He zoomed out until the screen filled with Warner's figure. "I can't see any wounds, but her hands are dripping blood, so she may be injured in a place we can't see."

Downs studied the image for a second and tried to uncover something else he could use, but it would have to wait. It was time to act, not think. "The slower she is, the better. Let's get moving, people. We're wearing our quarry down."

KRISTA RUBBED HER HANDS in the dirt and shook off the bloody mud. The weird tingling feeling had faded, but her vision had gone swimmy again and the dizziness had returned. She'd just gotten to her feet when she heard the distant clamor of the mob down the road. Gunfire rattled from the tree line above.

She stumbled to the car and fell into the front seat. "Okay, I did what you asked. Now what?"

"Just go."

"Go where?"

"Straight ahead." Ada pointed at the truck while wearing a smug smile. "We can go now. Trust me."

Krista slid the shifter into drive. When she pressed the gas pedal, the engine wailed under the hood and the car crept forward. Her bumper touched the pickup truck and pushed it like it was nothing more than a child's wagon. "Well, I'll be damned," she said.

Ada's smug smile widened. "You needed a tank, so I made you a tank."

"Hunh?"

"Watch out ahead," Ada said. "That truck's gonna go over any…oh, there it goes."

The front wheels of the pickup were hanging over empty air. The heavy front end dipped lower, and then it slid down the hill and turned end over end until the fug swallowed it. A moment later, metal crunched far below.

Ada watched until the truck disappeared and then gave a contented sigh. "Why don't we go now? We have a gang of bloodthirsty hooligans coming after us."

Krista stepped on the gas. The engine wailed louder as the car sped up, and the transmission shifted gears with a chunk; the car shuddered with each gear change until it finally reached overdrive. The engine still screamed, though, and Ada clapped her hands over her ears. "We're going twenty-five miles an hour!" Krista yelled. "This is it? This is our mad getaway run?"

"Stop griping! We're moving, aren't we? Look, I can change it if you want, but you'd have to stop the car for a few minutes! We need to put some distance behind us first!"

"This noise is driving me crazy! A few more miles then, but you've got to fix this!" She stuck a finger in one ear and steered with the other hand.

"I didn't *break* it! I modified it!"

A few minutes later, the road descended to the river, and a sign appeared on the right that said JOHNSON'S LANDING VISTA POINT. Krista steered the laboring car into the lot and stopped beside a stand of trees. The engine powered down with a rumbling whine, and the car grew quiet even though Krista still heard the reverberations. "I don't want to be an ingrate, but…" She wriggled her little finger in her ear. "I'm actually hearing stars. Is that even possible? Anyway, thanks for that little touch of magic back there. How'd you do that?"

Ada grinned and reached for the computer screen. "Bicep drivetrains are configurable if you know how to hack the tuning module. I used to do it to Mom's Bicep all the time, and it drove her nuts. By the way, while I'm changing this back, get me some painkillers. I'm really feeling it now."

"We should work on those wounds first –"

The strange bass sound roared overhead. "No time for that. That drone's back, and we need to hurry. Just give me painkillers. That should hold me."

Krista scanned the empty parking lot. "I've got no idea when something else will jump out and yell boo. It's been that kind of day. You make the car go fast again, and I'll go get the kit."

She climbed out and walked to the trunk. In better times, it would be a place of beauties; she heard the river rushing past a small meadow beyond the lot, and the views would be inspiring on a fugless day. On a dark fuggy night, though, all she could do was imagine.

What she saw at the rear of the car almost made her pass out again – the hatch was stitched by a row of bullet holes, and the lock was blasted away. She pulled the handle, but the latch wouldn't release, so she trudged to the passenger door and folded down a seat, finding two bullets buried in the back of it. After groping in the dark, she felt the medikit and the bag with the field surgery kit, as well as small, heavy pieces of metal lying on the trunk carpet. When she looked at the back of the trunk, she saw tiny pinholes of dim light.

Walking around the passenger side of the car, she saw even worse damage: Long swaths of paint were stripped from the metal, and Ada's door was punctured by ragged holes large enough to fit her thumb. She stuck her finger into a hole in Ada's seat cushion, found a matching hole in the driver's seat, and then looked at the fractured dashboard by Ada's knee. "That was close."

Ada reached down and stuck her finger in the shredded seat cushion. "How did these miss me?"

"Let's pretend this never happened."

Ada nodded and turned back to the screen, which was filled with a confusion of lines and numbers. Krista squinted at it and tilted her head this way and that, but it remained incomprehensible. "You can make sense of that stuff?"

Ada tapped at the screen a few more times. "Yeah, ever since I was four."

"Four?"

"I didn't become a genius yesterday. Jeez." A graph appeared on the screen, and Ada muttered a satisfied grunt. Her finger dragged a ragged red line around on the screen. "That looks about right. Did you say you wanted it to go fast?" Krista mumbled a reply as she opened the medikit, and Ada dragged the line around on the screen more.

"There. We're ready to go, but before we do, I want you to help me with something. It'll be quick, I promise." Ada gently pulled her jeans down to above her knees. "You need to pull this thing outta my leg. It's killing me."

Krista looked at a brown chunk of dashboard plastic protruding from her left thigh and nodded. Ada pulled a few packets of gauze from the kit and handed a pair of forceps to Krista.

"Yank it out fast. You have to do it fast, or it'll hurt even more. I'll take care of the rest, okay? On three. One…two…three!"

Krista pulled it out, and Ada yelped and blood spurted from the wound. She jumped up and slid her jeans down over her boots and then slapped a gauze pad over the gash. Swearing and pressing down hard on the wound, she sat back in the seat.

Krista examined the shard, a sharp triangle of plastic two inches long and coated in blood. "This was close to the bone."

She showed it to her, and Ada winced and fumbled for the bottle of antibiotic powder. "Thanks. I couldn't have done that myself." She grinned weakly and pressed a fresh wad of gauze down on her thigh, which immediately turned red. "Too much of a weenie, I guess. Maybe it's contagious." When she lifted the gauze off the wound, though, she spotted a small white lump among the clots. With her fingernail, she pried the object off the gauze, wiped the blood from it, and then held it under the reading light.

"What's that?" Krista asked.

"Dunno," Ada said as she turned it over. "This was in my leg. Why the hell –" She spotted a thin wire extending from one side of the cylinder and pulled it straight, and then she sat back and groaned. "Wonderful. A super high frequency antenna. I'll bet freakin Blue Ball implanted a tracking device in me."

"Who's Blue Ball?"

"Let's just say they aren't my best buds." She wrapped the chip into the gauze and handed it to Krista. "Crush it with the biggest rock you can find and throw it into the river."

Krista searched the edge of the lot until she found a watermelon-sized rock. She laid the gauze on a concrete curb, raised the stone over her head, and dropped it on the chip. To be sure, she did it again, and then she walked to the water's edge and flung the chip's remains far into the water.

She'd just returned to the car when a large engine roared by on the road. They ducked, and a few seconds later another vehicle rolled by.

"Federals," Krista said. "That's it – we've got to blow this burg right now. Rest stop's over." She ran to the driver's side and climbed in.

"You killed the tracker?"

"It's sleeping with the fishes now."

"Thanks. Now, about the engine," Ada said as Krista slipped it into gear. "I have to tell you a few things. First, it'll be a little…"

Krista stomped the pedal to the floor. G-forces slammed her body back into the seat as the car rocketed from the lot, and she gasped for breath and clutched the steering wheel. The roadside trees flickered into a blur, and the numbers on the speedometer changed too fast to read; the front of the car rose as if it yearned to leave the sorry Earth behind and fly.

When she finally caught her breath, Krista flung her head back and screamed a wild rebel yell.

THE WAY IT WAS

Day 32
Saturday night, September 19, 2043
St. James Anglican Church, Baltimore, Maryland

Sara Hogue parked her car on a residential side street and then strolled toward York Road. After a quarter mile, she slipped between two tall shrubs into the parking lot of a busy fast-food restaurant, where a nondescript black sedan sat idling. She climbed into the backseat.

The car pulled into the flow of traffic heading north. After two miles, it turned into the parking lot of an office complex. She climbed out behind the building, and the sedan returned to the road.

After it left, she walked to the rear of the lot and through an opening in a hedge separating it from a white clapboard church. As she walked through tall weeds to a rear door, she groped in her coat pocket and found a key.

At the door, she turned and scanned her threat environment. Satisfied that she hadn't been followed, she unlocked it and stepped into an empty robing room. After allowing her vision to adapt to the low light, she crossed the room and walked into the sanctuary.

The church had been stripped long ago of anything that wasn't screwed down, and all that remained was a large marble table swathed in eight years of dusty cobwebs. She stepped around it and opened a gate in a marble railing.

This had been her church, the place where four generations of Hogues had been christened and buried. She remembered it as a place of hope and life; faith had been unbreakable back then, and that certainty had bound generations of her family.

She peered down the nave, but she couldn't see as far as the entrance doors, since the air conditioning hadn't been used in years and the fug had crept in. It hung in the forlorn atmosphere and absorbed the dim light passing through the stained glass. Other than the altar, little remained to show that this had been a church; in a way, she was grateful for the fug because it obscured heartbreaking truths. She turned away and knelt on the frayed carpet in front of the rail.

The day the church closed had been filled with the hardest truth: The Archangelists had taken its parishioners and their money, and the church couldn't afford to keep its doors open. Father Kennedy and the rest of the staff became ex-employed that day; other Anglican churches across the country were struggling and couldn't take them in.

Angus Kennedy was sixty-four and had devoted his life to the Anglican Church. He had no job skills other than the ability to listen, empathize, and offer God's perspective on the meaning and challenges of life.

He kept in touch with his former parishioners, always believing that one day St. James would reopen, but everyone knew it never would. They'd all become Archangelists, and the Arkies excommunicated any member who stepped across the threshold of a competing church. In Washington, excommunication meant unemployment and a fate like Father Kennedy, so his flock just smiled and went along with his fantasy.

In time, he also accepted the truth and made his final confession. Life on the street was hard on him, and a year after the church closed, the police found his body in one of the confessionals.

Sara was one of the flock who had converted, but she'd become an Arkie only out of necessity. To her, Archangelism was a business deal, and a tenpez a year to keep her job at the National Tranquility Center was a small price. She detested the deal, though, and whenever she came here and remembered, she detested herself for selling out her faith so cheaply.

Even through the thick air, she could still see the marks where the crucifix had once been mounted on the wall. *Why have we forsaken you? Because the price was right. It's always been that way.*

With trembling hands, she reached into her purse and found a string of old and worn prayer beads, an heirloom from several generations back. She brought them to her lips and fingered them as she prayed.

Behind her, someone cleared his throat and she started; she'd arrived early to pray but must have lost track of time. She stood and turned to face the man, averting her eyes from the glare of his flashlight. She knew that behind the light was a well-armed young man, and without waiting for his order, she raised her arms and spread her legs. He patted her down thoroughly and then wanded her. "Okay, you're clean."

Shaking her head, she knelt at the rail again as four similarly dressed men searched the nave and galleries. She prayed, and then sensing someone beside her, she held out her hand. A strong, soft hand took it and caressed her fingers.

"I still remember the way it was," he said. "Despite the popcorn-gothic atmosphere, I still see it the way it was."

"I do too. I'm always reluctant to come here, but I feel better after I leave," Sara said. "I'm afraid I live too much in the past sometimes, but it's comforting. I see you here too. You know, back then."

He smiled. "Twenty years ago. Your cousin's wedding. You were the most beautiful bridesmaid I'd ever seen. God, I can recall every detail of that dress." He leaned toward her and whispered. "You gave me a fetish for purple right there on the spot. For months, I got an erection whenever I saw a jar of grape jelly. You were ravishing in that dress."

"I was twenty-six in that dress."

"You're still twenty-six. You always will be in my eyes, Sara."

She squeezed his hand. "That's why I keep you around, pal. You keep me young."

"It doesn't take any imagination on my part. You're more beautiful every year."

"You're even more handsome and dignified with each passing year. Age treats you so well. I hope the years treat me as kindly."

"No matter. Ever twenty-six, Sara, ever twenty-six. Remember that."

She sighed and stroked his hand. "I wish I could go back sometimes and stay there forever. I'd give years of my life to be twenty-six again, here with you on that day. The world went to hell on us after that, Gabriel."

"All we can do now is build a better one." He frowned as he pulled his rosary from his pocket. "And I've tried, but it slips away the more I try to get a grip on it."

He clicked a bead along the string and gazed at the back wall of the sanctuary, moving his lips in silent prayer. When he spoke again, his voice was barely a whisper. "The chances of a better world diminish every day. That infernal Containment Ring is slowing the spread of RVE so much that we'll need until April before Economic Selection is complete." He sat back with a tired, ragged sigh. "And I needed it to be done by January so I could implement fundamental reforms while the population was still stunned by the pandemic. By early spring, I'd hoped to show them an America reborn with a revitalized economy and democracy – an America where the damned Archangelists were marginalized once more." He glared at the spot where the crucifix had once hung. "The Profit Joe. Grandson of God, my ass."

"I'd love to put that claim to the test. How about Good Friday? What do you think?"

"Hah! Amazing idea! I have a lover in the NSF. I should ask her if they have a spare crucifix. They're into that kind of thing."

"Crucifix? That's so B.C.! Want me to talk to the boys in the basement and see what the latest tools are?" She nudged him in the ribs. "Come on. Let's do it. Let's see who his daddy really is."

"Oh God…the guy probably worked at a fast-food restaurant, and his name tag said Jésus. Maryann Heilmann wasn't too bright." He wiped his eyes and his laughter faded, ending with another sigh. He concentrated again on his beads and flicked them back and forth. "But whether the virus finishes its work in April or January may no longer be relevant, according to a report I received today from my Texarkana sources. They say the Archangelists have changed their schedule. They moved up their coup from April to the end of November."

Sara gasped and covered her mouth. "My God! Whatever for?"

"I don't know. Their political security is unusually tight right now, but I think the schedule change is tied to the California secession movement."

"California's seceding?"

"If the Arkies and the Reds have any say, yes."

"Oh, shit. Like we need Russia in this too."

"They're definitely in the game. CIA intercepts show that the Russian oligarchs have been transferring millions into Arkie offshore shell companies recently, so The Profit Joe's collection basket has a long handle that reaches into the despots' pews."

"The Arkies have been soaking their flock and the corporations for decades. Why do they need more money?"

"To fund their social media campaign instigating a California secession. My digital media team traced the money pipeline feeding Californians for Fair Taxation, and at the other end are the same Arkie shell companies the Reds are stuffing with covert rubles. That's their backup plan if the coup doesn't come together, I believe – to remove me from office for failing to quell a rebellion in the nation's largest state. Such an outcome would serve both the Arkies and the Reds."

Hogue hissed and then muttered a string of curses under her breath.

"Not all is lost yet, though. Their machinations have created a mild backlash among their Corporate-American co-conspirators, who have little desire to break up America, or more importantly their prime market. Of course, that doesn't stop them from sending money to the Arkies – spines of steel, they have – but I keep getting calls from chairmen who are distressed about the rising instability all this secession talk creates." He ran his fingers through his hair and looked at the ceiling. "Politics is not for the whole of mind. Only psychopaths deserve this kind of sentence. The voters shouldn't call for term limits but rather parole because all this is –"

"Gabriel."

"Yes, I digress. Anyway, the chairmen want me to push Gibbon to cut off the Arkies from their money. They hope that by choking the Arkie agitprop, California will see reason and towel off."

"So do it. I'll put together a team, and we'll deliver a few fifty-caliber restraining orders to Holy Joe and his ass-lickers. You cut off their bucks. They'll dry up in a year."

"That could be a major tactical error, Sara. If I cut the Arkie corporate money pipeline abruptly, they'll become even more dependent on Russian moneymen I can't control. And this is a dangerous time to make them bedfellows, being that their political goals are in tight alignment right now, much as mine were with the Arkies mere weeks ago."

"This sounds like a minefield. And you know the best way to get through one? Throw a couple grenades in it, wait for shit to stop blowing up, then stroll right through. Don't even try to tiptoe around mines."

"But I'm deep into this minefield already. It's rather inadvisable to blow shit up when I'm surrounded by explosives." He looked up at the shadow of the cross, a muscle in his jaw twitching. "Those damned oligarchs. They want to wreck this nation, as do the Arkies, who yearn to be the Messiah amidst the mess. And the oligarchs will merrily feed this beast as if nothing can happen to them, but I'll tell you this – the Reds will be experiencing a tragic epidemic soon, and when their billionaires come begging for the vaccine, they can crawl across broken glass on their knees and kiss my –"

"Gabriel!" she hissed. "The Secret Service can hear you!"

"Right, right. I'm sorry, but for some reason, I get a bit animated when discussing how the billionaires are cold-bloodedly stabbing me and Rutskoy in the back."

"C'mon, Rutskoy must know what they're doing. He's no fool, and what Russian would betray him anyway?"

"Dusan Nitskaya and his billionaire pals would. They're the ones funding the Arkies."

"I can fix that. I've worked with a mother-daughter sniper team from St. Petersburg. For ten grand and a basket of flowers, this Nitskaya dude's a corpse."

"Sara, please. Killing the man won't kill the movement, and Nitskaya is but one of a large group of hard-liners. I don't know who the rest are. Even Rutskoy doesn't. But he tells me about their skulduggery, and how he has to devise a Byzantine strategy with ten contingency plans just to get out of bed and take a leak. I sometimes wonder if using the bathroom is worth the risk too, what with the Arkies watching my every move, and I'm tempted to relieve myself *au naturel* in the Rose Garden to confound the devious bastards. Sara, could not have God burdened me with a sane and respectable adversary? Why did he inflict on me a mob of wall-eyed, gap-toothed dripspittles who see democracy as some drawn-out conspiracy concocted two centuries ago by a powdered-wig Founder who set in motion some absurd plan to crush their precious cult long before it was even born, but it's a conspiracy theory, and they can't resist one of *those*, oh no –"

"Gabriel."

"Right, right. Where I started, then. I think the Arkies pressed secession too hard, and now it's gaining momentum too fast and their backup plan could subsume their coup. Thus, they may be doubly ready in November, while I'll be waiting months longer for Economic Selection to bear fruit."

Sara's brows furrowed as she gazed into the fug, and then she snapped her fingers. "Governor Rodriguez! He was delaying the tenpez vote for you. Maybe he could buy you time."

"He's been losing his grip on the California Legislature for years now. Look how far the tenpez recall has gotten. Can I rely on him to quell the secession movement when he can't even delay a tenpez vote?" He sighed and rubbed his face as if trying to wipe it clean. "I'll have to pressure the legislature myself, but if they advance to a secession vote before November, I'll need to borrow a page from your playbook and toss a few grenades into the proverbial minefield."

Sara fingered her prayer beads for a minute and then threw them to the carpet. "Shit, I can't focus with that news. It's terrible. They could mess up everything!"

"They intend to, Sara."

"Those demented bastards. If it wasn't for them –"

"Don't blame the Arkies for being what they are," Cheyn said. "One can't blame the weed for taking root in the junkyard – one must blame those who built that junkyard. Forty years of failed presidencies ripped the political and economic center out of this country, and the Arkies thrive on polarization. Look at their nonsensical stance on population control – a limit of two children per couple, which pleases the liberals, but don't abort that accidental third pregnancy or you'll be slapped with murder charges. Arkie conservatives ejaculate at the prospect of killing criminals, so of course they'd want to create even more criminals and ejaculate constantly. Sure, they'd hang a thousand innocent women each year, but the entertainment value more than makes up for the injustice. After all, it's wholesome family fun killing girls on a fine Sunday afternoon, especially the brown ones, and then Mom and Dad can retire to the bedroom after and have great sex picturing the condemned twitching and kicking on the rope. That abnormative eroticism attracts the dripspittles to the Arkies, I think, who are conditioned to get an erection only when shown fetishized vengeance. That's why their birthrate is so low. If the dripspittles genuinely want to stop the Great Replacement, I have their answer – the Arkies should start a Snuff Video of the Month Club. That'll get the bastards in the sack and spitting out white babies –"

"Gabriel, chill." She picked up the beads from the floor and began fingering them again.

"Right, right." He drew three deep breaths and rolled his shoulders to relieve the tension. "I foresaw this problem, though. It was but a matter of time before I parted ways with the Arkies. Our only common interest was in culling the herd, and since that's underway, it isn't unexpected for them turn on me." He patted her leg. "I know this isn't fantastic news, but it's not terrible. In fact, this could be advantageous. If the momentum of the

California secession movement is pushing the Arkies to rush their coup, it may force them into unrecoverable errors. They're not ready to assume control now, nor is it likely by the end of November. My sources tell me they can't assemble a new general staff for the Navy and Air Force, and they believe they need their loyalty before executing a coup."

Sara noticed the string of beads in her hands – she'd managed to tie them in a knot in her nervousness – and tried to undo the mess as she talked. "Well, from the news, I'd agree with the Arkies on that. We're so close to nuclear war with the Soviet Bloc that they need to have the strategic forces on their side from the first minute. Hell, I'd want them to if they won this damned game. I saw their targeting assignments. I have a Ground Zero just two blocks from my apartment."

"Excellent! I'd hate to see you in harm's way."

"How can you be so insensitive? Every time I see car headlights flashing by my window, I'm sure it's the Bomb going off. I can hardly sleep at night. I'm thinking of moving, maybe out to the country."

"I recommend moving to Ground Zero. It's the safest place. I guarantee no Soviet Bloc missile can find it."

"Gabriel!" She wrapped her prayer beads into her fist. "I wish you'd take this seriously."

He laid his hand on her thigh. "There's no need to worry. There'll be no Soviet Bloc preemptive strike. No American first strike, either." Sara looked at him quizzically and he smiled back. "Premier Rutskoy has his internal problems – too many mouths to feed, breakaway states and dissidents, much like me. I rattle my saber to help him to keep the Soviet Bloc in line, and he's grateful for any assistance he can get. He's even distributed *Mushrooms over Moscow* inside the Soviet Bloc. Now everyone's scrambling to get under the Russian nuclear umbrella, and 'Patrick Henry' is becoming another word for 'Boogeyman.'"

"Huh." She sat back on her haunches. "Well, I guess it was a real bonus for him, then. That movie scared the living shit outta me. I can only imagine what it did to the Reds who saw it."

"Bonus? His Propaganda Ministry wrote most of it! Even Hollywood couldn't come up with something that frightening! That scene where the mother and her children melt as the nuclear inferno swallows them? That was their idea. If you want to play the fiddle of fear, you have to consult the old pros of the business. The Russians have been retailing fear for centuries."

"Damn. The whole movie was their propaganda, not ours?"

"Exactly. Rutskoy owes me big for that." He smiled a sly grin. "But in a way, he's already paid me back. His saber-rattling – like releasing his nuclear strike targets – keeps the Arkies thinking they need the loyalty of our strategic nuclear forces before attempting a coup, which they'll never get. The Navy and Air Force won't sign on to a government takeover. My loyals were burrowed deep into their bureaucracies long before I even approached the Arkies about Economic Selection."

She laughed and shook her head. "A classic Gabriel Cheyn maneuver."

"I'm rather proud of myself, but it gets even better."

"How?"

"Can you keep a secret?"

She snorted a short laugh. "Christ in Heaven, old man, you know what I do for a living! C'mon, out with it."

"In April, Rutskoy and I are planning a joint announcement in Warsaw. We're retiring eighty percent of the Lancet hypersonic stealth missiles on the *Henry* subs, and in return, they're decommissioning eighty percent of their ballistic subs. By the end of next year, neither side will have any significant sea-based retaliatory throw weight, leaving most of our nukes land-based and verifiable. Of course, we'll save a few warheads to toss at the ragheads."

She ran her fingers through her hair. "Wow."

"Nuclear tensions gone like that." He snapped his fingers and smiled. "We made that deal last May in Rio. I've been itching to tell someone about it ever since."

"That's fantastic news! I haven't slept soundly for weeks. Maybe tonight I will." She sighed and rubbed his hand. "How'd you get President Gibbon to go along with it, though? The Lancet missile is his baby. He even has a model of a Joe Slick in his office."

Cheyn took a deep breath and let it out slowly. "Bill has a terminal condition, I'm afraid. He won't make it until April."

She looked at him sharply, but his eyes were impossible to read. She chose her next words carefully. "What condition does he have? Or have you decided that yet?"

Amusement flickered across his eyes, and he turned away. "How goes the hunt for Warner?"

Sara frowned at him, but his expression was inscrutable. "Don't change the subject."

"I'm sorry, but I've forgotten what we were discussing. A consequence of age."

"Fine, whatever. Well, we almost got her a few hours ago in Ohio. We know where she is now, though, and we're tightening the noose. Even someone with my escape and evasion training couldn't dodge this dragnet. On top of that, Dickhead Downs has a personal grudge against Warner, and he's committed to getting her come Hell or high water."

"The high water's already here. Is Hell next?"

"You know what I mean!"

"How could the man develop animosity to anybody? He never leaves the NTC."

"She came to the Watch Room once, and they became mortal enemies or something. I really don't know what happened. That's good, though, because the Dickhead is a bulldog when he gets in that mood. He won't rest till he's gotten that tablet, and then the Paparazzo videos will disappear forever."

"I trust they will. They could be damaging if they were released, especially right now. I'll be called to account for the RVE Initiative someday, and when I am, I'll have enough information to make the virus release look like an Arkie act. But now…" He looked up at the altar and puffed out his cheeks. "Do the Watchers suspect that you know about the Transition and the RVE Initiative?"

She shook her head. "I keep a low profile, Gabriel. They think I'm boring and dutiful. They certainly don't suspect I listen in on their podium conversations."

"Listen, if Hayborn threw a stick, Downs would fetch it. He wouldn't hesitate to kill you."

"I have a Go Plan, and I'm much better at this game than the Dickhead. Don't worry about me."

"Good." He clasped her hand tight, but she felt him trembling.

"Don't worry, we'll get her, Gabriel, and then this'll all be over. We know she's around Columbus, and we're flooding the area with all the assets we can spare. There's a huge price on her head too, so it's even possible a citizen will get her first. A million eyes are watching for her. Just give it time."

"Time again. I always need more than I have. As I get older, I get more aware of the clock, and perhaps that's my problem." He puffed out his cheeks and rubbed the back of his neck. "Warner. I didn't think much of her in grad school. I thought she was just another vapid, unformed brat. Had I known what a troublemaker she'd become, I would've killed her myself back then."

Sara took his hand. "She's no trouble. We can handle this. Relax, okay?" Soft footsteps came from behind, and they turned to see a Secret Service agent approach.

"Doctor? Miss Hogue? We need to leave for the cabin now. This location isn't secure, and we've been here too long."

"Thank you, Jacob. Give us a moment, please." The agent nodded and backed away. Cheyn leaned toward Hogue and whispered in her ear. "Never enough time. Do you see what I mean? It's a disease, trust me."

REBEL WITHOUT A PAUSE

Day 32
Saturday night, September 19, 2043
Two miles north of Waldo, Ohio

Ada arched her back and moaned through gritted teeth.

"I'm sorry!" Krista said. "I'm not trying to hurt you."

"Maybe it wouldn't hurt so much if I still had some Spectracain left."

"I'm so sorry I used it all up."

"You're not the only one." Ada laid back, looked at the ceiling, and breathed deep. "Okay, try it again, but do it fast this time."

Krista pushed the needle through her skin. She squinted in the greenish light of the carwash and pulled at the end with the forceps, and Ada gasped again. "Jesus, how many times do I have to tell you, don't pull it straight up! The needle's curved!"

Krista mumbled more apologies and pulled the rest of the needle through. "All right, I'll hold and you tie it again." Ada's nimble fingers fluttered over the suture, and then she collapsed with a groan across the front seats. Krista covered the gash with gauze and then bandaged the constellation of smaller wounds higher on her thigh.

The flow of blood was much less now that the wound was sutured. For the last hour, she'd been concerned that Ada would pass out from blood loss because she couldn't slow the bleeding. In desperation, Krista pulled into the carwash and volunteered to play surgeon.

Her knees popped as she stood. She'd been squatting for more than a half hour, and she walked around the carwash a few times to loosen her joints. The bright lights turned the fug outside into an opaque, swirling wall; if goons with guns were lurking out there, she'd never see them.

They needed to move on, except that she didn't know where to go or how to get anywhere. It was also nearly eleven at night too, and she was so tired that she'd stopped caring if they were at risk.

It's time to trust someone, Miss Kellen. You can't continue this way.

"You've got a point there, Figment." She reached into the pocket of her sweatpants and opened her tablet. After scrolling through her mail, she found the message from Aaron and memorized the Witness's phone number.

Ada was sitting up again when she returned to the car. "We can't run anymore tonight. I was thinking that we oughta find an abandoned barn or something and hide in there."

"That's an idea," Krista said. "But the trail mix is gone, and we've got only two protein drinks left. We need food and shelter, and I've got an idea where we can get it." She picked up her tablet and dialed the number. "Hello? Is this Jack Ripley? The Editor gave me your name...that one, yes...he said I should say that 'gold is old, but blue is new' and you'd know what that means..."

Ada tried to hold back a giggle but failed, earning a sharp look from Krista. "The red crow flies at midnight!" Ada snorted. "You really sound like a spy, sorry, but it's funny."

"Will you zip it?"

Still snorting, Ada covered her mouth, and Krista returned to her call. "No, not you, that was someone else...a little brat...well, that's complicated, but I don't want anyone to know she's with me...Oh, he called you? Good, I really need food and shelter..." Krista made a writing motion in the air and pointed to a pen in the console. Ada grabbed it and pulled out the atlas. "Maryville, got it, left on Main Street, first alley on the left...okay, thanks, Jack, I can't tell you how much I appreciate this. Things are a little desperate right now...you're right, I should go. Bye." She slid the tablet into her pocket. "I hope you got all that."

Ada nodded, running her finger across the atlas. "We need to go north twenty-one miles. It's on this road. Who was that?"

"He's a *Midnight Sun* Witness. I know the editor, and he gave me Jack's name in case I needed help. I didn't think I'd need it, but Columbus changed my mind."

"Do you know this guy?"

"I don't."

Rebel Without a Pause

"So how can you trust him?"

"Witnesses are usually very anti-Administration. I doubt he'd turn me in, and besides, he has such a sweet voice."

Ada slapped her forehead. "Satan's supposed to have a lovely voice. Is this how you make decisions?"

"I've got a good feeling about this. Trust me for once, okay?" She backed out of the carwash and drove north under the open sky.

IN THE AIR A MILE BEHIND THEM, Spot sent a signal back to its base.

"Acquisition, Warner! '40 Bicep D4, 82 percent confidence. Two miles north of Waldo, Ohio."

"Put it up when you have a location," Raphael said to Ryan Beckmann, his Acquisitions Chief. Ryan ran his fingers across the monitor. A few seconds later, a map on the Wall displayed a dot on Route 23 in north central Ohio.

Raphael turned to his Tactical Chief. "You know what to do, Tom."

"I already have a unit coming from the north and one from the south."

"Two? Why only two units?" Raphael asked. "This is the highest priority."

"I know, but some of the teams worked a double shift today, and I allowed them to return to Fort Wayne. They're exhausted."

"The beauty sleep won't do them any good," Raphael said. "Why don't you give them a jingle and invite them to our shindig?"

"Yes, sir," said Tom. "It'll take thirty to forty minutes for them to return, though."

"All right. And don't call me sir." Raphael scrutinized the map of Route 23 on the Wall. "We need to tap the local resources. There's a small town ahead of them. Contact their PD and get them on the road. The mayberries can slow them down or give us a sighting."

Ari, the Intelligence Chief, broke in. "That's Maravelle. It doesn't have a police department. It was evacuated during the Cleveland Transportation for use as a staging point, and nobody came back after. It's been a ghost for years."

Raphael puffed out his cheeks. "Then let's hope two units can do the job tonight. Tom, launch the Talons in case we get a ping. I'd feel better with missiles in the air." He walked over to Acquisitions and looked at the radar image displayed on the Wall. "What the hell is that? A Rorschach test?" Raphael asked.

"It was taken at extreme range. Lots of interpolation and artifacts. We're trying to clean it up right now," Ryan said.

"Tom, maybe you should swing Spot around so we can get a better picture."

"Spot's returning to Dayton for refueling. If I move it over the target, it may have to land at a civilian airport."

"And we'd have to arrest everyone who saw it," Raphael said. "Forget it. Too much paperwork."

"I agree. Instead, I'm moving Fetch up from Columbus. Time over target fifteen minutes, and I can have Spot back on station in forty-five minutes."

"Excellent. You're reading my mind again, Tom." Raphael pivoted to Intelligence. "Ari, can you make anything of Spot's radar image?"

Ari rubbed his face. "You've got me. We're trying to correlate this image with the one we captured outside Columbus four hours ago, but I can't make any sense out of this visually."

Raphael stroked his chin and squinted at the image. "I can't either. It looks like a bunny with a goiter."

Ari laughed. "It does, doesn't it? However, I can draw other conclusions. Spot says this car's moving north at eighty-seven miles an hour. That road has a forty-five mile an hour speed limit, so this looks like panic flight. Wait…" Ari pressed his headset to his ear and listened. "There's a correlation in the bullet holes, Raf. They match in both images. This is Warner's car."

"Excellent work, Ari. Just excellent." Raphael whistled under his breath. "Eighty-seven in a forty-five. We should call her the Lead Foot Rebel." He smiled and snapped his fingers. "No! The Rebel Without a Pause! Whaddaya think?"

Ari smiled and leaned back in his chair. "Catchy. It's very Hollywood. If I might continue, though? If Warner's in that car, she's under stress. She's tired, she's wounded – perhaps seriously – and she also may be running out of gas. Her last recorded fuel purchase was September sixth, and unless she got some bootleg fuel somewhere, this car is at the end of its cruising range. We may not have to catch her. We might wear her out first."

"Even better," Raphael said. "Say, what do you think Downs would do if we caught Warner tonight?"

"He'd either kiss you or kill you."

He barked a short laugh and clapped his shoulder. "And that's why you'll tell him, Ari."

"Why would I do that? If he kills you, I get your job."

Raphael shook his head and grinned. "That's bloodthirsty, man. Just plain bloodthirsty."

JACK RIPLEY LUMBERED DOWN THE CREAKING STAIRS into a small room. He opened the door to his garage with a squeak from its rusty hinges and switched on the fluorescent light illuminating his messy workbench.

He might have a visitor if he was lucky, and he needed to make room for her. It took him a few minutes to pick up the boxes strewn around the empty parking space beside his pickup truck. When it was clear, he switched off the light.

The garage door was stuck, as it often was in the evenings, but he persuaded it to rise with a sharp yank. After poking his head out and looking both ways, he crept into the alley to check if anybody was around. The town was quiet tonight, but his heart wasn't – his pulse pounded in his ears.

He ran his fingers through his gray hair and frowned: This was a game for kids like Warner, not a fifty-six-year-old man with a settled life. He had no right to risk everything he'd worked to preserve over all those years of strife and challenge. He had no right to put Elise in jeopardy.

He had no right to be more excited than he'd been for a decade.

After taking in the night air, he sauntered back into the garage, sat in the front seat of his pickup, and rested his chin in his palm.

ADA FIDGETED IN HER SEAT as they rolled north on Route 23. "This is taking for-freakin-ever. Can I put on some music? Please?"

"I need you to navigate, not smash air guitars on an imaginary stage. Some other time, okay?"

She crossed her arms. "I oughta go on strike till you negotiate. This is inhuman. You have thousands of killer tracks in the car computer, and I can't hear a single one. I'm ready to just plug a jack in it and stick the other end into a vein and download straight into my bloodstream."

"But we'll be there soon. I'll get you a tablet, I swear it, as soon as people stop trying to kill me. Now how far away is it?"

"Three-point-one miles," Ada muttered.

Soon after, a brown sign appeared on the right, and Krista pulled over to get a clearer view. It was an engraved wooden panel, hanging from an arbor and covered in once-lush vines that had turned dry and brown. It said:

WELCOME TO MARAVELLE
POPULATION 312 YOU
"WE'D LOVE YOUR COMPANY!"

Krista rubbed her temples and moaned softly. "I said *Maryville.*"

"Right. Maravelle." Ada pointed at the sign. "That's where we are." Krista spelled the name for her and Ada's face sank. "Look, you have this accent and it's hard to understand when you go all leprechaun on me."

"*Ay, caramba!*" Krista sagged in her seat.

"Did he spell it for you? Maybe he said Maravelle instead of Maryville. I know Maravelle has a Main Street, so maybe this is where we actually oughta be."

"It's possible I just thought he said Maryville. All right, let's see if we can find his place since we're here." She pulled the car back onto the road. "This must be a big town. I don't see any lights yet. We must be far out."

"It doesn't look that big on the map. It's just a few streets near a railroad." Ada pointed through the windshield. "I see something ahead over there."

As they approached, they saw buildings lining the road behind shadowy street trees and antique light poles. The buildings were brick, but their windows were broken and the insides were ransacked. A stone sidewalk coated with thick dust ran into the distance.

"This doesn't look promising," Ada said, and Krista nodded as she peered at the road ahead.

The buildings ended at an intersection with a trash-bag-covered traffic light. "This is Main Street. Turn left here," Ada said.

The street was wide enough for four lanes of traffic, but it was empty except for a few tires and bags of trash scattered across the road. A yellow light glowed off to the right, and as they passed, they saw the remains of a collapsed grain silo in a graveled, weedy yard.

"Ahead on the left, between those two buildings. Is that an alley?" Ada asked.

"It looks like one. That must be our turn." Krista maneuvered the car into a narrow gap between two wooden houses; at the end of the alley, an empty field ran behind the buildings they'd passed coming into town. However, they saw no garage like Jack had described.

Krista stopped the car and peered through the windshield. "This is the wrong alley. This is the wrong town. This place is totally dead, kiddo." Ada punched her hard, and the blow caught her by surprise. "Oww!" she yelled, rubbing her right arm. "What was that for?"

"Stop calling me that." She snapped open the atlas and turned on a map light. "I'll try to fix your damned problem even though you don't deserve it. Just shut up and give the *kid* a minute." She ran her fingers up and down the map, squinting in the dim light to read the small letters. "Okay, don't get all snotty with me, but there *is* a Maryville. It's back the way we came –" She looked up. "There's a drone out there. I can barely hear it, but I remember that sound."

Krista lowered her window and nodded. "That's what I heard just before I got hit with that death ray or whatever."

"You got that too? Did you get the heebie-jeebies like me?"

Krista nodded, raised the window, and turned off the headlights. "We're hidden here. Unless it comes right overhead, it might not see us. It's almost like being in a carwash. Turn off the light."

They hunched down in their seats as the hollow bass sound grew until its echoes resounded throughout the town. The drone passed far to the left and then followed the highway north.

"I don't think it saw us, but that was a little too close for comfort," Krista said. "Time to blow this burg. Which way to Maryville?"

Ada opened the atlas again. "Go back the way we came, and after about fifteen miles, bear right on Route 614. That'll take us straight to Maryville."

"Nothing," Tom said. "The two ground units met up about ten miles north of Maravelle, but they saw nothing. Neither did the dash radars."

Ryan swiveled in his chair to face the podium. "Fetch acquired nothing too. No vehicles, no humans except for ours. That road is deserted."

"Did we miss the black hole in the middle of the road? Unless there's a black hole, folks, she's still on this Earth." Raphael turned to the map. "There's only one major road that connects to Route 23, this Route 614 here. Maybe she took that. She was south of it when Spot acquired her."

Ari drew across the map up on the Wall. "Fetch followed Route 23 a few minutes later and scanned for a mile down 614, so it's unlikely she took that route. Besides, it doesn't fit into the pattern of panic flight. Route 614 heads southwest. Why would someone in a panic turn around and go back nearly the same way she came?"

"Maybe she's more devious than we've assumed, Ari," Raphael said. "Maybe she isn't panicking at all." He looked up at the Wall and shook his head. "All this theorizing is meaningless anyway. She's probably hiding off the road somewhere, maybe in an abandoned outbuilding or even in Maravelle." He stepped up onto the podium. "Tom, bring your units south. Have one scope out Maravelle and have the other check any outbuildings within sight of the road. Bring Fetch down a mile west of Route 23 to scan that area, and when Spot arrives, send it down the east side."

"When do I turn?" Krista asked.

"At this speed, five minutes and forty seconds. Don't worry. I'm looking for road signs." Ada unscrewed the cap from the last bottle of protein drink and handed it to her.

"Sorry I popped off at you back there. The truth is that I'd rather have you navigating for me instead of any stupid satnav system. It never handed me drinks or lit my cigarettes for me. Or stitched my wounds, either. Thanks for all that."

"You're welcome," Ada said. "Buy me a tablet and it's all forgiven. I'll even be extra nice to you."

"You're really obsessing on that, aren't you?" Krista asked.

Ada nodded and pointed out the window at a road sign. "Route 614 in two miles. Watch for it. It's a small road, and it'll be easy to miss in this soup."

"Acquisition! '40 Bicep D4, Route 614, three miles northeast of Stenson, heading southwest at seventy miles an hour."

Raphael pivoted to Tactical, but Tom was already redeploying the teams. "I'm moving both units down 614, and I have another in Springfield moving northeast. Fetch is turning to pursue. I'll give ETA's when I have them."

"Excellent," Raphael said as the map popped up on the Wall. "Let's get in touch with the police departments along this road. Contact Stenson, Maryville, Standard, and Meconium. Get the mayberries moving."

KRISTA AND ADA ZOOMED THROUGH STENSON. They hadn't seen any road signs in the fug and were surprised when buildings flitted past the windows.

"And there goes Stenson," Ada said from the pages of the atlas. "That means we have another eight miles to Maryville, seven minutes and five seconds at this speed."

Krista grunted a reply as she glanced into the rear-view mirror. "Maybe I'm getting groggy and I'm seeing things, but I'd swear there are lights behind us on the road. Take a look for me, wouldja?"

Ada turned in her seat and peered out the back window. "It's hard to tell with your taillights on. They make the fug all red. Can you turn them off?" Krista clicked the headlights off, and Ada climbed into the backseat. "You're right. There's a glow back there and it's not getting smaller. It has to be a car."

"We're being followed. I thought so." Krista pressed down on the gas. "I'll leave the headlights off. They're useless in this fug anyway."

Ada climbed into the front seat and buckled her seat belt. "Five minutes and ten seconds now. When we get into Maryville, you'll need to slow down. Main Street is only three blocks in."

"If I use my brakes, I'll give away our location to this guy, and we've got to assume it's a Federal. I'll downshift and slow down that way, and I'll have to downshift to turn on Main Street too. This is going to be a little rough."

Ada looked over her shoulder and squinted through the back window for a minute. "Whatever. Okay, that's definitely a Federal. There are flashing lights on it, I think, or maybe my eyes are going screwy too. I'm pretty sure I see red and blue flashes…oh yeah. This guy's closing in on us, Krista." She turned and pointed through the windshield. "Someone's coming at us from the front too."

"I see it, I see it," Krista said through clenched teeth.

"Three minutes and twelve seconds."

"This'll be close. Look out and let me know when we're in the town, okay?"

Ada looked over her shoulder again. "He's only a few hundred yards behind now."

"Splendid! Now look for the feckin town, wouldja?"

Two minutes later Ada called out, "I just saw houses. We're in town!"

Krista shifted down a gear, and the car slowed slightly. "Shit, I'm still going fifty."

"Just passed Hooper. Two blocks to go." A few moments later, she saw tall brick buildings ahead lining both sides of the road. "This is Memorial. One block to Main."

Krista downshifted another gear and the engine strained to slow the car, but it was still going forty miles an hour as they approached Main Street. The lights of the Federal car were just a hundred yards behind, and another police car was a hundred yards ahead.

The wall of buildings ended suddenly. She downshifted again and yanked the wheel hard left, and the car screeched around the corner onto Main Street.

⊂━⊃━⊂━⊃

　　　　　　　　　　　　　　　　　　　　　Rebel Without a Pause

JACK RIPLEY SAT IN THE FRONT SEAT with his feet on the running board and his chin in his hands. He'd been waiting for more than an hour, and he was beginning to accept that she wouldn't show up.

Her chances were slim – half the country was looking for her, and the radio was broadcasting every sighting and every rumor. She didn't make it; that was the hard truth, and it was time to take it like a man.

He looked through the garage door at the dark alley and thought what the next workday would hold. Another eight hours on the Belt was grueling, but eight hours with dashed hopes would be worse.

He decided to give Warner a few more minutes. Growing up in Ohio, he'd learned early how to be patient and wait for something interesting to deliver redemption from small-town life's crushing dullness. As a teenager, he'd spent hours watching the phone and hoping it would ring, always giving it a few more minutes. Sometimes it rang, and a salesman was on the other end and not Becky, but he'd still listen to the man's pitch.

A half-smile crept across his face. Bouncing Becky – back in the Nineties when girls were still wild and cars were still fast and the horizon was so far away it didn't matter.

His feet tingled when they touched the concrete floor, and he danced an awkward jig in the dark garage until they felt normal again. He pulled up the pants that always slid off his skinny rear, cinched his belt tight, and then walked to the garage door and reached for the handle. It was time to give up.

As he started to pull it down, he heard the roar of a high-powered engine from somewhere up Route 614. He walked toward Main Street to see, and then tires squealed at the intersection and screeched down the street. He ducked beside a wall, but the car stopped and its turbines whistled down to rest. The smell of tortured rubber tickled his nose.

He heard the soft whir of the car's cooling fans somewhere on the fuggy street ahead but couldn't see it. It stayed motionless as the engine cooled down, and he wondered if the driver had been hurt when the car slid down the street.

He'd just started toward it to help when he heard more commotion from the intersection of 614 and Main. The fug flickered with red and blue lights, and then a pair of cars met at the intersection; men's voices filtered through the fug, and he heard the braying laugh of Officer Hollis, who always laughed like a donkey on nitrous. He was talking to another man in a much larger car that looked like a Silverback.

He squinted into the street, and in the glow of the cops' headlights, he barely discerned the rounded shape of a dark Bicep hunched in the fug, whirring softly, trying to be invisible while the cops chatted a hundred feet away. It looked like Warner's car, and his heartbeat stumbled and righted itself again.

Hollis was still talking, and Jack prayed that the Federal man wouldn't ask him about the Ohio State Buckeyes. The cops sat and babbled, oblivious of their prey a few feet away, and Jack's blood pressure soared.

After a few eons, a driver finally thumped his palm against the door, and the Federal vehicle moved down 614. Hollis and his mouth turned up Main. Jack watched the taillights recede and then turned to find the car, but the whirring sound was already passing him. Rubber crunched over loose asphalt as the car slid by, and he followed it down the alley. At the door to his garage, he heard the front wheels groan as the car turned in.

He ran inside, wiped his sweaty palms, and reached up for the handle. The door dropped with a clatter and threw the garage into complete darkness, and he stumbled to the workbench and flipped the light switch.

It shone on a slate-blue Bicep. It was filthy and battered, the front bumper and hood were bashed, and the paint was scraped off the front fender, but the phone had finally rung: This was *the* Bicep.

He tried to see inside, but bugs and dust spattered the windshield and the glare from the workbench light made it opaque. The car rocked as someone moved inside and thumped the driver's door.

It creaked open, and a woman with auburn hair climbed out. Even drawn and tired, she was gorgeous – big blue eyes, a sprinkling of honest freckles, lips built for long nights of kissing. His heart skipped another beat as he realized he was looking at Krista Warner.

She stood in the open doorway and eyed him warily for a long second. "I'm really hoping you're Jack Ripley," she said with a voice smoother than Irish cream.

He reminded himself to breathe, but he couldn't, so he just nodded. She smiled in return; her smile was the stuff of his teenage dreams, filled with unalloyed joy but also seasoned with shyness and vulnerability.

She ducked into the car and spoke to someone. The car jiggled again, and she stood holding a backpack and a small black tablet computer. Jack gulped at the sight – it was the most important tablet in the known universe, and people had died to get their hands on it. She slid it casually into a pants pocket and walked around the car.

"I appreciate your help, Jack." She wrapped her arms around him, and in her hair, he smelled strawberries, chocolate, gunpowder, and jasmine; the scents stormed his brain and short-circuited his lungs again so he could only nod in return.

The car jiggled again, and she walked to the passenger door and pulled it open. A small blonde girl climbed from inside. She moved awkwardly, and when Krista closed the door, he understood why – the girl's pants were shredded and bloody.

He cursed and ran forward to take her arm.

DISPATCHES

Midnight Sun
News Post of September 20, 2043

WARNER INVADES COLUMBUS, HUMILIATES NSF FORCES

Our Witness from Columbus reports he has escaped the city and found safety, and he also delivers the heartening news that the dissident journalist Krista Warner is still alive:

"I almost didn't make it last night. To get across the river, I had to go through Columbus. It was like that circle of Hell where they put the real bad ones: looters, goons, what have you, they were all out.

"I didn't shoot the looters cuz they were going about their business, but the goons were another thing. They were bustin and breakin and killin just cuz they could. I took out the ones I needed to, and you don't have to thank me for that. I underestimated just how many hostiles were out there, though.

"I got boxed in eight blocks from the LaSalle footbridge. I was hidin in a store, givin myself the last rites, when a blue Bicep pulled up. Bullets were zippin all around that street, but the gorgeous redhead drivin it just tosses her hair back like there was nothin to worry about.

"Krista Warner rescued me and got me outta that hole. And she got me to the footbridge and then – get this – she drove right over the damn thing! It's not even finished! It scared the shit outta me, the way that bridge was buckin and wavin, nothin but air on both sides, but not her. And when we got across, she vanished like a shadow in the night and left those Federal clowns lookin like the fools they are.

"They'll never get her. I been in combat and I seen this kind of bravery before. It's the kind you can't stop, the kind soldiers follow. If I was Gabriel Cheyn, I'd be pickin out my funeral suit."

NO BROTHERLY LOVE IN PHILADELPHIA

Our Witness in Philadelphia says the local population is preparing for conflict:

"A lot of people are arming themselves here. They're sure that there's gonna be a fight with the Federals again, and they don't want to be caught with their shorts down like the Rust Belt cities.

"Here's the ominous thing – just preparing for it makes it more likely. If the Federals don't bring the fight to the City, the City's gonna bring the fight to the Federals. There's just a bad feeling in the air, like the ax will drop soon.

"Walking these streets and talking to these people, I feel like the tipping point's already been passed. It's tense everywhere I go – everyone is quiet, watchful, expecting something to happen. Waiting for the starting gun, you could say.

"Everyone I know is watching Warner's escape, and one store has a clock in its window that shows how long the Federals have been hunting her. I'm looking at it now – it says 105 hours, 27 minutes. As long as that clock's running, Philadelphia's Own Daughter is still free.

"They call it the Freedom Clock, and people come here just to look at it. I think it gives them hope."

TOURNIQUET

Day 33
Sunday morning, September 20, 2043
National Tranquility Center, Fort Belvoir, Virginia

Raphael didn't turn when Downs stepped onto the podium; the custom was to let the relieving Watcher become oriented before breaking watch. He didn't have much to say because Downs had been fully briefed before stepping into the Watch Room. The two men watched the world flit by on the Wall for a few minutes.

"I hear you acquired Warner twice last night, Raf."

"It was actually exciting here for a change. We were hot on the trail of the Rebel Without a Pause for half the night."

Downs peered over his glasses. "Was that a joke?"

Raphael coughed into his hand. "It was until just now. Well, the Watch is yours, Bob. Good hunting." He stepped off the podium and hurried to the door.

Hogue was already seated at her station and taking charge of the Executive field teams. When she finished, she displayed the updated deployments of her tactical assets on the Wall. Downs scanned the list for a minute. "We're low on situated resources in a critical area of operation this morning, Miss Hogue. We have all the Special Activity Groups from West Virginia deployed, so why are we operating at less than half strength?"

"Sir, our teams worked far beyond operational parameters yesterday and through most of the night. Eleven of the twenty-four teams haven't slept in thirty hours. They need rest."

Downs looked at the map on the Wall, which showed a long oval shape encircling four small towns in central Ohio. "The most wanted fugitive in America is in there, so I don't care if the boys are a little groggy. Give them caffeine pills or something. We need two hundred men to tighten this cordon and execute the house-to-house search, and you show ninety-seven available for duty. This is unacceptable."

"Sir, tired personnel make unrecoverable errors. These teams are unready for any operation more than guard duty at this moment. I can release them in six hours, and in the meantime, the cordon will remain in place. Warner won't escape, sir. We can wait till we're ready."

Downs' face reddened, and he was about to snap a reply when Buta cut in. "Sir, we have two drones operating on visual acquisition. The fug is light today, and if it burns off more, we can employ the Blackeyes as well. Surveillance conditions are near optimal, and I'm confident we can keep a close eye on all movements within the inclusion zone until search operations commence."

Downs took a deep breath. "Very well. Initiate the search at precisely three o'clock this afternoon, Miss Hogue."

RAINBOWS OF GRAY

Day 33
Sunday morning, September 20, 2043
430 Springfield Road, Maryville, Ohio

Krista blinked a few times and gazed at the unfamiliar ceiling. Ada's arm was draped across her chest, and she pried it off and sat up on the side of the bed. She stood, stretched the stiffness from her bones, and stumbled to the bathroom.

It was as alien as a Martian landscape. The white wainscot, the tacky wallpaper, the plastic models of submarines on the shelf, the silly shower curtain with teen heartthrobs printed on it – she'd never seen them in her life. Standing on her tiptoes, she looked through the small window; the fug was no more than a haze and she could see far up the street, but the rows of brick buildings and stores were unfamiliar. The four black streaks of rubber on the roadway below tickled a faint memory, though.

A mirror hung over the small ceramic sink, and she saw Krista in it and breathed a relieved sigh. She was half-expecting to see someone else. She pulled a lock of her hair to her nose and sniffed it, and it smelled like strawberries and jasmine. That was her shampoo, so she'd showered recently.

She asked Krista what the hell was going on but just received a puzzled look in return. Giving up, she returned to the bedroom and the soft sound of snoring. Ada was pressed into the bed again and sleeping like the dead.

The floor outside the door creaked, and a wide woman with candy-apple red hair and a figure like stacked bowling balls walked through the doorway with a bundle in her hands. Her round face radiated happiness and contentment, and she smiled when she saw Krista. "Well, I thought you'd never get up, sleepyhead," she said.

"Where am I?"

"Oh, you're in Tala's room." She smiled again and dropped the bundle on the dresser, and then she sized up the prone Ada and walked to a closet. She rummaged inside and returned with an armful of clothes.

"And may I ask where Tala's room is?" Krista asked, and the woman blinked.

"It's right here, dear. You're in it. You still look a little off, not that you don't have reason to be. Some food will set you aright. As soon as Tala gets up, y'all come to the dining room. I'm making a nice breakfast for all of us. I hope you like bacon cuz it's all we have."

Krista forced a smile to her face until the woman left and then pulled aside the blinds at the bedroom window. The storefront windows across the street were papered with pictures of people wearing edgy haircuts; the sign over the entrance said BARBERY PIRATES. The store next to it was called MARYVILLE PAWNBROKERS, and down the street…Maryville! That's where she was. She sat on the bed and shook Ada until she grumbled.

"What do you have against sleep?" Ada mumbled.

"C'mon, slug-a-bed, shake a leg. We're in Maryville."

"I know. Jeez, you don't have to wake me up to tell me. We've been here since last night, don't you remember?"

"We've got to make sure we're safe. Get dressed so we can be ready to go if we have to."

"We're safe, the Ripleys are nice people, and I'm tired. Shut up and leave me alone."

"Some strange lady came in and –"

"That's Elise. You met her last night. Maybe you have amnesia or something." Ada pulled a pillow over her head and fidgeted under the covers, and then she sat up and threw the pillow at Krista. "You suck! Now I'm awake!" She climbed out of bed and limped into the bathroom, making sure to stomp her good foot, and slammed the door behind her. "And if we're in such a big hurry, why don't you get dressed, Lady Godiva?" she yelled through the door.

Krista swore and reached for the bundle on the dresser. Her clothes were washed and ironed; she pulled out her panties and sweatpants and found them starched stiff. When she finished cracking the starchy crust, she dressed and piled the clothes Elise left for Ada on the bed. "How are you feeling this morning? How are those boo-boos?" she asked when the bathroom door opened.

"They hurt like hell, but they oughta." Ada pulled a pair of jeans off the bed. "Are these for me?"

Krista nodded, and Ada scowled as she turned the pants over in her hand. "There's been a mistake. I only wear black, and these are brown. Brown went out of style five minutes after it was invented. Dork Factor Nine, Mr. Sulu."

"God, you're in a foul mood this morning," Krista said.

"Yeah, from lack of sleep." Ada slid into the jeans, which fit as if they'd been painted on. "They're hunormous! It's like wearing trash bags! I can't be seen in these!"

"We're trying not to be seen at all, so it doesn't matter. Stop whining and let's go eat."

"Wait. Before we go, I want you to check me over for scars. If Blue Ball planted one chip in me, they probably planted more. They're all about redundancy." She pulled off the pants and tossed them on the bed. "Okay, it's disgusting, but we need to do this."

"Who's this Blue Ball?"

"It's complicated. Please, check everywhere I can't see."

Krista checked her scalp, her armpits, every follicle and pore of her skin, and even the soles of her feet, but the only scar she found was under her left elbow, which Ada said she got when she broke her arm at the age of six. "I think you're clean," Krista said.

"Maybe they found a way to do it without leaving a scar."

"Maybe you're getting paranoid."

"Yeah, that could be." Ada pulled on her pants, and then her stomach rumbled. "I'm hungry. Let's eat."

The kitchen was right outside the bedroom. Elise worked in front of a range with three sizzling frying pans, and a mound of bacon lay on a serving plate next to her.

"Good morning, Aunt Elise!" Ada called.

"Well, good morning to you, Tala. Did you like the bed?"

Ada nodded and slipped a slice of bacon from the plate, and Elise smacked her wrist. "Why, you little sneak! Wait for breakfast, dear."

They walked to the other side of the room, where a small dining table sat in an alcove. "Was I asleep for a week?" Krista asked.

"No, just last night. Why?"

"Nothing. Hey, now *that's* a beautiful window." The alcove's small window was filled with a wonder of stained glass; colorful flowers, buds, and vines wove and glinted across the window and cast small splotches of colored light on the table. "It's a splendid bit of work."

A man behind her said, "I'm glad you like it. I made it."

Krista turned around and saw the man who'd helped them last night. "Oh, hello, Mr. Ripley."

"Call me Jack, please."

Ada waved from the other end of the table. "Hey, Uncle Jack."

Jack smiled. "Morning, little one. I hope you slept all right. Tala's bed was only built for one."

"I slept on top of the blanket and never felt the springs, just like you said."

"See?" Jack said. "I took a stroll 'round town this morning. Nobody's looking for you, so I don't think you'll have any problem staying here. You'll be safe here for a few days."

"Thanks," Krista said. "We need a little time to recover. Yesterday was absolutely horrible."

"Take your time. Stay as long as you need to. We're happy to help any way we can."

Elise set the plate of bacon on the table, along with a loaf of toast, and then clasped her hands and frowned. "I hope that's enough. I only made two pounds, but I can make more if anyone wants. It's no trouble."

"It's more than enough, Elise. Everybody sit. I'm starved," Jack said as he plucked bacon from the plate. "By the way, I always read your articles. You're a really good writer."

"Why, thank you," Krista said. "It's good to know my work is appreciated."

"Oh, it is. I especially liked your story about Bingo, that orangutan that…what's wrong?"

Krista was squeezing a piece of bacon into a greasy little ball, a dark look on her face. "Nothing, Jack. Let's talk about something else, okay?" She pointed to the stained-glass window. "You have a dazzling talent. That's absolutely beautiful."

"Thanks. I used to get a lot of commissions once, but around seven, eight years ago, the work dried up. I blame the fug cuz stained glass looks dead in hazy light. You need sharp sun to bring the work alive."

"It's gorgeous in the sun," Elise said. "On sunny days, I sometimes just sit here for hours and look at it." She looked at the empty plate and frowned. "We're out of bacon. I'll make more."

"No thanks, Elise. I'm stuffed," Jack said.

She looked at Krista and Ada, who shook their heads, and then she waddled back to the kitchen. A few seconds later, fresh bacon started to sizzle.

Jack leaned forward. "Look, she'll just keep feeding us if we stay here. How about we go downstairs? I'll show you where I make stained glass."

They nodded, and everyone got up from the table and thanked Elise. Jack walked through the living room to a flight of stairs, and then he stopped when he heard the Morse code of their limps behind him. "I'm sorry. That was thoughtless of me. Lemme help." He swept Ada into his arms and carried her downstairs.

"Really, don't bother," Krista mumbled to the empty room. She limped down the stairs after them.

Jack held open a door at the bottom for Krista. She walked into a large room with windows on two sides opening onto the street, and stained-glass panels hung in each one. Colors and shapes washed the floors and walls. A single large table sat in the center of the long space, surrounded by stools, and the back wall was lined with racks holding hundreds of pieces of glass. Small pieces of glass and lead littered every horizontal surface.

Krista walked along the window wall while Ada wandered to the racks. "Fallingknife Studio. That's an interesting name," Krista said, looking at a label on one of the pieces. "Where'd you get it?"

"My dad was Navajo, so he gave me that for a middle name. It sounded artsier than Ripley Studio, so I went with that."

"Interesting. You know, these are gorgeous." She stopped at a large panel of multicolored roses. "I absolutely love this one. And every one is different. Some are like Tiffany glass, but I like the geometric art glass you did too."

"I like to experiment," he said. "It sounds like you know something about the art."

Krista shook her head. "Not really. My mom was a raging Cathoholic, and she dragged me to the Latin Rite mass every morning. It was deadly boring, and I never understood a word, so I got to know the windows well. That was the only good thing I got from going to church, honestly."

"You're not the religious type, I guess?"

"I was, but the Church talked the faith right out of me. After my mom died, I asked the priest why God took her away. He said I shouldn't question God's bloody ineffable will unless I wanted a long stint in Hell. That was it for me. Any priest wants me to bend a knee to his god anymore, he'll have to kiss my feckin ass first and apologize."

"I'm almost there myself. I sometimes wonder if God…" Jack leaned against the worktable, crossing his arms. "Anyway, church work used to be a big part of my business, but once the Arkies started moving in, it dried up. Those folks are weird. I never met one I liked."

"Sure you have," Ada called from the back of the room, where she was looking at a shelf filled with glass bottles. "I'm an Archangelist."

"Are you now?" Krista asked.

"Yeah, and so's my mom. Everyone in Washington is, I think."

"Sorry, I didn't mean to be insulting," Jack said. "My mouth just runs on its own sometimes."

"Oh, I'm not bothered. We just go to the dunking every year. We don't go to services or act like we sleep in the freakin Shroud of Turin every night. I don't think they care if we show up as long as Mom pays the dues."

"They're a business, not a religion, but they're pretty harmless," Krista said.

Jack scratched his head. "You sure? They have that much money and power, and you think they don't use it?" He called out to Ada. "Hey, leave those bottles alone. That stuff's dangerous."

Ada held a small glass bottle in her hand and turned it over. "Don't worry. I've handled scarier goo than this."

"Just be careful. I use that for cleaning stained glass." He pulled two stools from under the table for him and Krista. "That's mostly what I do anymore – clean and restore installed glass that the fug eats away at. Not much of that work anymore, though, so it's good I have a day job."

"What do you do?" asked Krista.

"I work up at KLEPTCO Bellefontaine. It's a twelve-megawatt coal-fired generation plant, and I'm a beltman there. I was lucky to get the job because the plant's mostly automated. There's only five employees per shift."

"Klepco?"

Jack spelled it out for her. "It's short for Klean Power Transmission Company."

"Seriously? KLEPTCO? You must be joking!" Krista giggled. "Isn't that a little obvious, even for a corporation?"

He blinked his eyes a few times and then shrugged. "Sorry, I don't get it."

"Never mind. So what's a talented stained-glass artist do in a generating plant?"

"Like I said, I'm a beltman. I watch the Belt for eight hours a day trying to find Hot Rocks. You need a sharp eye for color and sheen to find those, so I was a natural for the job."

"What's a Hot Rock?" Krista asked.

The back door opened and Elise waddled through. "I'm getting ready to make lunch. What does everybody want?"

"Good lord, woman, I can still taste the bacon I ate ten minutes ago."

Elise smiled. "I just made more, so I was thinking I'd make a nice stack of BLT's for everyone. What do you say?"

"We don't have any lettuce or tomatoes, Elise."

Rainbows of Gray

"That's fine. We'll make do. Is everybody hungry?"

They protested that they were still too full to eat. Elise dragged a stool over, pulled a long cigarette holder from her pocket, and lit up. "Okay, I'll wait here till everybody's hungry. Go ahead and never mind me."

"All right. So what's a Hot Rock?" Krista asked.

"A Hot Rock is a bomb, dear," Elise said, and Ada walked to the table, her dark eyes glittering. "The coal loads are full of them sometimes. What's the record, Jack?"

"Forty-eight in one load last month, but that train came from Scranton. We expected it to be hot."

Krista shook her head and groaned. "Can we back up a little? I'm a little lost."

Jack took a deep breath. "The whole valley that Scranton's in is being strip-mined, and people there are resisting. Some dissident in Scranton is making these clever little bombs that look just like lumps of anthracite, except they're just a little grayer and a little duller. The Scranton trains come full of Hot Rocks, and there's no way to find them before they get into the furnaces except to have someone look for them and pick them out. That's what I do. They're sophisticated, too – they have heat-sensitive fuses, and they're made of some super-powerful explosive that's real hard to make."

"Which one?" Ada asked.

"I don't remember what the FBI said, sounds something like Tricky Dicky –"

"Triskadecagen?" she asked.

He pointed at her. "Bingo! That's it."

"That's crazy hard stuff to make," she said with a tinge of awe.

"Anyway, that's what I do. It keeps us afloat, and we did get the vaccine because I'm an essential worker, but I can't say it's a real fulfilling job."

"Y'know, sometimes Jack lets Hot Rocks go through," Elise said, leaning toward Krista. "Bo-o-om!"

"Elise!"

"Krista's one of us, dear. Who's she going to tell?" She turned to Krista. "My Jack's a little rebel too."

"I'm not a rebel if I just stand aside and let someone else do the work. Besides, they only blow up in the preheaters, which doesn't stop the plant.

Anarchista | *Alanson Rand*   71

But if one got into a furnace…" His eyes glinted and a smile barely came to his lips. "Okay, it's a small rebellion, but I'm a small man. It's all I can do."

"I'm so proud of him," Elise said to Krista. "He's doing all he can, and that's more than most people. There are so many small men, and if they all pitched in and fought, things would change. We'd stop getting stepped on."

"Wow. I wouldn't have pegged you two as revolutionaries," Krista said. "That's great."

"It'd be great if it worked," Jack said. "But it doesn't. Maybe people like me can slow down the Big Man, but we can't knock him over. If more people resisted, there'd be real change." Jack looked at her intently. "That might happen now that the resistance has a face."

Krista propped her elbows on the table and rubbed her temples. "I know, I know, I'm some marvelous hero now."

"You're more than that," Jack said. "You read *Midnight Sun* this morning?"

"You're practically the flag of the resistance, dear. As long as you fly, the dissidents grow stronger." Elise patted her hand. "You must be so happy. And all you have to do is not die and everything will be awesome!" She stood and the floor creaked in protest. "Now, I'm just plain famished. Tala, come help me in the kitchen, dear, it's time to make everyone lunch."

They sat in silence until they heard Elise and Ada moving around in the kitchen above. Jack reached under a counter by the window and pulled two beer bottles from a small refrigerator, twisted off the caps, and sat on the stool again. "You're not happy with this larger-than-life thing, are you?"

Krista lit a cigarette and watched the cloud dance in the hazy, polychrome light. "I never wanted to be a celebrity. I've seen what it does to people, and it's ugly. If I could become invisible, I would."

"That's no fun either, trust me. Try living smaller than life for a while." He waved his bottle around the room. "It's no treat being small and invisible."

"But at least your life is real."

He took a pull of his beer and smacked his lips. "Yeah. That's the part that blows, huh?"

"I don't think so, Jack. I always wanted the life you have – normal, predictable, happy. You're selling yourself short."

"Living in my own mausoleum and waiting for the end? This is the Jack Ripley Museum, Krista. I'm surrounded by everything that *was* good, not anything that *is*." He flicked a few droplets off the bottle, turned it around a few times, and read the label. "That's why I don't come down here anymore. Why remind myself that I'm less than I was?"

"If that bothers you, why don't you move on and chase a different dream?"

The floorboards creaked above, and he watched them for a few moments. "I hear that from Elise all the time, and I don't need to hear that from you."

"It's none of my business, I know."

"Damn right, it isn't." He emptied the bottle and threw it into a trash can. "Dreams, causes. Those are for children. Me, I'm just trying to get along without them anymore and not get squashed." He stared at the trash can for a few moments and ran his fingers through his hair, and then he suddenly slapped his palm on the table. "Look, your star is burning bright now. Burn as bright as you can while you can, all right? It doesn't last forever. Take your chances, take your risks. This is your time, and you have to live it to your fullest, and you're cheating yourself if you don't. Act larger than life and you might find out you actually are." He sagged and looked around the room. "You act smaller than life, you might find out the same thing."

Krista examined the ashtray for a few seconds. "I might get killed if I do that, Jack."

"But you might not. Don't let death scare you. Make it surprise you. It's no party seeing the end coming a long way off. How's that better?"

"Well, I wouldn't be dead, boyo! It's easy for you to wag your chin about how splendid this little adventure is because they're not shooting at your feckin ass. Sure as hell they're shooting at mine, and that sucks a helluva lot more than faded dreams ever will."

"You don't know what you're talking about. Get to my age and see how you feel about a wasted youth. Trust me on this."

She mashed her cigarette into the ashtray. "Don't go giving me advice you never followed. Get out and live your own life. Take your own chances."

His shoulders sagged, and he gazed at a corner of the room with unfocused eyes. "My starting gun went off a long time ago and I just stood there. I can't catch up now."

"My starting gun went off, and it was aimed at me, and I've been running my ass off ever since. Isn't that good enough?"

"It's good enough for you, but it isn't for the rest of us." He reached for the bottle of beer she hadn't touched and then took a hard pull. "Elise said it best – you're our flag. You've gotta wave proud and high, like that flag Francis Scott Key wrote about – as long as it flies, the fight's still on and we're still free. And the longer that flag flies, the more powerful a symbol it becomes, the more of a legend it becomes, the more people rally around it." He drained the bottle and banged it on the table. "You don't even have to fight. You just have to stand for something and endure. How goddamn hard is that?"

He's right, Miss Kellen. You're more than you think.

"Stop this bloody badgering, wouldja?" Krista moaned, and she bent over and pulled at her hair.

"Yeah," Jack said. "You're right. It isn't my place to comment on what you do. You're way up in the sky, and I live in the ditches." He stood and walked to the trash can.

"Jack, that's not what I –"

"It's all right. I'm sorry for stepping out of line, and I should stay in my place." He set the bottle in the trash without a sound. The floorboards above thumped three times, and he looked up at the ceiling. "Why don't we go get some lunch?"

ADA STOOD IN FRONT OF A WALL MIRROR and eyed her figure. "These pants won't be baggy anymore if I keep eating like this."

"I'm stuffed too," Krista said. "It's either feast or famine lately, isn't it?" She walked around the cluttered living room and checked out the photographs and knick-knacks on the walls. Even though it was the size of the dining room and kitchen combined, it seemed smaller because every surface was covered in memorabilia.

A wood shelf heavy with photographs was screwed to the wall, with a model of a black submarine sitting in the center. Krista maneuvered through the mess and glanced at the largest picture: It was a photograph of a young blonde woman that looked vaguely like Ada, except that she was much older and dressed in a Navy uniform. "Hey, lookie here."

Ada found a path through the clutter and looked at the photograph. "Is this their daughter?"

"That's our Tala," Elise said as she and Jack walked in from the kitchen. "She's beautiful, isn't she? That was taken two years ago when she got promoted to lieutenant commander."

"And it only took her two years to get to that," Jack said. "Tala's always been a go-getter. If Ennis Quinn gets command of the *Patrick Henry* next year, she'll become the youngest commander in the Pacific Fleet."

"That's impressive," Krista said. "What's she do?"

"She's the Strategic Warfare Systems Officer on the *Patrick Henry*," Elise said as Jack reached for the model. "Blue Crew, of course. Our Tala would never be a Gold Crew puke."

"If it comes to a shooting war, Tala will be launching the missiles," Jack said with a glowing smile.

"Bo-o-om!" Elise said, fluttering her hands in a pink mushroom cloud.

He held out the model for everyone to see. "This is her boat. SSGN-807 – the USS *Patrick Henry*, first of the most feared class of subs to ever slide under the waves. It packs thirty-six Joe Slicks. Each one can take out a city, and the only way you know they've been launched is when you hear the boom. And this boat is like a hole in the water. The *Henry* can surprise a mermaid."

"Isn't she a beauty?" Elise said, stroking the model and beaming.

Krista nodded and smiled; it was certainly submariney, but she couldn't find the beauty in it. "Isn't that the one from *Mushrooms over Moscow?*"

"Yep." Jack held it out proudly. "And everything in that movie was true, except they can't launch the missiles on their own. Only the president can."

"And there's no big red button that says 'Fire.' Our Tala says it's all done with computers now."

"That's quite an accomplishment," Krista said. "You must be proud."

"Oh, we are," Elise said, but then the smile slipped from her face. "But we hardly ever see her anymore. She's all the way out in Washington State, and they keep her so busy out there. We're lucky if we see her once a year." Her face sagged, and then the bright and happy smile returned. "Anyone like a beer?"

Jack said yes, and Elise trundled to the kitchen. He unleashed a salvo of minute details about the vessel that Krista couldn't understand, but Elise returned soon with a brown bottle, and he set his mouth to work on that instead.

Krista and Ada sank into the sofa, while Jack claimed a once-upholstered recliner and Elise plopped into a side chair with a bright floral cover. A smaller, identical chair beside it held a stuffed doll that looked somewhat like Ada. Elise picked it up and cradled it in her arms.

"Why don't you visit her sometime?" Krista asked.

"We would if we could," Jack said, "but it's a long trip. I work a five-day shift, so I don't get any annual vacation, and it's two days each way to Bangor. There's no way to do it."

"And flying is too expensive, so we just sit here and hope she comes home." Elise fussed over the doll's hair and rocked it to sleep. The room grew awkwardly quiet, with only the sound of Elise's humming to relieve it.

After a few minutes, Krista cleared her throat and spoke to Jack. "I love that rose piece you've got in the window downstairs."

"Thanks. It was fun making that one."

"I've got a house in Washington, near the submarine base, in fact, and it would look fantastic in the…umm, foyer. I'd like to buy it."

Jack put his beer on the arm of the chair. "Buy it? You can have it. Nobody else wants the damn thing."

"I insist. I'll give you fifteen tenpez for it."

Elise stopped humming but didn't look up; Jack took a swig of beer and kept his eyes on her. "That's ten times what it was ever worth."

"I'm including the delivery charge," Krista said. "You'll need to deliver it to Washington for me. I can't carry it in my car."

"I guess you didn't hear me, but we don't have the time to drive all the way out to Washington. We just can't do it."

"Dear, you don't understand," Elise said. "She's bribing us to go see Tala because she knows we're too bone stupid to go on our own." She smiled at Krista. "That's so sweet of you."

"I'd have to quit my job, Elise!"

"That's why she's paying you stupid money." Elise smiled beatifically at Krista again, who cleared her throat and blushed.

"We can't do it!"

"Well, you wear the pants in the family. Of course we'll do what you say, dear." She turned to Krista. "We love our squalid little hellhole. It's so gritty and authentic. We'll stay here till we die."

"All our memories are here. We raised Tala here. Thirty-seven years of memories are in this squalid hellhole!" Jack said.

"Good memories and bad, dear. Are there more good than bad? I honestly don't remember."

"We are *not* going, Elise!"

"Of course we aren't. I wouldn't dream of it," Elise said, rocking the doll again and rubbing her finger along its cheek. "You were such a naughty girl, Tala. You grew up even though I told you not to. Why should we drive out there to see you again?" She smiled at Krista again. "Did I tell you that Tala's boat sails in four days?"

"Doesn't matter. We won't be there," Jack said.

"I'll have to go over to Barbery Pirates to touch up my color before we go." She pulled a lock of her hair down and examined it cross-eyed. "The sex is so much better after I get a color."

"Elise, please…" Jack croaked.

"Well, it's not exactly a secret, Jackson. Everybody's seen you looking at Krista's hair." Krista's blush deepened even more, and Elise reached over and patted her knee. "I don't mind that you make Jack horny, dear. I'm the one he takes to the boneyard at night."

Jack hid behind the beer bottle and tried to melt into the recliner, and Elise examined a lock of Krista's hair. "I'd give anything to get this color. Did you know that I was a strawberry blonde before I had to start coloring?"

"I'm sorry," Jack said to Krista. "Elise isn't all there sometimes."

"But I'm everywhere else. That's even better." She got up from the chair and walked down the stairs humming.

He spun a finger around his temple. "It's hard to take if you don't know her. But she's harmless."

The color of Krista's face nearly matched her hair, and she waved Jack off instead of answering. Ada's face was red, too, but from holding back her laughter; she ran to a small covered balcony beyond the stairs and burst out giggling just moments before Elise returned with a cardboard box. She wrapped Tala's picture in a towel.

"Elise, I've made up my mind. We're not going. That's final."

"Absolutely, dear." She pulled down another photograph and wrapped it. Jack gulped from his bottle, and then a phone rang underneath a pile of papers on the table next to him. He rooted through it and picked up an old cellular phone.

"Hello? ...Hey, Rocko, how's it hangin?" His smile faded as he listened. "I dunno what they're looking for...Warner, you think...no...are they there now? ...I don't have anything to hide, do you? ...Yeah, okay, see you around, Rock, thanks for the call." He set the phone down and sat silently for a minute.

"What happened? That sounded like bad news," Krista said.

Jack nodded. "That was a friend of mine up in Stenson. The Federals just swarmed into town a few minutes ago, and they're going door to door. Searching for something, but he didn't know what."

"They won't find what they're looking for there. How long till they get here?"

"We have time. Stenson's not a big town, but it has a lot of apartments, and people have been bugging out lately, what with the virus and all. If they have to break down doors, that'll hold them up." He glanced at the clock. "Just after three now, so they might be here tonight, if they're working nights."

"Trust me. The NSF works nights."

"Yeah, I guess you'd know. Look, you'll have to leave before they get here. Say seven, seven-thirty at the latest."

"I'm ready now. Everything's still in the car."

"I'll go pack a nice dinner," Elise said as she headed into the kitchen.

KRISTA SCRAPED HER WINDSHIELD and pushed a gritty paste of dirt, blood, and bugs across it. She mopped it off with a wad of paper towels and polished the glass until it squeaked, but crud was still embedded in the groove the wipers had cut in the glass.

"I only have seven gallons of dino," Jack said. "Tomorrow's my ration day, and I can get as much as I want then, but that's all I have for now."

"The batteries should be charged, so seven gallons should last awhile. Don't worry." She sat on the running board of Jack's pickup as he heaved another red can of diesel from the back and placed it on the floor. The bullet holes in the passenger door appeared more frightening in daylight, and she shivered. They'd come close to dying last night, and she wouldn't risk Ada's life anymore. "Jack," she said.

He grunted as he pulled the can up and slipped the spout into her fuel filler.

"I'm going to die, Jack. I just have this feeling."

"Naw, we'll get you outta here. Don't worry."

"It just feels inevitable. No matter how hard I try, the end will be the same. If I run fast, I'll just die later down the road."

"I don't think that's true. Did you know there's a clock in Philadelphia that counts how long they've been hunting you? It was at 105 hours this morning, and that's a hundred hours more than anybody expected. You've got luck on your side."

"Right, and Fate on the other side." She sighed and laid her head against his door with a thump. "My mom died when she was twenty-seven, and all she was doing was standing on a street corner. My dad died when he was twenty-seven, and all he was doing was sitting in a plane. Now I'm twenty-seven, and a thousand people want me dead. It's not hard to see the writing on the wall."

"That's a dangerous attitude. It'll get you killed. You gotta believe you can win, and then you'll have a decent chance."

Krista sighed again. "I hear the pipes calling me, Jack. It's hard to be optimistic."

"Listen, I know a lot about luck. I know what it feels like when Lady Luck is screwing me over, but it feels like she's on your side right now. Everything's breaking your way. A thousand people are looking for you, yeah, but that's also a thousand people that haven't found you. Why's that?"

She stared at the holes in her door, unblinking, and listened to the diesel glug into the tank. "I hope luck's on my side, but I'm not betting Ada's life on that. Will you take her till things settle down?"

He laughed and picked up another can. "Elise is upstairs right now trying to bribe her into staying. I haven't seen her so happy for years. Of course we'll take her. The problem's gonna be giving her back."

"Just between you and me, I think her mother's dead. Her father doesn't want her either, so she's probably an orphan and doesn't know it." She looked up at him. "Don't ever tell her I said that, and don't you ever say that to her."

"Yeah, okay." He blinked back tears and turned back to refueling. "Poor kid's got luck like me. Listen, we're honored to have her, and fuck everyone else. They don't know what they're missing."

KRISTA LIMPED UP THE STAIRS and found Ada sitting on the balcony, her injured leg propped up on a pillow and an old, single-screen tablet computer in her hands. Somebody had printed 'Go Navy!' in blue marker on the back of the scratched pink case. The soft syncopation of *Rhapsody in Blac* oozed from her earbuds.

She waved her hand in front of Ada's eyes. "Hey, somebody got a new toy!"

Ada pulled out the earbuds and smiled. "The only problem is that the thing's older than I am. You need a freakin hammer and chisel to work it, not a stylus. Still, it plays music, so I'm not complaining." She tapped on it a few times. "It also has one of those GPS trackers in it, so if I make a phone call, the whole world will know where I am. I'd have to hack the firmware to turn that off."

"So don't go making any calls, then."

"I won't. I don't have anybody to call anyway."

Krista sat next to her, and Ada picked up a long cigarette holder from a table. She made an ostentatious show of lighting up and then blew a glamor-queen plume into the air. "Do I look sophisticated and elegant?" she asked.

"Let me think," Krista said. "Umm…maybe?"

Ada chuckled and waved the holder in the air. "Okay, it looks goofy, but Aunt Elise gets so tickled when I use it. She has a whole collection."

"It's sweet that you get along so well with Elise. It's like you two have known each other forever."

"She's so easy to get used to. She's funny and warm and generous all at the same time. I'll bet this is what it's like to have a real mom." Ada looked down into her lap at the tablet. "But you know what's sick? I'd give my right arm to have The Commander back again even if all we did was yell at each other. I'd ditch Elise in a heartbeat if my mom knocked on the door. If I could go back in time, there's so much I'd…" She bit her lip and concentrated on the tablet again. "So. This was Tala's tablet, and it still has all her music on it. Lots of boy bands and Keriana and other crap, but only one Blac Sac song. I can't wait to get down to your car and download your collection."

"You're welcome to it." Krista looked out over the rooftops and tried to avoid Ada's eyes. "You should do it before I go."

Ada stopped tapping. "Before *you* go?"

"Listen, I –"

"Don't try to explain. I know how this works. Nobody puts up with me for long unless they want something."

"This isn't because of you."

"Of course it is," Ada said. "I'm the disposable girl. I'm a one-use friend. I'm used to that, okay?" She sniffed and looked away. "Why'd you have to be like everybody else?"

"Oh, c'mon, that's not it. We make a fabulous team, and if I could take you with me, I would."

"Then why are you dumping me?"

"This trip is getting dangerous, and I don't want you to get hurt. You almost got killed last night, Ada."

"*That's* your problem? That's all?"

"That's all? Isn't that enough?"

"C'mon, this is no big deal. It's just a meat wound." She pushed down on her stitches, suppressing a hiss, and forced a shaky smile to her lips. "See? I'm better already."

"We were just lucky last night," Krista said. "Next time, we might not be. This isn't your fight, and there's no reason for you to risk your life. It's best you stay here."

"So now you make the decisions for me? You don't bother to ask what I want? I don't get a say?"

"It's my car and it's my fight and what I say goes," Krista said. "I've arranged for you to stay with the Ripleys, just till things get settled, and then you can go back and lead a normal life."

"A normal life?" She stabbed her cigarette into an ashtray and sat up in the chair. "What makes you think I can have a normal life? You don't know what you're talking about! It's the worst thing you can do, sending me back to that, sending me back to find out I'm an…that my mom is…" She slammed her hands into her lap and squeezed them together until they were white. "I'm probably an orphan, okay? And if that's not bad enough, now the freakin Blue Ball boys will grab me and that's the last freakin daylight I'll ever see, and…and…" She clasped her hands to her face and unleashed a muffled scream. "I can't tell you why I can't go back! You don't know one freakin thing, sister, oh no, not one, and you're making decisions for me like you were my mom! Well, you're *not* my mom and Aunt Elise *is not* my aunt and none of you get to decide what I do!" She stabbed her chest with a finger, her face turning red. "It's *my* freakin life! Not yours, mine! I'll make the decisions for once! ME!"

"Calm down. Nobody's going to force you to do anything you don't want. We just want what's best for you, and getting shot isn't best for you. Isn't that obvious? Why on Earth would you want that?"

"I don't *want* to get shot, you stupid freakin twit!" Her eyes grew wide, and she brought her fist to her mouth and limped to the balcony rail. "That was mean. I'm really sorry. The Commander would slap a patch on me for that, and I'd deserve it."

Krista walked to the rail and wrapped her arm around her shoulders. "Well, I've been called a lot worse than that, kiddo. Just don't go making a habit of it. Now you calm down, okay?" She rubbed the muscles of her neck, which felt like knotted piano strings, but they slowly loosened under her touch. "So who are these Blue Ball Boys?"

"You don't wanna know. Listen, Krista, you just can't walk out and leave me alone. I can't handle being alone, I really can't, not after ten days in that rest stop, please."

"I'm not abandoning you. I wish you could see that I'm just trying to keep you from getting hurt."

"It'd hurt more if I didn't go with you. Don't make me explain why."

"I'm so sorry, but this is the way it's got to be." Krista hugged her, and Ada sank into her shoulder and sobbed gently.

Suddenly, she looked up with her eyes bright and a small smile at the corners of her mouth. "If you want me to be safe, if you want Jack and Elise to be safe, you have to take me with you!"

"Hunh?"

"That drone saw me, Krista, and they might know I'm with you! And what if they found out I have my mom's briefcase? If they come and find me here, then all three of us might get arrested!" Her smile grew wider, and she poked Krista in the chest. "Hah! The safest thing is if I go! It's true, it's true, you have to admit it makes sense!"

Krista rubbed the bridge of her nose and then flopped into the seat. "Well, damn. You're right."

She strummed her air guitar and then whipped around to Krista with her eyes narrowed. "And don't you ever talk down to me again!"

"Easy, girl." Krista shrunk back in her chair. "I thought it was the best thing."

"I know, you were just wrong, like most people. I'm used to it." Ada sat and picked up her tablet. "So when do we go?"

"Another hour or so, around seven-thirty."

Jack's footsteps thudded from the stairwell, and then he ran onto the balcony. He stalked to the edge, checked up and down the alley, and then turned to them wearing a worried expression. "I just saw Silverbacks coming down 614 from Stenson. They stopped up on Hooper, and a bunch of them got out and started knocking on doors."

"Oh, crap," Krista said. "Now we're stuck. Are we stuck? Can we still get out of here?"

"Maybe. You can go out Main in my truck and take the harvest access road. Bet they don't even know it's there. I could take your car for a joyride, tell 'em I found it outside town. That would throw 'em off for a spell, but we'd still need a diversion so they don't see you go. I was thinking that I'd go pull the fire alarm down at the corner. That might distract them."

"Now there's a good idea!"

"A good idea to shoot into the sun, maybe," Ada said. "These guys aren't total morons. They'll know that's a diversion. You'll just confirm we're here."

"Okay, how about this?" Jack said, pacing back and forth. "How about I make an anonymous call and say I saw your car north of town somewhere?"

Ada fidgeted in her chair. "You have to pull a Kobayashi Maru on these guys, Jack, something that changes the game and knocks them off-balance. If you call in a false report, they'll just send a car or two to check it out. They won't stop searching."

"Okay, let's try this then. I'll get my truck and run up –" Ada stood while he was talking and stomped down the stairs to the studio. "What's up with her?" he asked Krista.

"She's just wound up. We don't have time to deal with her now. So what was your idea?"

THEY SETTLED ON THE JOYRIDE PLAN and got to work: Krista loaded the car while Jack swallowed a few swigs of whiskey and splashed drops on his shirt. They were ready to go twenty minutes later, except they couldn't find Ada. She wasn't in the apartment, so they checked Jack's studio.

Elise stood at the large worktable, sliding Krista's rose panel into a cardboard box. Jack walked to the front window to check the street, but Krista stopped at the table. "Have you seen Ada?"

"Oh, yes, yes. She just left. She was down here for quite a long while, just playing."

"Where'd she go?" Krista asked.

Elise's face beamed happiness. "She went to deliver her playcake a few minutes ago, that little dear. She's so adorable. Y'know, my Tala used to –"

"A playcake? What's that?"

"Well, that's what I was saying, dear, before you interrupted. Tala used to make them too, and she'd use the silliest things. One time she made a cake out of foam rubber! And she frosted it with paint! Mostly, she made them out of mud, though." Elise's eyes went soft as she smiled at a distant memory. Krista looked around the table; spread across it were a pot of ice, a glass measuring cup, a dropper, and several bottles. The pungent smell of nail polish remover hung in the air.

"And she was singing that lovely Pizza Song while she played. She sings like an angel, y'know." She clasped her hands together and sang, "*A small dash of this and a small dash of that, in pro-poor-tion!*"

Krista sniffed the air and smelled something acidic. "Elise, I know Ada, and she's not a playcake kinda kid. This doesn't sound good."

"I know! I'll have that tune in my head for weeks!"

Jack walked to the table. "A Silverback just parked down at Memorial, and a buncha guys are knocking on doors. We don't have a lot of time. Where's Ada?"

"Elise says she left a few minutes ago. I don't know where she went."

"We'll have to leave her here. Getting you out has to be the first priority." Jack walked back to the window, and Krista joined him, but they couldn't see Ada anywhere on the street.

"She picked a splendid time to take a walk," Krista said, and then the rear door crashed open. Ada limped through breathing heavily. "Where have you been? We've got to go now!"

Ada looked through the window. "Five seconds. Duck."

Krista searched the sky for waterfowl, but Ada crouched and jammed her fingers into her ears – and then bright purplish-white light flashed as if lightning had struck next door. The entire street shook and the window glass cracked.

"The hell was that?" Jack asked, peeking over the windowsill. A flaming tire rolled past and wobbled to a rest on the curb outside.

"That Silverback down the street exploded," Ada said.

"How'd you know…wait, this is the perfect diversion!" Jack said.

"I know," Ada said, "That's why –"

"Everybody to the garage, now!" Jack said. "C'mon, let's move it while we have the chance!" Jack and Krista ran to the back door, and Ada limped after them.

At the door, Jack turned around. "Well, c'mon, kid! We gotta move!" He ran into the garage.

"Kid?" Ada rested her hands on her hips. "Aunt Elise, did he call me a kid?"

"Yes, he did, dear." She hummed to herself as she taped a corner of the box, and Ada stalked to the rear door muttering. She slammed the door behind her, and a second later, she opened it again. "Bye-bye! See you in Washington!"

"Bye-bye, Tala! You have a nice trip, dear." She blew Ada a kiss and taped down another corner of the box.

KRISTA CLOSED THE GARAGE DOOR and walked back to the pickup. The sunset was a watercolor of pink clouds and soft golden light, and she felt a whisper of peace.

However, she had no time for wonders. She straightened Jack's tractor cap, tucked her ponytail into his plaid flannel shirt, and climbed into the truck. Ada sat on the floor with a clipboard across her knees and her tablet in hand.

Krista shifted the pickup into drive, and at the end of the alley, she stopped and glanced up and down Main Street. "There's a roadblock in both directions," she said.

"How far?"

"Right at the end of town, maybe six or seven blocks away." She looked to the left and squinted. "I hope Jack made it through."

"He left four minutes ago, so maybe they just arrived. If they're not making a fuss over there, then I bet he did."

"It looks like they're just sitting there." A drone flew over and Krista felt a slight tingle. "I wish they'd stop shooting off that ray gun. I'll get brain cancer or something, I just know it."

"That's a high-power radar. Just keep your windows rolled up, and most of the energy will reflect away." Ada picked up the clipboard and wrote a note. "That drone was a lot closer than the first one. I'll need to time them and find a gap we can use. Okay, make a right here and go down to 614. Gawk like an innocent citizen."

Krista turned and coasted up to the intersection. A police car blocked the road to the right, and beyond it, the twisted black chassis of a Silverback lay smoking on the roof of a three-story building. Small piles of smoldering debris ringed a crater in the road, which firefighters sprayed with extinguishers. Men in gray shirts stood on the sidewalk, talking to each other and pointing at the wrecked Silverback. "I hope Elise will be all right," she said.

"She'll be fine. She'll just feed the Federals till their tummies explode. Make a left here on 614."

Krista rolled the pickup forward but braked just in time to avoid getting clipped by a fire truck, which roared across the intersection and rolled to a stop halfway down the block. Once the road was clear, she turned onto Route 614 and looked through the center of town. "There's a roadblock up there too, maybe eight or ten blocks ahead. I can't tell exactly."

Ada squinted to see her clipboard in the dark footwell. "That's okay. We're turning on Van Kampen in five blocks, so we'll miss it. Just drive like an ordinary Joe." They heard a drone pass overhead again and Ada swore quietly. "Four minutes. They're orbiting quicker than I assumed. Have you heard the second one yet?"

Krista felt a tingle in her scalp again, nothing like the blast she'd received in Columbus but enough to trigger the memory of it. "No, but I'll let you know if I do."

When they were a block from Van Kampen, Krista heard a distant buffeting sound. With a sudden burst of light and noise, a helicopter flew over a house, turned on Main Street, and headed toward her with its spotlight sweeping the street. It hovered slowly and scanned every building as well as the few pedestrians on the sidewalks. Two men leaned out from either side, each holding a rifle.

"A helicopter's coming. Try to squeeze under there." Ada crawled under the dashboard and pressed her body into the firewall as the spotlight swept over the car. Krista watched the helicopter hover down the street and illuminate the rooftops of the buildings on Jack's block, and then she turned on Van Kampen. It was wide open and free of Federals.

Ada reached for the clipboard and read the map Jack had drawn. "This street turns right at the end. Just follow that till we find the entrance." The faraway thrum of a drone filtered into the car and Ada made a note. "Okay, we definitely have two drones in concentric orbits. The outer one has a period of seven minutes and the inner one is four. I just have to do a little algebra and I can figure this out."

"Ahh, so there's a use for algebra?"

"Math is the language of life, sis. It whispers sweet somethings in your ear. Don't knock it." Ada blinked once. "Okay, my math was right. After it's gone over us three more times, we'll have the maximum window, which is only four minutes and seven seconds, so we have to get to the park in less than fifteen minutes and eleven seconds. Jack will miss all the drones, too, if he stays on the schedule I gave him."

"I'm seeing the end of the street, so we're close. We should be there in less than five." She followed a curve in the road and drove a few more blocks to the park entrance, which looked like the driveway of a long-abandoned house. The two rusted posts flanking the road confirmed that it was the old park, though, and she turned onto a lane crowded by trees.

The light had already abandoned the driveway. Krista didn't want to use her headlights, so Ada climbed out of the footwell and aimed a flashlight ahead to light their way. After a minute, they rolled into a parking lot overgrown with vines, brush, and stray corn plants from the nearby fields. The wheels snapped and crushed the floor of dry branches carpeting the lot, which was covered by a dense canopy of old trees, the only light filtering into it from the cornfield on one side. The building they were trying to find was supposedly next to the field, and Krista drove the truck up to the curb and coasted until she saw it ahead – a brick building with a faded wood sign that said FIELD OF DREAMS TICKETS. To one side, a wide red-brick sidewalk extended from the curb and stopped at the stand of corn. "Okay, so this is where the old ball field was. How long do we have to wait?"

Ada looked at her tablet. "Nine minutes, nine seconds. But once we leave, we'll have just four minutes to run a half mile, and we have only two good legs between us."

Krista puffed out her cheeks and exhaled slowly. "All right. All we can do is try. Do you have all your stuff ready?"

"Yeah." Ada nodded and checked her tablet again. "Nine minutes now."

"Stop it. It just makes the waiting seem longer."

They sat in silence and listened to the whirring of the ventilation fan.

"Say something," Ada said. "This is driving me nuts."

"Sure. This is going to be the longest nine minutes of my life. How's that?"

Ada lit a cigarette and stared through the window. "That's all you've got?"

"Right now it is," Krista said. She lit up and peered into the cornfield.

"So you don't believe in God?" Ada asked.

"I don't. But if I see him, I'll be sure to kick his ass."

"You don't believe in God, but you believe in His Almighty Keester?"

"Maybe God is just an ass floating on a cloud. I don't care," Krista said. "And I'm in no mood to take crap about it from some Arkie-atheist-scientist, or whatever smorgasbord of beliefs you've got."

"I don't believe anything. I only accept what I can observe, and I've never seen any evidence that God exists or doesn't. I'm keeping an open mind. But from what I've seen, there might be a God of some sort."

"You? Miss Science? You believe in God?"

"Maybe," Ada said. "The evidence suggests it but doesn't prove it."

"Seriously?"

"Yep. Each quark in the universe behaves like it's aware of other quarks, some of them unimaginable distances away. They even respond to changes in each other's states when they shouldn't. On a higher level, I've seen overt patterns of quantum organization where I should see chaos. That means there's probably a universal consciousness, or what I call the Unicon, that communicates among its parts. If there's a God and a Heaven, that's where I'd find them."

Krista yawned and looked through the window.

"That's all I get? I crush centuries of scientific and theological presumptions, and all I get is the ole ho-hum?"

"It's nothing new. Your Unicorn sounds like the Life Force. You just used fancy words, that's all."

"Unicon."

"Unicorn."

"Whatever. The Unicon is nothing like your Life Force. Your notion of the Life Force is just a mash-up of Buddhist and Wiccan reward structures. But the Unicon doesn't have any values to reward, and it doesn't care whether we live or die. It only wants order. Kinda like some cosmic Department of Motor Vehicles clerk." She glanced sideways at Krista, who was staring through the window with her lips tightened into a line. "C'mon, that snark was right outta your toolbox. You won't even give me a snicker?"

Krista looked at the dashboard clock. "How much longer?"

"Seven minutes." Ada gazed at the parking lot, whistling tunelessly. "So do you really have a house by the Navy base?"

"I don't."

They listened to the fan whir for another minute, and Ada checked her tablet. She whistled tunelessly again for a few seconds and then rechecked it. "Could you please stop ignoying me?"

"I'm not ignoying you. I'm just worried. I hope Elise is okay, and I hope Jack made it, and I hope we do too. That's all that's going through my mind right now."

"Jack just has to avoid the roadblocks. He'll be fine. Stop worrying."

Krista looked into the corn and imagined what lay beyond. "He took a big risk. I wish I could thank him for it."

"You left a pile of tenpez on his workbench. Most people would be thankful for that."

"That was just a payment for the glass," Krista said. "He coulda gotten two thousand tenpez if he'd turned me in. Fifteen tenpez wasn't enough thanks, not for the danger I put them in."

"Don't worry about it. They're leaving tonight. Aunt Elise said she can play Jack like a piano, and that they'd leave right after we do and be at the sub base the day after tomorrow."

"Really? Good. I hope they stay safe." She gazed through the window and then snapped her fingers. Wearing a wicked grin, she reached over Ada and pawed through the glove compartment.

"What are you looking for?" Ada asked.

"Scissors." She found a penknife and opened a small pair of scissors, and then she turned the rear-view mirror toward her.

The outer drone buzzed over the cornfield, but its sound was lost when the inner drone flew over; Ada peered up into the sky and then wrote another note. "I just saw third drone up there carrying missiles."

Krista looked through the window with wide eyes. "Oh, crap."

"As long as those observation drones don't pin down our location, we'll be safe. That weapons drone is carrying the Hades-7 missile, which couldn't find the ground unless somebody sent it the coordinates."

"How do you know all that?"

"Jeez. It's the most common standoff air-to-surface missile system there is, Krista. Don't you read the SatNet?"

"Right, right. Slipped my mind, that's all."

Ada turned off Tala's tablet and dropped it into her bookbag. "So once they pass over a second time, we've gotta bolt or we'll become coordinates. You don't have time for a haircut."

"Just a little off the top. I need to cut it all someday soon, though. It's dangerous to be so noticeable."

"It's dangerous to be so out of fashion," Ada said. "Everybody knows that if you wear it below the shoulder blades, you think you're a princess."

Krista snorted. "I never heard that."

"That's cuz you're ancient and out of touch. It's good you have me around to tell you this stuff. You'd be warping through Galaxy L-7 if it wasn't for me."

"I'm twenty-seven!" Krista said. "Since when is that old?"

"Tell me, were dinosaurs hard to ride?" Krista scowled and pulled up a lock from the crown. "Just wanna know. Scientific curiosity, that's all."

"Well, they were easy to ride, but getting the saddle on was a real bitch." She snipped the lock and draped it over the rear-view mirror.

"Eww. That's like hair porn, Krista. That's a little sick."

"He'll like it, and truthfully, I just don't care," Krista said. "We rebels are supposed to do weird stuff. We're all bold and glamorous and deadly and whatever."

"Yeah, but Elise will get pissed off when she sees that," Ada said, and then she saw Krista's laughing eyes. "Omigod, you're right! She'll probably rub it in his face!"

"Can you picture those two in the sack?" Krista asked, and she shivered. "Buh-bye, libido. It's been swell."

"Thanks for coming."

"I might as well just go find a nunnery now."

Ada's stomach rumbled. "I'm getting like Pavlov's dog. I think of Aunt Elise and I get hungry."

The thrumming sound returned, and they sat still as the drones passed overhead again. "Good. Now it's only the longest four minutes of my life. I'm going outside to limber up before we go," Krista said. She slid out of the truck, walked back and forth and swung her arms for a minute, and then bent over and tried to touch her toes. She yelped and staggered back to her seat holding her hand over her leg.

A few minutes later, they heard the drones approaching from the west again and picked up their bags. After the aircraft passed, they jumped from the truck and ran into a gap between the corn stalks.

Ada stopped after a minute and grabbed her leg. "It feels like I'm stabbing myself every time I put my foot down." She tried to run again but fell to the dirt.

Krista grabbed her arm and took some weight off the injured leg, and they hobbled across the field like a three-legged race team. The stalks thinned ahead, and they stumbled into a stubbly clearing just as the *basso profundo* tones throbbed again in the western sky. They looked for the wooden barn, but it was still hundreds of feet away. They couldn't get there before the drones returned.

Ada pointed to a stack of white plastic boxes beside a rusted-out truck and pulled Krista along. The boxes were the size of a car, but there was a space between two of them. They slid into the gap as the sound of the drones reached its peak.

Krista had just rested against a box when her scalp tingled. The box behind her shook, and hundreds of small animals chittered inside. She squealed and tried to get up and run, but Ada grabbed her arm and pulled her down.

The chittering stopped, but the creatures were still agitated, and they shook the boxes around and above them. A box overhead shifted and creaked, and Krista squealed again and bolted across the clearing. Ada crawled out and limped behind.

Krista had run halfway to the barn when she realized that she was alone. She ran back and grabbed Ada, and they stumbled together to the open door. Once safely inside, they sagged back against the wall.

Krista's car sat idling by the far door beside bales of hay. Jack climbed out and ran over when he saw them. "Did they see you?" he asked, and they shook their heads. "Okay, good. So far, so good. We're doing good."

"You've…gotta go after the next pass," Ada said. "Boxes…good hiding place…if you don't mind rats."

"Don't like them much, but they don't faze me. Thanks for the advice." He took the hat and shirt from Krista and put them on. "I only have a few minutes, then. Okay, you remember what I said? Follow the map. Drive straight ahead and take the harvest access road on the left into the field. And this whole farm's automated, so watch out for the Producers."

"Got it," Krista said. "What are…" Her throat caught on some dust and she coughed, and Jack slapped her on the back until she found the air to tell him she wasn't choking. "My throat's just dry. Thanks."

"Hey, you coulda warned me about that car. I didn't know Biceps had such giddyap and go. I was gone before the Federals even showed up. Never had to use my drunken joyride story. Thanks."

Ada heard the drones coming again and hugged him. "We have to go. Bye-bye, Uncle Jack. See you in Washington!" He smiled and shook his head.

"I might not ever get a chance to thank you again." Krista wrapped her arms around him and kissed his cheek, and he pulled off his cap, held it over his heart, and smiled.

She limped to the car, wrenched open the creaking door, and fell into the front seat. The sky had grown dark fast, and she squinted through the windshield trying to see the harvest access road. At the end of the field, she spotted a gap in the corn rows. "So what are Producers?"

Ada watched a countdown on her tablet, and then she punched an icon. "Go!"

Krista honked the horn, and Jack sprinted from the barn. The wheels spun on the Bicep as they fought for traction, and then the car sped across the open field toward the road.

"I've been doing some calculations," Ada said.

Krista turned the wheel hard left, and the car slid into a dark, narrow lane bordered by rows of tall corn. "I'm glad you know math. I couldn't figure this out myself."

"Yeah, well, I figure that if you stay at twenty-two miles an hour, we'll be outside the inner drone's range in about a minute. We'll be outside the outer drone's range in about six minutes, but anything less than that and, well, we're screwed, to use the mathematical term."

Krista looked at the speedometer. "No problem. We're going thirty-five." She heard the cornstalks swish by outside the window but couldn't see them.

"The outer drone comes over again at 6:51, more or less. We need to be at least a mile –" The front of the car dropped suddenly and then rose again, and the underside scraped across the dirt. The front end flew into the air for a split second and the engine roared, and then it hit the road and the wheels bit in again.

"That was a helluva rut," Krista said. "I hope the whole road isn't like this." The front of the car bounced over smaller ruts and Krista fought the steering wheel for control, but the surface smoothed out again.

Ada picked up her clipboard from the floor. "That shook my fillings loose. Listen, you can slow down to twenty-two miles an hour. My math is right. We don't need to go any faster. It might make it easier to handle this road."

"I want to get out of here, and anyway, this thing doesn't go slow anymore ever since you broke it."

"I *modified* it. Wanna stop and I'll modify it back?"

Krista grinned at her. "Nuh-uh, sister! I like speed!" She sped up to forty miles an hour, and for another minute, they sailed through a sea of corn with the wind at their backs. Except for the weak beam of Ada's flashlight lighting the stalks on both sides, though, the road was completely dark.

Ada looked at the clock. "It's 6:47. Four minutes and we'll be –" The front of the car dropped into a rut again and rammed into the dirt on the other side, and something popped inside the dashboard. The impact threw Ada against her seatbelt, and the mirror flew from the windshield and hit her injured leg.

Krista pawed at a plastic sack hanging from the steering wheel. "Is this an airbag?"

"Yeah," Ada said. "Are you okay?"

"I'm a little rattled, that's all. How about you?"

Ada rubbed her chest. "That reset me to my factory settings."

"I know, right? I wish I could see this feckin road."

Ada rubbed her sore leg with one hand and groped around on the floor for her flashlight. "Look, if you use headlights, you'll give away our position. C'mon, we need to get going. We're still in range of the drone."

"I'm trying to move." She slipped the shifter into reverse and backed up a few feet, but then the car shook and slid sideways. Krista looked around outside, but she couldn't see why it was moving by itself.

Ada heard hissing outside and peered into the darkness. "There's something out there, something huge."

She lowered her window, and then a horn blasted and the car shook. The movement stopped, and this time Ada heard loud, mechanical whirring outside the window. She picked up the flashlight as the air horn blasted again.

Ada played her light across something outside. "It's like a giant mechanical beetle or something. I see solar panels, and the front of it has these things like pincers…Uh oh, here it comes again!"

The machine slammed into the car's side and pushed it hard enough that the front wheels pulled out of the rut. Krista pressed the gas and the wheels spun, but the car didn't move. The machine continued to push the car and turned it perpendicular to the road. After doing its damage, it whirred away, ripping off the mirror as it went.

Ada watched a wall of black metal glide by the window, followed by a wheel taller than the car. Another wheel followed, and then another. "It's an automated harvester, I bet." She ran her flashlight up and down the machine's side. "This has to be a Producer. God, that's a magnificent machine. I wonder what kind of guidance system it has. I'd love to get inside that thing for a few minutes."

"We don't have time to be curious," Krista said. She pointed at the clock, which read 6:50 PM. "We need to get out of here." The wheels felt like they had traction, but they wouldn't turn. "Crap, my tire's bumping up against that thing. I can't turn the wheel."

Ada looked up at the machine. "Just stay here in its radar shadow till the drone goes by." She shined her light under it. "I've gotta get me one of these."

The black wall passed, trailing behind it a large cart with three white plastic boxes like they'd seen in the clearing. An irregular thump came from inside them. "It's harvesting corn," Ada said. "All by itself too. It's a robot. Wow." They felt the pins-and-needles sensation at the same time and groaned. "That was the radar. I didn't feel it very strongly, did you?"

"I didn't, but it still gave me the willies."

"We didn't get a full blast. I'll bet that drone didn't pick us up." She watched as another cart rolled past; this one was like the first, black metal with a curved solar panel at the top, but it also made a hissing noise. Ada watched it approach and then gagged when she smelled what it was spraying.

"What's that smell?" Krista asked.

"Fertilizer!" Ada squeaked. A foul brown liquid sprayed across the back window and side of the car.

"Shit, that stinks!" Krista pinched her nose and tried to raise Ada's window, but it wouldn't work. "Screw it, we're outta here!" she yelled. She punched the gas pedal, and the car bounced out of the rut and raced south along the bumpy road, trailing a cloud of dust.

THE PRESIDENTIAL SUITE

Day 33
Sunday night, September 20, 2043
St. Elizabeth's Hospital for the Indigent, Washington, DC

The third-floor physician's locker room was empty, as it usually was at midnight. Returning to the locker was just a small risk for Victoria because it was assigned to Tommy Talbott, not her. Since his wife hadn't known about their affair, he probably hadn't told the NSF that he'd given his lover the combination so she could change clothes after a weekend fling at his cottage.

She spun the dial while listening for boots stomping in the hallway. The lock unlatched, and she found her weekend bag inside, which held one of her navy blue skirtsuits and a pair of handmade Italian shoes.

She examined her suit but couldn't find any cleverly hidden tracking devices. It was a risk wearing them, but she had to take the chance; she needed her street clothes because strolling off-campus wearing brown orderly scrubs would attract attention. They were the perfect camouflage on-campus, though, since they identified her as a lower-class drudge to be ignored. Her only problem was that she couldn't hide the pistol in them, but her shirt concealed the knife she'd used to kill Dr. Timmons perfectly. That was all the weaponry she needed on hospital grounds.

Outside the locker room, she slid the weekend bag onto the lower shelf of a morgue table, draped the bedsheet over the side, and then pushed it down the corridor and stopped at a supply closet. She fumbled in the pocket of her lab coat for her passkey and reflected on how grateful she was to have friends, especially ones who owed you their lives. Thinking about her escape from the NTC, she was grateful for her ex-lovers too.

She locked the supply closet door when she finished and pushed the cart to the north stair, where she parked it next to others in a side corridor.

After checking the dome mirror on the wall and seeing nobody but herself, she grabbed her bag from the cart, creaked open the door, and padded down to the tunnel level.

The tunnels were now dark because she'd removed most of the lamps. She didn't need light; she could navigate the place in darkness, which could be a critical advantage if everything went to hell again.

She shuffled through the corridor to the old iron door, which opened with its familiar creaky groan. After going back and forth on whether to oil the hinges, she'd decided to leave them as they were because they made a useful warning system. The fluorescent light still worked in the long hallway beyond, one of the few she'd left untouched.

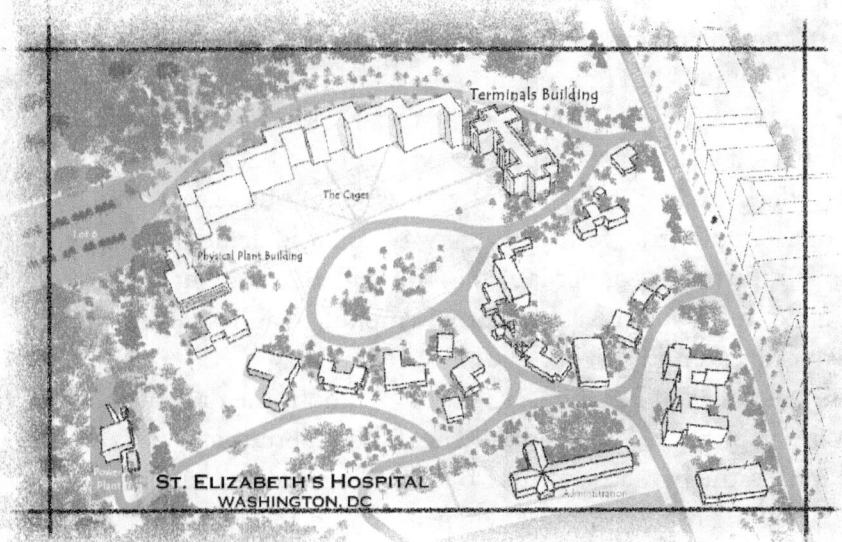

ST. ELIZABETH'S HOSPITAL
WASHINGTON, DC

She walked down the narrow hallway, careful to avoid puddles or plaster dust that would leave footprints, and stopped at the fifth door on the left. She'd named this room the Presidential Suite because it was dry and had a light and a working door. The next one she'd named the Vice-Presidential Suite because that was where she'd execute Gabriel Cheyn.

If I make it that far, she reminded herself. If she found Ada, though, revenge and retribution wouldn't matter because they'd go to Canada, start over, and get far away from anything American. If she found Ada, someone else could take up the sword, someone who didn't have a child, someone who loved war more than life.

Ada…

Her face twisted, and she brought her fist to her mouth to stifle the rising wail. With a shaking hand, she steadied herself against the doorjamb until the feeling passed, and then she pulled the door open.

She yanked the string and turned on the ceiling light, illuminating a cell furnished only with a ripped rubber mattress and a small cart, both found in the pile of furniture in the tunnels.

From a lower shelf on the cart, she pulled out a chromed bedpan and looked at her reflection. Wearing the brown wig she'd bought the previous night, she looked completely different; she took it off and put it on a few times, marveling at how it transformed her face.

She removed the wig and toweled her hair dry. As she did, she noticed that the bandage over her missing ear was getting bloody again. She peeled the bandage off and gingerly cleaned the wound. The cut was already healing, but it itched. Fighting the urge to scratch it was maddening; when she was reading Warner's posts in the orderly's lounge this evening, she caught herself pawing the empty air where it had been. Fortunately, none of the orderlies had noticed, although it wouldn't have mattered if they did. Most of them did stranger things anyway, and the tic helped her fit in.

From the pocket of her lab coat, she pulled out the handful of syringes she'd filled in the supply closet, some wrapped in adhesive tape. She set them on the cart and reached for her weekend bag.

As she polished her shoes, she thought about the days ahead: Walking five miles in designer pumps would be difficult, but that would be nothing compared to the barefoot sprint from the National Tranquility Center to here – five long hours, running when she could and walking when she must, all to get here before sunrise. All to get to the last place anyone would expect her to hide.

The day after tomorrow, she'd again do what nobody expected, and her bleak deadlock would break. Things would change, maybe for the better but more likely for the worse. However, she'd be freed from this tormenting purgatory, and that was all she wanted.

She was putting off the difficult part, and she berated herself for succumbing to distraction when she needed to focus. Squaring her shoulders, she opened the weekend bag again. In a zippered pocket, she found a roll of dollar bills and a photograph of Ada.

She gasped and staggered back to the mattress; her throat felt tight, almost too constricted to breathe. It hurt seeing her; she'd known it would, but not that it would hurt so much. It hurt more than her bruised ribs, her twisted ankle, her phantom ear; it hurt more than every pain she'd ever felt, experienced at the same time.

Holding Ada over her heart, every harsh word she'd ever said pierced her. Every missed opportunity to hold her or comfort her pummeled her soul. Every missed chance to say that she loved her child gripped her heart and shook it in her chest. She regretted too much, far too much for one person to bear, and she rocked herself in her prison cell until exhaustion claimed her.

TO NOT BEING DEAD

Day 34
Monday morning, September 21, 2043
Four miles south of June Bug, Kentucky

The light in the old carwash couldn't make up its mind. It would burn bright for a few minutes, suddenly turn off, and then struggle to burn again. Krista preferred that the carwash remain dark so she couldn't see her damaged car. "I kept the thing spotless for four years. You know that it's got only fifteen thousand miles on it? It's practically a baby, but then I take it out for a little road trip and this happens."

Ada pawed around inside a plastic bag. "And that Producer squirted diarrhea all over the back too."

"I'm calling it the Scatmobile from now on." Krista shifted to find a more comfortable position against the concrete wall, settled back and grinned. "Well, at least I've got insurance!"

"You should tell them you accidentally drove into a live-fire demolition derby. That's the only story they'll believe."

Krista took a sip of water and shook her head. "And the feckin thing still runs, that's the amazing part."

The ceiling light shimmered to life again. The bullet holes and stripped paint were unnerving, but the Producer's damage was even worse. The rear fender was crumpled back over the tire, and bits of important-looking metal things stuck out around the wheel, making the car look like an extraterrestrial rover.

"A little bondo and some paint, and it'll be good as new," Ada said.

Krista looked from bumper to bumper once more and sighed. "I never liked the color anyway."

"That's the spirit! Now you can get a color you want."

"I'd like the Invisibility Black right now," Krista said. "We can't drive this beater around much longer. It looks like it's been through a war zone, and people will notice. Can you steal a car for me?"

"Sure," Ada said, pawing through the plastic bag again.

"We'll find one tonight and then drive this one into the woods. I wouldn't want anybody to find it right away and tell the NSF where we are."

"But that would take two drivers, and I can't drive," Ada said.

"It's easy. I'll teach you how."

"The last time Mom tried to teach me, I drove the car into a ditch five minutes after getting behind the wheel. She had to call a tow truck and get the airbags replaced."

Krista smiled. "I've got the perfect car for you to learn on, then." She pointed to her car, and the light went out at the same moment.

"Okay, that's bad," Ada said. "That's an omen."

"It'll be fine, just trust me." Krista stretched and yawned. "I need to get some sleep. The sun's coming up soon." She looked around the carwash. "We'll be safe here today. The cash box has been ripped off the wall, and somebody stole all the hoses, so nobody's coming to wash their car. In fact, it doesn't look like anyone's been here for years."

"I could use some sleep too. How about dessert before bedtime?"

"Mmm. What did Elise give us?"

Ada pulled a greasy strip of meat from the bag. "Bacon!"

"This is what's really wrong with America. Forget that the fascists are killing everybody. The real problem is that there just aren't enough smoked-pork desserts in this country."

"Let's be trailblazers!" Ada said.

"We'll do what rebels do – be unexpected, break the rules, challenge the system!" They tapped their bacon strips together in a toast. "Cheers! To not being dead tonight."

Ada laughed. "I'm getting to like this not-being-dead stuff. I could get used to it."

Krista smiled and patted her leg. "Kinda grows on you, doesn't it?"

IT'S DOWN TO MAGIC

Day 34
Monday morning, September 21, 2043
National Tranquility Center, Fort Belvoir, Virginia

"Day-o, Bob," Raphael said as he heard footsteps on the podium.

"How's it going, Raf?"

He shrugged. "Busier than usual. We raided a house up in Scranton an hour ago, but it was just a Base-M lab, so our coal bomber remains at large."

"The coal-fired plants will be unnecessary soon anyway," Downs said. "After the Transition, energy demand will plummet, and the coal plants will get shuttered. Why waste resources trying to destroy them?"

"But the bombers don't know that, so they keep trying. Hey, did you read the report from the Maryville bombing?"

"Of course, right after I woke up," Downs said.

"I was busy with the raid, so I didn't get a chance. What did it say?" Raphael asked.

"The lab found traces of triacetate and aluminum on and in the truck's fuel tank. Their theory is that someone made a multiple dual-binary explosive, an unusual combination we've never seen. The upshot is that this person built a powerful bomb from easily obtained compounds we'll never be able to trace."

"All right. Now give me the bad news."

"Raf, that *was* the bad news."

Raphael drew a deep breath and exhaled slowly. "I was thinking last night that Warner was headed to Maravelle, but then she turned and went in the opposite direction for Maryville. The two names sound alike. I think she never saw the name but heard it from someone."

"I've been wondering about that too. I think she has confederates, and one of them told her to go to Maryville, which also turns out to have a talented bombmaker in residence. I'm starting to believe there's more to this Warner woman, Raf. She might be heading a dissident cell, or at least be linked with one."

"I think so too. Ari also found another tasty morsel last night." Raphael paused and looked at Downs.

"And…?"

"Maryville is home to four employees of the KLEPTCO Bellefontaine plant, which suffers more Hot Rock detonations than average."

Downs stroked his chin.

"Methinks there are too many coincidences centering on that town," Raphael said, mimicking his chin stroke.

Downs paced the podium a few times. "We'll take the direct approach and round up these employees. We'll cognitive-map them and find the connection they have to Warner and Scranton – and maybe even find the connection *between* Warner and Scranton. It's not out of the question that she could've always been involved with the dissidents."

"Not at all. Why don't you drag them in today and find out?"

Downs nodded and stared at the Wall, lost in thought.

"How goes the hunt for Lang, by the way?"

"I just hope she's dead somewhere. We can't find anything at all. The searches along her escape route have turned up nothing so far, and we've had no sightings. I'm banking on her surfacing to pick up her daughter."

"This could be bad, Bob, really bad." Raf looked around, but the staff was wearing headphones and couldn't overhear their conversation. "She could be more damaging than Warner. That package has damning data in it. She's not just carrying around a little picture show."

"I know it could be bad, believe me."

"Well, it's your worry for the next twelve hours. I've hauled my load of bananas for the day. The Watch is yours, Bob." Raphael stepped off the podium and sang as he headed for the door.

Downs nodded and scanned the Wall, and then he turned and called after Raphael. "Kopelli's doing his little magic show at 2045 hours tonight. Why don't you come in early and have a look?"

"So we're down to using magic now." Raphael smiled. "Okay, cool. I'll bring my trick cards and we'll have a party."

DISPATCHES

Molle's Hill
NewsHub Political Affairs Channel
Broadcast Transcript of September 21, 2043

Molle: We're visiting again with America's Doctor, Surgeon General Mae Esteban. How are you, today, General?

Esteban: It's good to be here, Arista. Thanks for having me on your show.

Molle: A few days ago, you mentioned that you were investigating the Recombin shortage. Has your investigation produced results yet?

Esteban: We've been unable to reach any definitive conclusions. We've encountered nothing but obstruction and obfuscation from both the HHS and Chalys Pharmaceuticals. As a result, I'm meeting this afternoon with President Gibbon to discuss further measures we can take to advance our investigations. Specifically, I'll be asking the president to issue a National Security Directive waiving the corporate privacy protection of Chalys Pharmaceuticals.

Molle: Isn't that unconstitutional? Corporate-Americans are private citizens, and their privacy is protected by the 32nd Amendment, isn't it?

Esteban: There's no 32nd Amendment to the Constitution, Arista. You're referring to the 31st Amendment, which allows the veil of corporate privacy to be pierced in matters of national security, which this certainly is. I hope to persuade the president to act.

Molle: Well, you're a bulldog when you set your sights on a goal, General! Still, since the Neovirus isn't spreading anymore, why are you pursuing this so aggressively?

Esteban: It's premature to say that Neovirus has run its course, Arista.

Molle: The Department of Health and Human Services says so. Their spokesperson said this morning that it hasn't been detected past Columbus, Ohio. They don't expect it to spread any further.

Esteban: The HHS has been obstructing our investigation, and their guidance should be disregarded. To be blunt, they're liars, so the opposite is probably true. Anecdotal evidence confirms this. Reports from hospitals in central Ohio indicate that the virus has mutated toward even higher transmissibility and lethality than before. It's lunacy, perhaps even manslaughter, to recommend that vaccinating the population is no longer necessary. We should produce as much Recombin as we can, and Chalys Pharmaceuticals has stopped doing that. A National Security Directive would help us find out why.

Molle: It seems like an indirect approach if it's so important. Why don't you just send in your troops, General?

Esteban (mumbling): You bloody twonk.

Molle: I'm sorry, I didn't catch that.

Esteban: You weren't meant to.

Molle: All right. General, there are many who say the Neovirus was an act of nature meant to cull the herd, or even divine retribution intended to punish the lower classes for their irresponsible ways. What do you think? General? Why are you looking at me like that?

Esteban: I'm trying to diagnose your condition. I've concluded that the simplest diagnosis is the correct one.

Molle: What do I have? Is it anything serious?

Esteban: I doubt you can have anything serious, Arista.

Molle: That's comforting, but I see that my producer is telling me to discuss this off-air. Now, on an unrelated topic, I understand that you were a classmate of the fugitive Victoria Lang at Johns Hopkins. She apparently went berserk and killed three unarmed NSF doctors.

Esteban: The word 'berserk' doesn't fit Dr. Lang. Controlled, squared-away, disciplined, committed – that's more like it. I also don't consider her case to be unrelated to the Neovirus outbreak. One, she was the first physician to isolate and identify Neovirus. Two, she was present at the death of the Washington index case, John Durant, and she administered Recombin to a nurse there before development of the vaccine supposedly even started. Three, that nurse swore under oath that the Recombin vial

Dr. Lang showed her was dated April fifth of this year. If that date is correct, then –

Molle: My producer tells me that Senator Pendeha has arrived. There you are, Senator!

Pendeha: Arista, you look lovely! Where *did* you get that beautiful suit?

Molle: I got it at Frick and Frock, and what a deal! You know, Senator, I don't understand why more women don't shop there. They have the latest brands at affordable prices and a convenient layaway...

THE REBEL COMMANDER

Day 34
Monday afternoon, September 21, 2043
Four miles south of June Bug, Kentucky

Dad sat on the stool by her bed and sang a gentle lullaby: *Keira Love, Keira Lune, asleep below the rising moon…* His voice was beautiful, and she loved the rough and throaty sound. She even loved the way he looked at her, his thick glasses full of eyes, and how he laughed when she called him Dowdie. It was her secret love name, and no one knew it but them, not even Mom.

She burrowed deeper under the covers and hugged her plush unicorn as her eyelids grew heavy. Everything was wonderful and everything was possible, but the wonders would have to wait until morning because she was so tired. She hoped she'd dream of the zoo again – it was her favorite place in all the world – and she sighed happily, thinking about all the delights the next day would offer.

Dad sang some more, but then she heard a guitar, too, and playing musical instruments was against the crabby building manager's rules even in the penthouse. He was earning a grown-up time out, which was going to be bad, but he kept playing louder and louder. She recognized the silly bop bass line of *Another Freakin Love Song,* which would be a smash hit in another two years when he'd write it, and she hoped he didn't go wild in the bridge and make a lot of noise the way he did in concerts. She turned her head to shush him, and the music grew softer and tinnier, which was odd. She opened her eyes to see what was going on.

The ceiling of her car swam into view, and the reek of cow manure caught in her throat. She closed her eyes and tried to jump back into the dream, but it was gone.

The music was still playing, though, and she looked for the source. In the passenger seat, a young blonde girl snored and snuffled, wearing earbuds turned up to full volume. Beyond her, greasy fug swirled past the cracked concrete wall of a decrepit carwash, and tendrils of the murk invaded the car through three bullet holes in the passenger door.

She lay back in her seat and stared at the ceiling. However, her bladder wouldn't leave her be, and she opened the door and stumbled just outside the carwash. She wouldn't go any further because they'd found stiffers with bloody eyes in the weeds last night. However, most of the locals had probably escaped; the village of June Bug had been empty when they'd driven through it the previous night, the doors on a few houses hanging open as if the residents had run for their lives. They'd become feverish a few minutes after finding the stiffers, so she hoped the townspeople had run early and fast.

She shuffled back to the car and took her tablet, cigarettes, and the small bag of food from the console. Sitting against the carwash wall, she opened the bag and ate one of the two remaining pieces of bacon while checking her tablet. It was already after five in the afternoon.

She read the news and laughed at Friendly's account of their escape from Columbus. The report was an outrageous fabrication, but she knew well-crafted propaganda when she read it. The problem with his fantasy was that she wasn't the person the world wanted her to be.

Or maybe they're not fantasizing and they're right, Miss Kellen. Maybe Jack is right, and your life is larger than you assume.

"Oh, shut up and don't be such a feckin nag," Krista said. "I'm sick of your constant preachin. Bloody Figment. You've got a mouth like a fidget spinner, that you do."

Miss Kellen...

"Grow a pair of lips and zip it, wouldja?"

"Who's Figment?" Ada asked, walking around the front of the car.

"Oh, you're up! You were sound asleep a few minutes ago."

"That was before you started slamming car doors. So who's Figment?" Ada asked.

"Umm...here, I saved the last piece of bacon for you!"

Ada gave her a puzzled look and then grabbed the bag. "I'm starving. We need to get more food soon."

"Not around here we won't. This place is dead," Krista said. "We need to head south and outrun this virus. Maybe we can find food if we get to Tennessee tonight."

BY SIX O'CLOCK, they were driving southwest through a broad valley in Kentucky. They'd passed through a few empty towns since leaving June Bug, and the isolated rural houses they'd seen also appeared dark and abandoned. Cars rocketed past from the north, but they'd seen none from the south for hours.

Ada navigated their course through the valley. As they approached Lexington, she turned on the map light and looked at the atlas. "We need to avoid Lexington in case it's another Columbus. We oughta go around it, although it'll take longer."

"No way I'm going through another city," Krista said. "I'd rather live. Tell me when to turn."

Ada gave her directions, and they were soon driving down an empty two-lane road that passed through more small towns. Like the others, these places were abandoned. The towns weren't just devoid of people; they were also devoid of cars, meaning that everybody had fled. They stopped outside a few stores, but the lights were turned off and the doors were locked.

"Maybe we oughta cruise through Lexington and find a car," Ada said.

"This one works for now, and I don't see any reason to take that chance. If we can find a safer place, that's fine, but I'm not going into a city that could turn out like Columbus."

"We also need food. I'm graying out over here."

"I am too," Krista said. "How much food could we have gotten in Columbus, though? You wouldn't have gotten out and shopped with all those zombies walking around, wouldja?"

Ada shook her head. "Forget that. Let's go out to the sticks and break into a house or a store, see if we can find anything there. Somebody had to leave food behind, and really, I'd even eat Meals under Wheels right now."

"Meals under Wheels?"

Ada snorted. "Y'know, roadkill?"

"Sweet Jaysus, I hope we don't get to that."

Krista turned onto Bluegrass Highway and headed southwest. Ada searched for a town or an isolated house to ransack, but the area seemed devoid of anything human, dead or undead.

RAPHAEL STEPPED ONTO THE PODIUM. "Hey, Bob. I hope I'm not late for your magic show."

"We're just getting ready to start, Raf. A few more minutes at the most."

"So I hear you made progress with the Maryville bomber today," Raphael said.

"Yes and no. We found the bomb materials in the workshop of Jack Ripley, a KLEPTCO employee, and Warner's and Ripley's fingerprints were all over the room. They also lifted prints from the equipment that belong to an Amy Lichtblau of Bisbee, Arizona."

"Ahh, so our bomber has a name now!"

"And it's a false identity. Bisbee Unified High School shows her registered as a junior, but nobody can recall meeting her. FBI agents checked her home address, but the apartment has been vacant for years. And the rent is being paid from her parents' checking account – Hans and Gretel Lichtblau."

"Seriously?"

"Raf, have I ever made a joke?"

"Not intentionally. You know, I like their style, telling us right up front the whole gig's a fairytale and daring us to crack it."

"I don't. It implies organization and confidence."

"And what organization is that?" Raphael asked. "I'll run it through the Engine tonight. So, do you think Kopelli can pull this trick off?"

"Yes. The little freak says so, at least."

Raphael glanced into the conference room, where Anton Kopelli fussed behind the glass wall. The room was packed with mounds of equipment he couldn't identify, but Kopelli and his assistant knew what each did. They moved back and forth, caressing and twiddling the knobs and levers in a strange mechanical foreplay. "What do you have against him? Are you bigoted against short people, or is it his eyes, or both?"

Downs grimaced. "Kopelli doesn't have eyes. He has marbles."

Raphael laughed. "Get over it, man. Lots of people are blind, and lots of them have glass eyes. Really, as far as glass eyes go, he's got an amazing pair. You can't tell the difference."

Downs grunted. "I can."

"Since when did you become so sensitive, Bob? He's just blind." Raphael waved at the conference room; Kopelli didn't wave back, of course, but his assistant Mihalic did. "He says becoming blind made his ears into fine instruments, which is why he runs six companies and became a multi-millionaire. Ease up on the guy, would you?"

"I think dark sunglasses would've accomplished the same thing."

"He didn't have a choice. He went blind after a car accident in college."

Downs stared at the Wall and recalled his junior year at MMU. That May, Kopelli met him out on the Quadrangle and showed him a selection of glass eyes. He asked Downs which matched his natural eyes best, and not knowing the reason behind the request, he picked a pair. When he saw Kopelli in September, he was wearing them in his eye sockets. Kopelli told everybody he'd lost his sight after his car got rear-ended by a tractor, and he'd spent the entire summer in Intensive Care, but Downs knew what he'd really done.

Later that year, when the college offered Downs eye surgery to correct his rubella-damaged vision, he swore for the first time in his life and stormed out of the office. Rather than explain his outburst and admit that he'd naively enabled a man's act of self-mutilation, he accepted ejection from the Field Practicum. He'd never told anybody the true story of Kopelli's so-called accident, and he wouldn't today, either.

Kopelli wandered through the desks and up to the podium as if he weren't blind. He didn't need a cane because he had the hearing of a bat and could hear any obstructions in his path. He stepped onto the podium and chatted with Raphael for a few moments; Raphael told him a joke, and he rolled his marbles when he heard the punchline. Downs turned away and studied something, anything, on the Wall.

"You can look at me, Bob. I don't mind," Kopelli said.

"I'm standing the Watch, Dr. Kopelli," Downs said, tapping his foot on the podium. "I like to *see* what's going on in the world."

Kopelli laughed. "You still resent me for that?" He leaned toward him and turned his face to Downs as if trying to capture his gaze. "Well, look me in the eye. Let's work out our problem, Bob."

"I don't have a problem, Kopelli, you do. You suffer from Chronic Lead Deficiency. By all that's holy, I dream of giving you the cure."

"Evolve, would you? That's all I did. I jumpstarted evolutionary organ specialization, and thank you for assisting –"

"You're conflating evolution with perversion!"

"The unevolved always see a successful adaptation as strange. Maybe you should try –"

"I WILL NOT!" Downs roared. "One more word and I'll drop you where you stand! Get off my podium before I throw you off, you demented homunculus!" Everybody in the Watch Room turned to see what had made Downs erupt, and he pinched the bridge of his nose. "Return to your station and prepare for the operation. We begin in thirteen minutes."

KOPELLI SAT IN HIS CHAIR AND HUFFED. Mihalic asked, "Is something the matter, Doctor?"

"Rest assured that nothing is the matter, Miklos," Kopelli said. "I merely encountered the small and narrow military mind, which always upsets me. Did you know that I studied to be in the NSF? What a disaster that would've been! Now, please run down your checklist again."

Kopelli slipped on a pair of headphones and turned a control on his console. He heard Bob Downs reading the test script – that brusque and Okie-flat voice – and he fingered the filter dial until his voice faded, and the foul man vanished from his world.

Next, he called up Warner's voice from a phone intercept captured the previous month. She was talking to a boyfriend – a clownish and insincere man, he could tell – and she was having a playful conversation that clearly was an invitation to sex although her doltish friend wasn't picking up the hint. He turned the dial and her voice faded out, leaving only the background noise behind. Her speech was complex and hard to filter, and it had taken him three days to purify her audio stream.

But it hadn't been all work; in reality, he could have finished in a day, but he'd dawdled because her vocal tones were sultrier to him than the hottest phone sex. The faint Irish lilt in her overtones and her delightful

The Rebel Commander

glottal T's were erotic enough, but even better, her consonants were guttural and clipped like the hard rhotic sluttiness of an unrepentant Manhattan bitch. But she also exaggerated her long vowels like a Philadelphia lady holding court at a Society Hill brunch, and the luscious contradiction drove him wild, so much that he'd been sporting an erection for three days.

He replayed her phone call, cuddling into her soft, round vowels like a baby between a mother's breasts – then she cracked off a stinging consonant that lashed him like a dominatrix's whip, reminding him that this lady could also rock leather and stiletto heels. He felt himself stiffen again.

In his mind, he imagined her face: A fair and flawless oval, perhaps with a sprinkling of girlish freckles, a wild mop of curly red hair and big green or blue eyes, a soft mouth built for blowjobs. Choosing blindness had been wise, he thought, because every woman wore the face he pictured. He was never disappointed.

"Doctor, the checklist is complete. I confirm the readiness of all systems," Mihalic said.

Kopelli's mental image shattered, but it didn't matter. She couldn't look anything like he imagined, and in fact, she probably looked like a mule. Soon, she'd look like a dead mule.

KRISTA LOOKED AT THE CLOCK: It was 8:45 PM, and they hadn't seen even a darkened house for ten minutes. "Is any civilization coming up, or are we driving off the edge of the feckin world?"

"We'll be crossing a river in a few minutes, and about ten miles after that, there's a highway that connects with this one. There should be some sort of life around there, or afterlife, or whatever."

Krista peered through the windshield but didn't see a glow anywhere in the fug. "Okay, I'll take your word on that," she said, and then her tablet rang. "Who'd be calling me now? I'm a little busy running from the law." She read the screen:

"What the hell? Is this code or something?" She showed the tablet to Ada.

"Probably a telemarketer. You gonna pick it up?"

"I will not. Why should I?" She pushed the END button and laid the tablet on her knee. "Now what does that stand for? It sounds familiar..." She stared through the windshield for a moment and then snapped her fingers. "Domestic Intelligence Command, National Tranquility Center?"

"Whoa, spacegirl, fire your retros! The Federals just called you?"

Krista nodded. "Why on Earth would they do that?"

"To track you. Do you have the geolocation turned off on your tablet?"

"Of course. I'm not an idiot."

"Maybe they think you don't," Ada said. "Or maybe they want to just say hello. Dunno."

"Huh, well, that was weird." Krista tapped her fingers on the steering wheel, and then the tablet rang again and displayed the same screen. "All right, this'll kill me if I don't find out." She tapped the speakerphone button. "Hello?"

"Miss Warner, this is Bob Downs. How are you this evening?"

DOWNS LISTENED FOR A REPLY, but all he heard was wind rushing past an open window. Then Warner laughed and said, "Hey there, Stalker Bob! Look, you've got to cut this out. I told you I only like handsome and dangerous men."

"I'm sorry to hear that," Downs said. He noticed Hogue's shoulders shaking and made a mental note. "I'm surprised you still think I'm interested in your type."

"What type is that? Female?"

"No, unclean," he said, tapping his foot.

"Bobby, Bobby, Bobby. If you're this desperate to get laid, I know a blind girl..."

"Miss Warner..."

"…she's actually not blind, just really nearsighted, but if I tell her to leave her glasses at home, you *might* have a shot –"

"Warner!" he bellowed. "Enough! Much as I'd enjoy trading sophomoric barbs, the purpose of this call is only to conduct government business. Please respect that."

"I'm doing my business, boyo. I'm still alive and free, and you've got your head so far up your ass, you can count your tonsils. It's going well."

"Not so well for you. We picked up your dissident friend in Maryville a few hours ago. And he's telling us so much about your movement."

"My movement?"

"Yes, of course. We know you're not doing this alone."

There was silence on the other end of the line followed by a short, stifled laugh. "So what? My movement has no shortage of dissidents, Downs."

"And we have no shortage of ammunition, Warner. We'll be happy to use it, starting with your friend Jack. Mr. Ripley begs you to turn yourself in."

"Is that so? Then tell me what was hanging from the rear-view mirror of his pickup truck. Then I'll believe you have him."

"I wasn't on the scene, and I haven't received an inventory of the vehicle's contents yet."

"But your thugs didn't report that I left like a pound of my DNA in his truck? Now, wouldn't that be the kind of thing they'd phone home about? Don't they teach that at your feckin Nazi Camp?"

"This isn't –"

"So you *don't* have him, then! Omigod, you bloody wheezers couldn't even catch an old man in a rickety pickup!"

"Warner –"

"Put your daddy on the phone, wouldja? I've got grown-up stuff to talk about."

"How funny. I wonder if Jack will laugh when we blow Elise's brains out."

"Oh, golly gosh, you're *so* scary! Listen up, boyo, send the A-Team next time if you've got one. We're getting bored playing these schoolyard games."

Downs' face had blossomed into a shade of red and was deepening into purple. "I admire your spunk –"

"Want me to send you some? Sounds like you're tapped out."

He lowered the tablet and took a slow breath until his anger dissipated. "Thank you for that outburst and for the valuable intelligence it revealed. We've known for some time that you were a member of a resistance movement, but now you've confirmed that it's evolved into a criminal rebel organization."

KRISTA'S MENTAL SPIN MACHINERY WAS BUZZING as she realized how easily Downs could be played. All she needed to tell him was the lie he wanted to believe, but it was just beyond her grasp.

Then it came to her, the stand-out whopper that capped a career of lies, and the audacity of it jolted her so hard that she barked a short laugh. "Jaysus, Bubba, how obvious have I gotta get before you'll take the hint? I've been working to take down this bloody government most of my life. I was recruited by The Activity in college, and I've been the DC district commander for the last three years."

"The Activity? Such a rousing name."

"Sure, and it's so generic that your snoops didn't pick up on it. That's called operational security. Heard of it?"

"I'm familiar with the concept."

"But not with the practice. You let one of The Activity's commanders walk right into the NTC to spy on you, boyo. You even offered to tell me all your secrets."

"At the time, it was the most appropriate tactical decision. That time has passed, as has yours, Miss Warner. Now you must give up, and I'm prepared to negotiate the terms of your surrender."

"Hah! That's a good one. So why do I keep wanting to tell you to go fuck yourself? Explain that."

"I figured a mouth like yours was built for profanity."

"It really isn't, but I've been swearing like a sailor ever since I smeared your two gorillas in Washington. I think they gave me Tourette's or something. Is that an airborne disease?"

"Miss Warner, may we return to the subject at hand? We aren't interested in you, as you know, but rather your tablet. If you'll surrender that, we'll escort you to the international gateway of your choice. You'll be allowed to fly to any nation you wish, as long as it's outside North America."

"Like I believe you."

"I'm an honest man."

"You're neither."

"I'm making this offer in good faith and to serve our interests as well as yours."

"Jaysus, you guys must suck at your job. You even suck at groveling. How pathetic is that?"

DOWNS IMAGINED THROTTLING WARNER'S THROAT until her face turned blue and she shut up. He bit the inside of his cheek, though, and forced himself to be calm. "This is a matter of budget, not skill. We've spent over twenty-three million dollars pursuing you so far, and we need to cap our expenses. As a taxpayer, you should support a government agency's efforts to be efficient." He turned to the Cybermeasures quadrant; Mochyn and his team seemed agitated, meaning that the trace worm they were trying to insert into the voice signal hadn't worked yet. Over in the conference room, Mihalic spun his finger over his head, signaling for more time. "The alternative is to keep running. We'll catch you, you'll die, and we'll take your tablet, but you'll be in fear the entire time, all alone in a big scary world where everyone wants to kill you. You'll spend the last days of your short life in constant terror, always waiting for the bullet or the knife to strike you down, always tired and hungry and dirty, slowly becoming the savage animal you pretended you never were. And in the end, you'll want to die, Warner. They all do in the end."

"Hmm. It sounds like you enjoyed saying that. Did it make you hard? Is little Mr. Downs up?"

He drew a slow, deep breath. "In the meantime, we'll seize all your trust's assets and sell them to defray the costs of your pursuit. Everything you own will disappear. You'll become penniless, incapable of buying the food or the fuel to continue this futile evasion. If you accept my offer, you'll retain your assets."

"My trust is a corporation, Bobaloo. You can't seize its assets. 31st Amendment, remember?"

"We can waive that by presidential decree, Warner."

"Oh, Bobby boy, you've got a gift for the absurd, I tell you. But you know what you can do with that decree? You can set it on fire and brew a nice cup of hemlock tea over the flames, a nice big cup, because Gibbon's gonna make you commit seppuku if you show up with that decree. He won't sign something that'll wipe twenty million bucks off my bank's balance sheet, boyo. They paid for half his campaign. They've got the deed to the man's soul in their back pocket!"

Downs started to reply, but Warner was howling so loud on the other end that he couldn't hear his own words.

THE TRACKING SIGNAL FROM DOWNS' TABLET pinged back from SatStream Nine four seconds after the call connected. Mihalic overlaid the satellite's uplink area on the NSF map of Warner's maximum travel radius from Maryville, Ohio, and he constrained his search to that. The map displayed on the Wall as well.

From Warner's purchase records, they knew that her tablet was a foldable triple-screen Advanced Heuristics AE-35, which came standard with superb stereo microphones. As Kopelli tuned into the background, he heard a whistle that a phone caller would say was faint; to his sensitive ears, it was as loud as a freight train horn. The whistle came from the bullet holes in the door, he concluded, and he turned a small dial to filter out the distracting tone.

He and Mihalic listened intently to every remaining sound. They already knew the make and model of Warner's car. They'd also found its approximate mileage in her dealership's maintenance records and therefore knew the condition of her tires. From this information, they'd assembled the sound profile of the tires at different speeds and on different surfaces.

Kopelli tuned his headphones to pick up the tire sounds, which told him that the cracks in the road were irregular and the car was traveling over exposed aggregates. To make a buzz at the pitch he heard, the pavement had to be old but not too old; he didn't hear the telltale sound of large crack repairs, either. "Stone matrix asphalt pavement, five to ten years old," he said.

Mihalic clicked on his monitor and filtered out the older pavements in the target area. Most of the road network on his screen grayed out, leaving 147 possible roads.

Kopelli pressed the headphones to his ears and turned two dials until he heard a match. "Speed 45 to 55 miles an hour, exclude speed limits under 35 and over 65," he said. The number of possibles dropped to 122.

He heard no water hiss. "Dry pavement, filter precipitation minus eight hours." After a few seconds, the map updated, but the number of candidate roads only dropped to 116 because the region had been dry for the previous day.

The background sounds didn't change for a minute, and Kopelli prayed for a conclusive marker sound because he'd determined little of value so far. He had a reputation to protect, and Dickhead Downs would pounce on any failure, so he raised the volume on his headphones and listened for higher frequencies.

He heard the tidal sound of breathing, but it wasn't Warner's – her respiratory pitch was deep and slightly raspy, where this subject's pitch was high and clear, meaning it had the small airways of a child or young adult. However, he'd merely been tasked with finding Warner's location, so he filtered it out.

Her tires thumped over something, and then again a half-second later; Warner's car had driven onto concrete, and he decided it was bridge pavement given the sound resonation. Mihalic heard it as well and motioned that he was clocking the bridge's length and updating the map. Twenty-one possible roads remained.

Kopelli pressed his headphones to his ears and concentrated; he thought he heard a faint train whistle, so he turned the volume up to maximum and strained to pick up the sound.

KRISTA GRASPED FOR THE WITTY RETORT that would finally crush the man, but then she spotted an accident ahead and turned her attention back to the road. Near the end of the bridge, a small truck had hit the concrete barrier, and a highway wrecker 'bot was prying it off. The robot wasn't finished cleaning the mess, though, and green liquid oozed across the roadway. When her tires hit the slick, the car slewed sideways, and she turned into the spin with one hand while holding the tablet with the other.

The car skidded through a mist of greasy spray, coating the windshield and making it nearly opaque. The rubber on her windshield wipers had worn away, though, so she leaned out the window to see the road – just as Ada tapped the wiper lever and metal screeched across glass.

KOPELLI HEARD A BRIEF WHITE-HOT SHRIEK a split-second before his eardrums ruptured and blasted apart his middle ears. He ripped off his headphones, screamed wild wails he couldn't hear, and stumbled back to the glass wall. Dizzy and unbalanced, he fell hard against the thick glass and cracked his skull.

With a barely visible smile, Downs watched the bloodied Kopelli slide down the glass. In the Watch Room, men and women rubbed their ears and flung headsets across monitors and desks.

He ended the call and wrung out his ear with his little finger. From the deployments board on the Wall, he saw that Hogue had been moving her teams into place as Warner's position became clearer. Before the screech, Kopelli and Mihalic had narrowed the possible locations to eight three-mile stretches of road, most of which were in northern Ohio and Indiana, with one far to the south in Kentucky.

"Hogue," he said, and receiving no reply, he yelled, "HOGUE!" She pointed to her ear, and he strode to her desk. "Have you covered those sites?"

"Yes, sir. Teams are deploying to the northern locations, and we have the Blackwings in the air for surveillance. This one in the south is in a coverage gap, though. I tried to contact the PD's in the Lexington area, but none have responded yet." She pointed to the map on her monitor. "We have one asset here, somewhere around Nashville. It's an off-duty Executive trainer in transit to attend a conference in Washington. He's about fifty miles south, and he could be there in a half hour or so. I'm trying to contact him by phone because he's driving an administrative vehicle with no radio. I haven't gotten through yet."

"No aerial assets?"

"Not in that area. It'd take more than an hour to get them there from Ohio."

Downs pointed to the dot in Tennessee. "Who's this?"

"Mike Miller. He teaches at MMU."

"He's a good man. I trained under him. He's a one-man war zone, and he can handle anything that comes his way. Send him there when you get through."

KRISTA STABBED THE 'END CALL' BUTTON and wheeled around to Ada. "Oh, that was feckin brilliant!"

"I didn't know!"

"It's *my* car, okay? If I wanted to turn the wipers on, I woulda done it myself!"

"I was just trying to help!"

"Stop trying to help! They don't bloody work!"

"Well, *now* I know that, okay? They sell new wiper blades in every store on the freakin planet, y'know," Ada said. "Don't blame me cuz you didn't fix the damn things!"

"Look, I've been a little too busy lately to keep the car up. Is that all right with you?"

"It's not fair." Ada crossed her arms, glared through the window, and then reached into her bookbag and pulled out her tablet. She plugged the earbuds in, and then she ripped them out a second later and glared at Krista. "*And* you're worth twenty million dollars, and I have to use this chickenshit tablet?"

"I own an office building in Georgetown. I left in a hurry and forgot to pack it, okay?"

"Well, stop being a freakin Ebenezer and get me one like yours!"

"What? My tablet cost six tenpez, and that was on sale!"

Ada cupped a hand to her ear. "What's that I hear? Is somebody playing *Hail to the Cheap?*"

"Oh, zip yer feckin gob and gimme a second of crickets, wouldja?"

"Hunh?"

"Just shut up. Please, you're giving me a migraine."

They rolled down the road for another few miles in silence, driving through an area devoid of houses and life. The car filled with a sickly-sweet smell from the liquid they'd driven through on the bridge, and while it was nauseating, at least it overpowered the liquefied manure stench.

Ada opened the atlas and turned on the map light. "We have another five or six miles till we get to that intersection with the highway."

Krista grunted and looked through the side window.

"Hey, I'm sorry I hit the wipers. I didn't know. It's all my fault." She laid her hand over Krista's. "Can we be okay again? Please?"

Krista's face softened. "Sure. I'm sorry I popped off at you back there. I was stressed from the phone call. I wasn't really mad at you."

"That's okay," Ada said. "Hey, that was one slayin takedown, Commander Krista!"

"You liked it?"

"You got all in his face," Ada said. "You must have a pair of stone *huevos*."

Krista shook her hair out and smiled. "I improvised. I remembered something Jack told me about pretending to be more than I was, so I tried that. The funny thing is that Downs thinks I'm more than I am too. Who am I to set him straight?"

"Not you! You're the Rebel Commander!"

"And why shouldn't I say so? The Big Lie Principle works for politicians, so why shouldn't it work for me?"

"What's the Big Lie Principle?"

"You didn't study this in history?" Krista asked.

"Are you kidding me? I cut every class."

"Well, I can't blame you for ditching it. History's boring as hell."

"Yawn Factor Nine."

"Anyway, here's how it works," Krista said. "Don't tell small lies because most people can spot those. If you're going to lie, tell absolutely colossal whoppers and constantly say they're the truth. Before long, everyone will believe you."

"Does this actually work?"

"Sure. Hitler came up with the idea, and it's been behind every war since. That's how Clune talked us into that Persian war – he said the Caliph's mad scientists had cooked up some sorta miracle goop, changed crude oil into beer or something, and they'd squirt it into all the white folks' oil wells if we didn't flatten Tehran."

"That's bullshit. Cracking a complex hydrocarbon takes –"

"But the facts didn't matter, doncha see? All the scientists called bullshit on it too, but he kept repeating the lie until the jingoism boiled over, and all America wanted was war. And America adores wars, even stupid ones. They make us feel special or something."

The Rebel Commander

"Huh," Ada said. She watched the trees flit by the window for a few moments. "Is this Downs guy an Arkie?"

"He is. Why?" Krista asked, watching her tap her fingers against her lips. "You're putting out that brooding genius vibe again."

"This isn't brooding, it's spocking." Ada lit a cigarette and gazed through the side window. After a few minutes of furious puffing, she flicked her cigarette through the window and sat back in her seat. "Okay, I figured it out. You will *so* shart your shorts."

"I will?"

"Yep." Ada crossed her arms and grinned. "Downs wants you to start a revolution."

"What? Are you serious?"

"Well, yeah. He just didn't say it out loud. Arkies believe there's a sentient Satanic thing called the *Foetidus* that stalks them and messes their shit up. I think they actually get a chubby for fighting it cuz that makes them feel worthy, and they all have low self-esteem. And that's why you can get Downs to buy your Big Lie without even breaking a sweat – he wants the end-times, good-versus-evil conflict you're selling. Not only that, fighting the *foetidus* commander of some evil Activist army will make him feel all good and noble. And getting his ass whupped by an ordinary girl would just make him feel like a dumbass, so he'll work pretty hard to convince himself you're a dreaded commander."

"Because getting his ass whupped by Generalissimo Warner is almost respectable."

"Well, natch. He wants to fight the good fight, Krista. He'll delude himself that you're a passionate rebel *anarchista*. Most Arkies I know are masters of self-delusion."

"Anarchista. I like the sound of that. It's so French Revolution."

Ada pumped a fist in the air. *"Viva la Activity!"*

"I could do so much with this. It's like putting a boogeyman under the Boogeyman's bed. You really *are* a genius." She kissed Ada on the top of the head. "Y'know, playing the anarchista is the natural extension of my muckraker brand. And I'm the perfect person to pull that off – *everybody* will buy the stereotype of some temperamental Irish rebel. I think I was purpose-built to gaslight this feckin world, that I do."

"You might not have to fake anything," Ada said. "You might start an actual revolution if you keep saying The Activity is real. If the Big Lie can start a war, why not a revolution?"

Krista laughed and patted her head. "Oh, kiddo, I sure wish I could, but it's impossible to get people to put down the remote and get on their feet. They're so bloody blue-pilled, I've got to pull off the most ridiculous antics just to get them clicking on my site. Revolution? No feckin way..." She noticed the screen on the car's console, where a yellow exclamation point was blinking. "Uh-oh. That's never good." She tapped the icon:

PRIMARY BATTERY DEPLETED
SWITCH TO RESERVE BATTERY?

"Don't worry, I've got this." She touched the YES button, and another message displayed:

RESERVE BATTERY DEPLETED
SWITCH TO PRIMARY BATTERY?

She sighed and puffed out her cheeks. "Oh, crap. Now what?"

Ada tapped a few commands on the screen and numbers appeared. She studied them for a few seconds and frowned, and then she reached into the glove box and pulled out the flashlight.

"Your charging circuit is dead, and I think it's because a control wire from the computer was damaged back here." She shined the light into the blasted hole in the dashboard. "Yep, it's a mess in there. I can see a wiring harness that got blown to crap. There's your problem."

"I've only got a quarter tank of fuel left. I won't go far on that without batteries. Can you do some magic with the computer and make it work?"

"No, I can't configure around a hardware problem." She called up the wiring schematics. "But I could bypass the computer and hook the battery directly to the alternator. I just have to switch two harness connectors under the hood. Pull over. I'll see what I can do."

Krista saw a pullout ahead, coasted into it, and parked on the shoulder. They walked around to the front, and after a minute of searching for the latch inside the crumpled hood, it finally opened with a pop. Krista shined the flashlight into the engine compartment, which was a tangle of wires and hoses even more confusing than the schematics. Ada looked at it with a frown, hands on her hips.

"What *is* all this stuff? It looks complicated, Ada. Are you sure you can figure this out?"

"Oh, this is nothing. I built a thermonuclear device in the sixth grade. This is a piece of cake compared –" She clapped her hand over her mouth. "Forget I said that."

"That's all right. I'm not the type who…whoa! You made an atom bomb?"

"No, I made a *device*. It's only a bomb if you plan to detonate it." She stood to her full five-foot height. "Which I didn't, by the way."

Krista sagged onto the bumper. "I don't think many people would see much difference at all."

"Yeah, that's what the Nuclear Emergency Search Team said too." She sat on the bumper next to her. "It was just a little one – way under ten kilotons and smaller than a gallon jug of milk. It was nothing to get worked up about, but they got all up-against-the-wall with me and Mom."

"You were arrested?"

"Well…don't repeat this, okay? This is Q-Level Compartmented Information. I could go to jail for telling you."

"Who am I going to tell?" Krista waved at the emptiness around them, but that only made Ada frown and cross her arms. "All right, I promise. So you were arrested?"

She nodded. "They took us straight to a ranch in the middle of Bumfuck Wyoming and wouldn't let us go till I agreed to work for them after I graduated – for the rest of my life. Mom fought them for three weeks, but in the end, it was either that or life in prison."

"Wow. The government did this?"

"Yeah. We never knew their names, but after Mom signed the agreement, they said they were from Los Alamos, the nuclear weapons lab," Ada said. "They have people who look for destructive little brainiacs like me. When they find us, they make us an offer we can't refuse. It's called Project Blue Ball. I'm one of about thirty kids they snagged."

"That's illegal! Nobody can enforce a contract like that! Take the bastards to court and get it nullified!"

"Mom tried. We went to this National Security court up in Philly that handles secret legal issues like mine. The douchenozzle judge told me I don't have any rights cuz I confessed to a felony, and that I was lucky Blue Ball didn't just take Baby Bang Bang and toss me in jail – or worse. He let that last part hang in the air. I figured he was hinting I should be grateful they let me live."

"Would Blue Ball have killed you?"

"No, not Blue Ball, no way. They work around the clock just to keep us alive. We're a seriously unstable bunch, y'know. Everybody there has a suicide buddy."

"Do you have one?"

"But it all worked out okay. The job pays crazy money, and I get to do lab work, which I love. And it's fun hanging with the Gamers. They can break into any computer that's plugged into a wall. One night, me and Poe Morton got ripped on some ace apricot brandy, and we backdoored through the energy management computer into Nizhny Novgorod's mainframe and scrambled all the launch codes in the Russian Atomic Munitions Inventory and the CIA was purpleface pissed cuz they'd wanted to do that for decades –" She clapped her hand over her mouth again.

"Forget you said that, right?"

"Big time, yeah, totally forget that."

"I'll do my best."

She sighed and looked down at the ground. "I always thought I'd do good with my gift, like crack the problem of time travel or develop a source of unlimited energy. That's actually why I built Baby Bang Bang – I was proving that strong fission works so it could be used to generate cheap energy. A strong fission reactor would generate about twenty-one times the energy of a conventional weak-fission reactor, and it'd be a cinch to retrofit them. You just need to add an initiator array and a few pumps and turbines, and then you're pumping out so much juice that you could shut down all the coal-fired plants and half the gas-fired ones. And that would cut our carbon emissions by half."

Krista snorted and looked at the swirling blanket of acidic fug. "That's like trying to put the pus back into the blister, now isn't it? Look at this soup."

"Okay, so the climate's already changed a lot. Does that mean we oughta give up and turn this into Planet Sauna? Taking two billion tons of carbon out of the atmosphere is still worth doing."

"All right, all right," Krista said. "But why build a bomb to prove you could make a better reactor?"

"Because bombs get attention, and a badass bomb will get you funding and labs and resources. If I made a perpetually self-powered teakettle, what would I get, some As-Seen-on-TV deal? To make strong fission viable, I needed to get the government's attention." She shrugged. "And boy, did I ever. Now I'll have to build little nukes for the rest of my freakin life. That's my clandestiny. Goodbye, dreams." She watched the fug swirl in the headlights, lost in her memories. "Sorry I went all coldwar and said you were a Red spy. That's ridiculous, thinking you were a spook."

"It's all right. I'm sorry I thought you were a paranoid little kid with an overactive imagination."

"Paranoia? What's that?"

Krista shrugged. "Dunno. Some screwball theory, I guess."

"Listen, I needed to be extra careful. I didn't want to wake up in bumfuck Siberia. Bumfuck Wyoming was bad enough. That's why I gave you my whitename –"

"Your what?"

"My whitename. Amy Lichtblau. Blue Ball made up an identity for me to use if I ever got caught by a Red extractor. If anyone tries to find out who Amy actually is, they'll go to Defcon Level Freakout cuz it means I've been captured. And I can't be captured. I've seen stuff so secret, it's illegal for me to even think about it. Oh yeah, Blue Ball will go all madmonkey on somebody's ass, that's for sure."

"Wow, they really watch out for you," Krista said. "So this is a stupid question, but is Ada Lang your real name?"

Ada looked down at her hands. "I'm pretty sure."

"You're not sure?"

Ada shook her head. "The Commander says so, but she could be lying. I had another last name till I was two, but she won't tell me what it was. So who can say I'm Ada Lang? Maybe I really am Amy Lichtblau, I dunno." She looked out past the headlights for a moment, her lips so tight that they turned pale. "I wish I was Amy, honestly. Ada is a real bitch."

Krista took her hand. "That's not true."

"Yeah, it is. Blue Ball makes sure of it. They manage all my social media, and I think they make me out to be a dragon or something. Some days when I show up at school, everybody shuns me like I've got the syph, and I think that's Blue Ball's way of making sure I don't have friends that aren't other Blues. I mean, I'm a social retard to begin with, but poisoning my puny social life on top of it?" She let out a disgusted huff.

"Wow. They post for you and all?"

Ada nodded.

"So what do you say, or what do they say you say?"

"I actually don't know. I can't get on any social media site, not a single one. They block me from everything."

"Now that's just cruel." They sat on the grille for a few minutes, listening to the engine tick as it cooled, but Krista couldn't think of anything to say that would lighten Ada's mood. Finally, she said, "I'm sorry, but it's a little hard to believe that a kid actually made an atom bomb. Where'd you get the…what's it called…the uranium for it?"

"Plutonium-gallium alloy. Uranium ore is about as fissionable as cheese."

Krista rolled her eyes. "Okay, so where did a sixth-grader get plutonium?"

"Plutonium-gallium alloy. Elemental plutonium is unstable at room temperature. You don't want to be in the same county as that stuff."

With a whimper, Krista bent over and pressed her hands to her temples. "So where did a sixth grader get plutonium-gallium alloy?"

"I was only in the sixth grade. Where would I get that?"

Krista sat upright and slapped her hands on her knees. "Jaysus, Mary, and Joseph!"

"What?"

"You're so annoying! Listen, if the bomb wouldn't have blown up, what was the bloody problem?"

"Oh, it would have detonated. I used a lithium-moderated polonium dioxide core instead of plutonium. Polonium is used in medical research, so the lab had a lot and I could liberate a few kilos pretty easy. It's not normally fissionable, but it'll give a good pop with strong-fission triggering inside a fusion event. Maybe six kilotons, I'd guess."

"Hunh?" Krista tried to shake the confusion from her head.

"If I had plutonium alloy, the effective yield would approach ninety kilotons cuz the dual-detonation characteristic amplifies the shockfronts. That's why I named it Baby Bang Bang. The first shockfront was just a massive hadron jetwave, but the second one – pow! Instantaneous gluon decay is profundo blastissimo, sister."

Krista stiffened. "Jaysus, girl, you're proud of it?"

"Why not? It's not like it was dangerous or anything."

"A nuke isn't dangerous?"

"Nope. We never use them, Krista. They're just a deterrent. They're more like physics test platforms than bombs."

"I've got to be honest with you – nukes are feckin dangerous. If you say they aren't, you've gone over the rainbow, and that's the truth."

Ada looked at her hands again and clasped them together. "You might be right. I get these ideas sometimes, and if I don't do something about them, I go a little nuts. But if I *do* do something about them, shit blows up." She lit a cigarette and gazed into the fug, blinking back tears.

Krista lit up too, and they collected their thoughts for a few minutes. "So *that's* why that truck exploded back in Maryville. You made a bomb, didn't you?"

Ada's eyes glittered, and a smile of true joy brightened her face. "I always wanted to make an amplinergic tetrabinary, and I knew it'd give a decent pop, but I never expected…" She noticed Krista's jaw hanging open, and then she looked down at the road, her shoulders sagging. "There I go again. Listen, I can't help it. I have weird hobbies, and I have a seriously weird mind. People look at a glass of water and see water, but I see worlds in it, Krista, wild and beautiful places with infinite potentialities." She flicked her cigarette deep into the fug and shrugged. "Is any of that real, or is what I see in my mind a hallucination? Am I sane or insane? I don't know how to tell sometimes, and that's when I think The Commander was right when she called me a dangerous monster."

"Well, you built an atom bomb, for chrissakes. Anybody's going to get stressed out about that. I'm sure she didn't think you're a monster, and I don't either." Krista reached out and turned Ada's face to hers. "You saved my life back there, and you saved Jack and Elise's lives too. You were dangerous when we needed you to be. You're a blessing, not a monster."

Ada searched her eyes in the faint light for a sign of insincerity. "You really mean that?"

Krista put her arm around her shoulder and hugged her. "I do." They sat on the bumper, Ada nestled into Krista's shoulder, and listened to the sickly croaking of tree frogs from a distant hollow. "How'd you build it without being caught? Didn't somebody at school catch on to what you were doing?"

"Oh, no, I couldn't build it at school. I needed an engineering lab, so I made it at Chalys. I had the whole summer off and a lot of time to kill."

"Chalys? You mean Chalys Pharmaceuticals?" Krista asked.

"Yeah. Mom's a director there, and she gave me access to the Creation Labs."

"You never told me she worked at Chalys! They're the maker of Recombin, the vaccine for the virus that's killing everyone. The vaccine there's not enough of!"

"Are you serious? *Chalys* makes the vaccine?" She jumped up and spun around in the headlights' fuzzy beam. "That's what's in the briefcase! Mom discovered something dirty about the vaccine, and the Federals want it back!"

"And that's why they wanted her so bad!"

"I have to open that thing!" Ada ran to the car, opened the back door, and pulled the metal briefcase toward her.

Krista had just turned to follow when tires hissed to a stop on the road beside her. A spotlight snapped on and caught her in its beam, and she blinked a few times, raising a hand to ward off the glare. A man's brusque voice called from the fug beyond the light. "Don't move. Put your hands on your head and spread your legs two feet apart, ma'am."

She did as she was told, and large hands grabbed her and twisted her arms behind her back. Something hard and cold encircled her wrists, and then he shoved her forward into the light.

ADA HEARD THE TRUCK STOP TOO. She crouched and looked underneath the car, and she saw big, knobby tires on the other side. A light flashed on, and a man talked to Krista.

She reached into the passenger seat and slid the briefcase out. As quietly as she could, she crept to the front bumper. A big Silverback was idling beside the car, and on the other side of it, the man was still talking.

Unsure what to do, she assessed the situation: No other lights glowed in the fug, so this was the only vehicle; she heard one voice, so just one man was out there; he was standing in the spotlight, so his eyes weren't adapted to the darkness; and finally, he didn't know she was here because he hadn't searched for her.

She held every advantage, and she even had a weapon – the briefcase weighed at least fifteen pounds, enough to knock a grown man down. She slipped off her boots, and she'd just started moving toward Krista when the Silverback's tailgate chirped and whined open. The voices moved to the back of the truck, and Ada crab-walked over to it and crouched by the rear wheel, listening as the voices approached.

It sounded as if Krista was pleading, but she couldn't hear the man's voice since he was facing away. A sound cracked in the air, and for a moment she thought he'd shot Krista, but then she heard the rustle of plastic sheeting being spread in the trunk.

Krista made a strange sort of dance; Ada couldn't see her in the fug, but it appeared as if she was stamping her feet on the road. The sound would cover her footsteps, though, and she tightened her grip on the briefcase and peeked around the rear of the car. The man still had his back turned, and Krista protested that her name was Sue McConnell, and that she knew nothing about a tablet. His hand moved toward a holster on his hip.

Her pulse pounded and her breathing came fast and shallow, and heat bloomed in her arms and chest. She grasped the briefcase with both hands, and then she jumped around the corner and swung it at the man's head with all the strength her small body possessed.

The briefcase hit him with a thud, and he fell over sideways. However, she lost her grip on it, and her momentum carried her into the trunk, where she landed on something soft. She raised her head and saw that she was lying on a large, dark-skinned man with yellowish eyes staring blankly at the ceiling. Shrieking, she scrambled out of the trunk but tripped over the briefcase. She stumbled into something and spun around, ready to fight – and saw Krista wearing a puzzled look. "Ada? What happened? I heard a whistle and a thunk, and there you were. And there he was…"

She stood and dusted herself off. "I clobbered him. I figured somebody had to take care of this goon. You were doing absolutely freakin nothing."

"What could I do?" She turned around and wiggled her hands. "I'm in handcuffs."

Ada glanced at the cuffs and then rifled through the Federal's pockets. He still stared at the ceiling, but he was blinking his eyes, so at least he was alive. He didn't react when she pulled the keychain from his pocket, though. "Well, you coulda run or kicked him or something," she said as she unlocked the handcuffs.

Krista shook the blood back into her hands. "What good would that do?"

"What! He was going to shoot you! Just do something, don't just stand there!"

"I don't like hitting people. I'm a non-violent person."

"So you'd let him blow your brains out? It's okay for some cold-blooded bastard to get violent on you, and you don't do anything? Why do you treat him like he's human? What the hell's wrong with you?"

"Ada, calm down, wouldja? I'm seriously grateful..."

"For saving your damn ass again cuz you can't lift a finger to help yourself! Are you French or something?" She whirled around, stomped to the side of the Silverback, and punched the side door a few times. "It's like going into war leading the freakin Buddha Battalion! *Ohh, we are veddy non-violent!*" The thumping grew louder, and the truck rocked from side to side. "What the fuck does *that* mean when someone's got a gun to your head? What sorta rebel are you?"

"Please don't pitch a fit, all right?" Krista sat in the trunk and rubbed her wrists. "Jaysus, what was I supposed to do? Strap bandoliers across my chest and yell *'Viva Zapata'* and fire my pistols in the air?"

"It's a start! It's better than this lipstick-to-a-gunfight shit!" A loud thump came from the side of the truck and Ada grunted. "Oh, fuck, my toe!" She limped back to the tailgate, pushed the Federal's leg to one side, and sat next to Krista, muttering things both incomprehensible and unwholesome. "Okay, I never said I wasn't an ass," she grumbled, rubbing her foot.

"You're just wound up. You need to calm down," Krista said. "Hell, *I* need to calm down. How'd he find me?"

"He tracked your tablet somehow. Are you certain you turned off the geolocation on it?"

"I did. Not only that, it was a satellite call, which is untraceable. You've got to figure this out before we get killed."

"Not now. I can't think," Ada said. "We oughta bounce. We've been here too long."

"Right. Get your things from my car. We'll take this truck."

Ada nodded, ran to the car, and slipped into her boots. She grabbed her bookbag and whatever else she could hold and threw them into the rear seat of the truck, and then she returned to the tailgate to get the briefcase. Krista reached under the seat of her car and pulled out a small but heavy leather bag. She dropped it into her backpack, which she tossed into a rear seat of the Silverback, and then yelled for Ada to climb in.

"But what do we do with this guy?" Ada asked.

Krista walked around to the trunk, where the Federal was lying half in and half out. She pulled down the tailgate, but it closed on his legs.

"Coulda told you it wouldn't work," Ada said.

"It was worth a try. Well, better out than in, I always say." They each grabbed a leg and pulled, but he was too heavy and didn't budge an inch. They yanked harder, and Ada skittered out into the fug holding the man's boot.

"He's not moving," she said as she trudged back. "Let's just push his legs in and leave him back here."

"What if he wakes up?"

Ada pulled the pistol from his holster. "I'll shoot him."

Krista pursed her lips. "Okay. Good plan."

DOWNS READ THE MAP on the Wall; five of the eight target roads were checked and cleared already, but the dot in Kentucky was still blinking red.

"Hogue, any news from Miller?"

"He hasn't checked in for twenty minutes, sir. The last call we had, he said he was turning east on Bluegrass Highway and hadn't encountered any vehicles yet."

"Hmm. Give him a call and get an update."

Raphael sat in a spare chair with his feet propped on the side of Cochon's desk. "Bob, I love it when you do my work. I can just sit here, relax, and watch the master in action. It's like Sunday afternoon football."

"Don't get too comfortable, Raf. I'll end this hunt soon."

Raphael sighed. "Fine. Hey, you guys got any beer?" Cochon pushed his feet off the desk, and he grumbled.

Hogue swiveled around in her chair. "Sir, no answer after twenty rings on the Miller tablet. The phone is receiving and ringing, but he's not picking up. We'll try again in case he's away from it."

"Mike's never away from his tablet," Raphael said. "I trained with him for an entire year, and it never left his hip. I think it was grafted on."

"That's what I remember too," Downs said. "Try it again, Hogue."

Hogue turned back to her monitor. A minute later, she said, "That's weird. This time someone picked it up and disconnected."

Downs and Raphael looked at each other quickly. "Cover that area now," Downs said. "Divert the Blackwings. Launch the Talons from Dayton. Contact any PD in the area and have them respond. And get a team rolling down there now."

"This is really luxe," Krista said. "Wow, talk about roomy. This isn't a car, it's wheel estate!"

"Hello-o-o over there!" Ada called. "Hey, I wonder when the flight attendant is coming with the sandwich cart."

"Better be soon. The service on this flight sucks."

To Ada's delight, the truck had a satnav system. She'd set it for Paducah, in the southwest part of the state, to avoid the traffic cameras on the interstate highways.

Krista was driving at eighty miles an hour, relying on the Silverback's dash radar to warn them of traffic. Even if she hit something, the truck would get the best of anything it met on the road short of an eighteen-wheeler.

"Do you hear something beeping?" Ada asked.

Krista listened and heard a chirping sound. "I do. Where's it coming from?"

They listened and swiveled their heads to find the source. "It's from the back," Ada said, unbuckling her seatbelt. "It's the goon's tablet. I'll be right back." She picked up the pistol and walked down the aisle to the trunk.

"I'll bet it's not for you," Krista called.

"Of course not, Commander Obvious. I just want to mute it." She stumbled and bumped into a shotgun on one of the seats, and she wriggled the numbness from her hand.

The Federal was in the same position he'd been in for a half hour and didn't move to answer the call. In fact, he made no moves of any kind. His eyes were still open, though, and he was staring at the ceiling the way living men didn't.

She placed her fingers on his neck, but he had no pulse. She dropped the pistol, climbed onto the trunk floor, and tried to remember how cardiac massage worked. Crossing her palms as her mother taught her, she leaned over his breastbone and pressed down with all her weight. She heard a sound as if someone had stepped on a wet sponge.

She pressed down hard three more times. *Squish, squish, squish.* From behind his skull, blood trickled across the plastic sheet and meandered to the tailgate. "Oh, fuck," she said.

"Whatcha say?" Krista called from the front.

"Umm...I said it's stuck!" Ada sat back, and the tablet in his pants pocket rang again. She reached in and pulled out a rubberized metal tablet; its screen displayed the same gibberish that Krista's had shown when Downs called. She tapped the REJECT NUMBER icon and then walked shakily back up the aisle, collapsed into the seat, and buckled in.

"How's he doing?" Krista asked.

"He's, umm...resting peacefully." Ada reached for her cigarettes and showered the car with them as she opened the pack.

"Here, I'll help with that." Krista reached over and took the pack from her. "You're getting a delayed case of the jitters. That happened to me too. After the garage incident, I blanked out for a while, and I couldn't keep my hands from shaking for hours." She settled back in the seat and took a long puff. "At least you didn't kill the guy. That feels terrible, and I can't help but think about that sometimes. I mean, they were bad guys, and I did what I had to, but they were still some mother's baby once. A mother held that little boy and nursed him and sang to him and dreamed of all the wonderful things he'd be, and I –"

Ada threw the cigarette out, grabbed her tablet, and then rammed the earbuds into her ears.

"What? What did I say?"

HOGUE PULLED OFF HER HEADSET and turned in her chair. "I tested the phone lines. Miller's tablet is rejecting the call, sir."

"That's Warner. Are you sure you can't locate the truck or the tablet?"

"Yes, sir," Hogue said.

"Sir," Cochon said. "Some of the newer trucks have built-in hijack beacons as standard equipment. This may be one of them."

"Get on it, then," Downs said.

A minute later Cochon called out. "It has a beacon, sir. I'm trying to activate it now. I'll feed the output into the map." He tapped the monitors and then pointed to the Wall, where a red dot blinked in central Kentucky. Bearing and speed data appeared on the screen. "The truck's traveling southwest at a high rate of speed, sir. That's opposite the direction Miller should be going. This is flight behavior."

"Agreed," Downs said. "Hogue, when will we have assets in the area?"

"First response will be the Talons in approximately eighteen minutes, followed by SAG Nineteen in twenty-one minutes, sir."

"When will the drones be in range to fire?"

"If that truck keeps moving at that speed, about sixteen minutes, sir, depending on winds aloft."

"Excellent. When we have a lock, light that target up."

KRISTA FIDGETED IN HER SEAT. "How about we stop, maybe take a little stroll?"

"How about we don't?" Ada asked. "The further we go, the better I feel."

"We should pull over. I'm getting antsy, maybe from caffeine deprivation or something. I've absolutely got to get out of this feckin car."

Ada spotted a metal canopy ahead on the roadside. "That looks like a gas station. Maybe we can find something to eat."

"That's perfect. I'm starving, and I wouldn't mind finding a working toilet." She slowed and eyed the darkened building. It had only two islands and four rusted pumps, and a banner stretched across the canopy advertised cold beer and juicy nightcrawlers.

"And I left my banjo at home," Ada said.

"It'll be okay. I've got a good feeling about this. But what do we do with the goon while we're inside? If you give me the gun, I guess I can stay out here and watch him."

"Don't worry," Ada said. "He won't wake up anytime soon."

"Are you sure?"

"Yeah, trust me."

Krista pulled under the sagging canopy and up to the entrance. A darkened neon sign over it said EMINENCE SPEEDIMART. No other buildings were in sight; the place was surrounded by fields of tobacco plants and nothing else except a side road.

She pulled the parking brake and then glanced at the truck's thumbpad. She wouldn't be able to restart the engine if she turned it off, so she left it running and climbed out. "Behold the city of Eminence!" She heaved her heavy pack from the backseat and walked around the back of the truck. "Now where'd I put my bucket list?"

Ada was already standing at the front door. She swung the briefcase behind her and rammed the glass door with it, but it bounced off. "What the hell kinda glass is this?" she asked.

Krista swung her backpack at it, but the glass didn't even crack. "This backpack weighs about twenty pounds. If that won't break it, nothing will. You've got to pick the lock."

"Why pick the lock when you can bust the glass? That's way more fun." She turned and ran to the truck, opened the rear door and rummaged inside, and then returned carrying a black shotgun with a drum underneath the barrel.

Krista stood back. "What are you going to do with that?"

Ada slammed the butt of the rifle into the glass, and the gun thundered and bucked out of her hands. They dropped to the ground and covered their heads with their arms.

Krista opened one eye and saw the shotgun lying on the sidewalk, a curl of blue smoke drifting from the muzzle. "Damn it! You didn't turn it off first?"

"I guess I didn't," Ada said, rubbing her ears. "Wow, was that ever loud!"

"You could kill somebody! Find the off switch before you pick up that damned thing again!"

"Well, you show me where the off switch is!"

"What?" Krista looked at her blankly. "Mother of God, I'm sure I've gone stone deaf. All I hear are whistles." She walked back and forth trying to shake the sound from her head. As she passed the truck, she spotted a constellation of small holes in the rear fender. "Jaysus, look at this!"

"Shut up, already. It's stolen."

"That coulda been me!" She cupped her hands and looked through the back window. "At least the noise didn't wake up the goon."

Ada found a small button near the trigger. "Here's the off button."

"Splendid, just splendid."

Ada banged on the glass another time, but it wouldn't break.

"Just pick the damn lock, for chrissakes. It'll be faster."

"No." She walked back a few paces, waved Krista away, and raised the gun to her shoulder.

"Uh-oh," Krista said, covering her ears and cringing. "Don't do it, don't do it…"

Ada squeezed the trigger, and the weapon bucked in her hands three times, obliterating the glass in the door and the window next to it. Inside the store, a cloud of shredded cardboard and paper fluttered to the floor.

"You're dangerous, girl," Krista said as she rose from her crouch.

Ada smiled back. "Oh, yeah." She flipped the safety and ran her hands along the barrel, which had the name 'Maussner' engraved on it in ornate letters. "You shall be my Scepter of Power, Mickey Maussner." She hoisted the shotgun onto her shoulder, picked up her bookbag and briefcase, and climbed through the blasted door. "I have a new best friend now. Mickey knows how to fight back, at least."

"I'm so bloody happy for you two. Let me know when Mickey can drive a car, wouldja?"

The racks near the door were wrecked, and the newspapers on it were pockmarked and shredded. The rest of the store was mostly empty, though.

They walked to the restrooms. Krista finished first and started searching the darkened store for anything edible. The coolers still held a few bottles of juice, which she stuffed into her backpack, but the shelves in the middle of the store were empty. She walked to a coffee urn and flipped the handle. Nothing came out.

Under a hot dog rack, she found a stale bun and ate half, pocketing the rest for Ada. She checked the soda machines, the sandwich displays, and even rifled through the trash can, but the only food in the store was the meager bun.

Ada walked out and set her briefcase near the door. "Find anything? My stomach's already rumbling."

Krista shook her head and handed her the half-eaten bun. "Only this." They walked to the checkout, where Krista searched the shelves under the cashier's counter. She pulled out a box and found two chocolate bars. "Oh, here we go! Two Rhesus Chunky Munky bars –"

Ada snatched a bar from Krista's hand, peeled it, and swallowed it in one bite. "Gonna eat yours?" she asked, and then she licked her lips and eyed Krista's bar. Krista slipped it into her hoodie.

Ada walked to the clerk's side of the counter, gnawing on the stale bun, and then she knelt and pulled something from a drawer. "Hey, guess what I found." She dropped a jar of instant coffee on the counter.

Krista's eyes widened, and she twisted the lid off so fast that it hovered in the air a second before falling to the counter. She licked her little finger, dipped it into the jar, and sucked the furry digit. "Mmm, come to Mama," she moaned.

"That's revolting," Ada said.

Krista nodded and dipped her finger in again.

"I can't watch this." Ada turned away and searched the countertop next to the broken window. "Jubilations! They have Kamelles!" She grabbed every pack she could find, shook the broken glass off, and stuffed them into her bookbag until it could hold no more. "You want smokes?"

Krista pulled the finger from her mouth. "Absolutely. Get me some Breathless Menthols, wouldja?" She dipped it back into the coffee jar.

"I don't see any, but they have Reapers," Ada said, holding up a fluorescent orange pack of cigarettes. She waved her hand over them in prize-show model fashion. "You know what they say: 'Go for the Burn.' They have a killer kick."

"Blech. I tried those once and hacked up chunks for days. It's the Breathless or nothing."

"I'll look." She searched again and found a small cardboard rack leaning against a piece of unbroken window. "Oh, here they are." She stuffed a few handfuls into Krista's bag, and as she was reaching for more, she glanced through the window and froze in place. The truck was gone.

She dropped to the floor. "Get down!"

"What?"

"I said get down! Now!"

Krista crouched behind the counter and Ada duck-walked from behind it.

"What's the matter?" Krista asked.

"The truck isn't out there!"

"Huh?" Krista blinked a few times. "Where'd it go?"

"How the hell would I know?" Ada slipped the shotgun from her shoulder. "The Federals might've taken it, and we have to assume they're out there right now." She crawled to the end of the counter, pulled her briefcase over, and peeked around the corner. "I don't see anything, but then I wouldn't expect to. They're probably concealed."

"And if they *are* out there, we're trapped."

Ada nodded slowly and clicked the shotgun's safety off. "We might have to fight our way out."

DARL SCOTT WAS HAVING AN AWESOME DAY. He knew it would end splendidly because he'd awakened with an erection this morning, and the portents of morning wood were powerful. The rest of the day was frustrating, but this made up for it.

He tossed his dark ponytail back and forth, his huge white smile glowing in the light from the dashboard: *his* new dashboard in *his* new ride. When he'd pulled up to the Speedimart a few minutes ago to emancipate some diesel, he was a small man driving a small car – and then he looked on the other side of the pumps, and the angels sang and danced. There it was, a big-ass Silverback with the engine running, just waiting for him to get in and go.

This truck would set him up for the big time. The trunk could hold a ton of Base-M, and now he could move product anywhere he found a market, and nobody would touch him because this looked like a Federal truck.

He could even move product right outside the elementary schools, and fifth-graders were always an easy mark for a slick sell. All it took was one rock of the stuff, and the little brats would be buying it by the pound a week later. Each new kid he hooked would be a steady buyer for at least five years. Then they'd die, but more would take their place. The world wasn't about to run out of fifth graders.

He'd fill the truck from Boone's lab and make a run from Cincinnati to Louisville to Nashville in one week, and then he'd fill up and do it again. He'd be driving a lot, but this was a comfortable cruiser; he could even sleep in the back if he wanted, although he knew he wouldn't. No, those days were gone. He'd be staying in five-star hotels from now on and eating like the king he always knew he was.

Cash would be a problem, though. He'd make tons of it, and he couldn't carry all of it with him. He started thinking of places to make buried stashes.

"Why'd I listen to you?" Krista asked. "We should've tied that guy up."

"Why'd I listen to *you?* I didn't want to stop."

"I bet he got up and drove off." Krista slammed her fist on her knee. "Damn it. One little slip and we're screwed."

"He didn't drive off, trust me."

"Maybe he was faking unconsciousness, and he was waiting till we were gone to take the car back. It coulda happened."

"He didn't drive off!" Ada said.

"How can you be so sure?"

"Cuz he was dead!"

She stared at her blankly. "Dead?"

"Y'know, kevorked? Living-challenged? Returned to sender?"

"Dead?"

"Yes, dead. The not-driving-cars kind of dead, Krista. Somebody with a pulse was just here. They took the truck." Ada peeked around the corner. "There's something out past the pumps. I'll go check it out, but I need you to see if any Federals come out of those bushes across the road, all right?"

"He's dead?"

"Can you focus for a minute?"

Krista nodded and crawled to the doorway. She crouched by one side while Ada pressed against the counter opposite her. "I'll run to the first island. You let me know if anything moves, okay?"

"Right, got it," Krista said.

"But you have to promise me something first," Ada said. "Promise me that you'll never tell Mom what happened tonight."

"I promise. It's just between us," Krista said, and then Ada reached over and held out a bent little finger. "Pinky swear? You can't be serious." She felt a laugh rising but stifled it when she saw Ada nod solemnly. "Right, okay. I pinky-swear it."

Ada nodded and ran through the doorway, stopping at the first row of pumps. She pressed against it and looked back at Krista, who stood and scanned the fields surrounding them. "No movement so far!" she called out.

Ada winced, laid a finger on her lips, and gestured with the other hand.

"Okay, got it," Krista said to herself. "Like we're secret agents or something."

Ada ran to the second row and disappeared around it. A few seconds later, she stood, swore a few times, and kicked a gas pump so hard that pieces fell off into the dirt. She stomped back to the store with the shotgun over her shoulder and a sour look on her face.

"What is it?" Krista asked.

"The Federals weren't here. Someone just stole the truck, that's all. They left their car, keys and all."

Krista sagged against the wall. "At least we don't have to shoot our way out now. Let's get our stuff and go steal *their* car."

"You won't like it."

"It drove here and it can drive away, and that's all I'm wanting right now," Krista said. They picked up their bags and walked out, but Krista stopped short when she saw the car. "Well, this is a piece of crap."

A tiny, rust-red hatchback missing a front fender idled by the pump. Looking closer, she noticed that the car's paint had worn away, and the rust-red color was real rust. The windows were coated with greasy yellow film; the hatch was taped shut and wire held the rear bumper on. "What the hell is this? Did this fall out of a gumball machine? This isn't a car, it's a car charm. It should be hanging off a key ring."

"It's a Hugo. Two seats and two cylinders. It's the worst car in the world," Ada said. "But it drove here, and it can drive away, right?"

Krista groaned and leaned against the pump. "Are you sure it even runs?" She stopped and turned to the east, where a familiar bass sound rumbled. "Uh-oh. I've heard that before."

Ada heard it too, and she ducked between the pumps. "Get in here before it sees you!" She tugged on Krista's arm and pulled her down.

Krista peeked around the pump after it passed and roared down the highway. "I didn't feel even a little tingle, so I don't think it spotted us. It must be searching this road. That means they've got some idea where we are, and I'll bet a truckload of Federals won't be far behind."

"Yeah, we need to get outta here, and we won't be able to take Bluegrass Highway anymore. We'll take this side road."

Krista nodded and stood, and then the fug around the drone brightened. A second later, it lit up again, and they heard a whooshing sound.

"Missiles. That's the sound of rocket motors." Ada looked into the western sky and snapped her fingers. "There was a tracker on that truck, I bet. And now they're going to destroy it cuz they think we're in it."

"They're close. We've got no time to waste." Krista watched the lights recede and rubbed the back of her neck. "Wow, if we hadn't gotten out of that car, we'd be dead."

DARL'S IMAGINATION WAS RUNNING WILD. There were so many things to do now and so much money to make. He'd need an accountant, a shady one who knew the Base-M trade and could launder money. Maybe he'd incorporate, too, and someday buy a baseball team and have his own suite. In his own stadium.

He saw the glow of twin headlights in the rear-view mirror, and like the gentleman he now was, he lowered his window and waved for the motorist to pass.

THE SKY LIT UP A FEW MILES AWAY, and then the double concussion of the explosions shook them. The fug glowed white and then faded to yellow, and a boom echoed off faraway hills.

Krista rubbed her neck again and puffed out her cheeks. "On second thought, I prefer the Hugo."

"Yeah, it's perfect, now that I think about it."

They loaded the little car and drove onto the side road heading north. They were a mile up the road when a gray Silverback flashed down the highway, roaring toward the fire's glow.

GOOD MORNING, DAVE

Day 35
Tuesday morning, September 22, 2043
Oxon Farms, Oxon Hill, Maryland

Victoria Lang waved to a guard in the faux-colonial gatehouse and continued down the sidewalk. The gate was supposed to be the only way in and out of Oxon Farms, but Dave Eggie once told her about loose boards in his back fence that the property manager had never repaired. For what she planned to do, that was the ideal entrance.

Her feet were killing her, both heels were blistered, and the floppy hat and mask she wore to confuse the NSF aerial cameras was making her pour sweat. She was almost there, though, and she'd be driving back to St. Elizabeth's if her plan worked.

Boulders ringed a thick stand of trees just ahead, and Dave's property was beyond them. She scanned her perimeter, and finding it clear, she sprinted into the woods and stopped at a high, wooden board fence. She looked in both directions and saw a section with warped boards a hundred feet to one side.

They pried off quickly with a stout stick, and she made an opening large enough for her to squeeze through. Trees crowded the fence on the other side, but she spotted a clearing past them and picked a path toward it. A few minutes later, she stood at the edge of a thick green lawn behind the house, with an in-ground pool and a large patio to one side.

She crept alongside the house to the front. The building imitated a Colonial mansion: Every surface was brick, a high colonnade covered the entrance, and a brick driveway curved up from a distant street to the front porch. On it sat Dave's Good Ole Boy truck, a ten-year-old silver pickup. She reached into her pocket for the lock-picking pins and silently thanked Ada for the lesson in crime.

My little felon. I should've thanked you for so much more, and if I ever have you back, I'll thank you every day for every small thing. I pinky-swear it.

She dug a fingernail into the wound on her arm; she was weakening again, and it was the wrong time to lose her situational awareness. Back in her cell, she could cry through the night if needed, but not here, not now.

She heard no sounds inside the house, and the front door was closed. At just after six in the morning, Dave was probably still getting ready for work, so she'd have at least twenty minutes to prepare.

However, she needed to confirm his whereabouts first. She crept along the front of the house and peeked into the windows. Nothing moved inside, so she slipped off her shoes and padded up the marble steps to a thick oak door. She heard nothing beyond it, but through the sidelight, she glimpsed a husky man with blonde, brushy hair walking to the kitchen in the back. A morning newspaper lay on the porch floor too, so he'd just begun his day.

She pushed back her hat and stepped away from the window to run through her options. He'd be a while if he was starting breakfast, so she decided to break into his truck first and set it up for the interrogation.

Just as she started down the steps, though, the door opened and she heard a cry of surprise; without thinking, she wheeled around and hooked her leg behind Dave's knee. Before his body hit the floor, she'd slipped her combat knife out and was leaping to his side. As he opened his eyes, she pressed the knife point into the base of his neck to let him know that the knife was sharp and she was serious. "Good morning, Dave."

"The hell?"

"I slit a man's throat with this knife a few days ago, and I won't hesitate to slit yours if you piss me off. *Capische?*"

He nodded and gulped. "Tori?"

"It's Dr. Lang to you."

"What are you doing?"

"I'll ask the questions. You'll answer them or die. Simple, no? Now, slide back to the door and sit up." She kept the pressure on the blade as he shimmied back and propped himself up against the door. "Good. Now we'll have a little chat."

He barely nodded. With her left hand, she felt in her coat pocket; the tape had fallen off the syringes, and she couldn't tell which of them held the sedative she needed. If she used the paralytic by mistake, she'd have to drag

Good Morning, Dave

his bulky corpse to the truck, being watched the whole time by the NSF cameras. She'd be arrested within minutes.

"I heard you went nuts a few weeks ago. I guess this proves it." He cleared his throat, and as he gained his composure, a look of indignation crossed his face. "What makes you think you can come on my –"

She pressed the point a little harder and he stopped. "Dave, shut the fuck up. You're helpless as a baby right now, and it doesn't matter at all that you're a vice president. You'll bleed like anyone else. Now, if you talk back to me again, I'll end this conversation fast." Her dark eyes bore into his, and she leaned forward, speaking barely above a whisper. "I'm coming off the worst two weeks of my life, and all I want to do is kill something. Right now, that something is you. You can change my mind by giving me the answers I need."

"Why should I? Why don't you just kill me now? Rance will do it if I talk. I have nothing to gain by cooperating."

"Have you forgotten that I have a knife to your throat?"

He sneered and sat up straight. "All that gets you is a standoff, you stupid bitch. Use it and you don't get any answers."

Victoria slid the knife across the skin and raised a thin line of blood, and he shuddered and winced. "You'd still be dead, so don't get macho with me, pal. But you want to play mind games? Okay. I have a few syringes of pancuronium bromide in my pocket, a respiratory paralytic –"

"I know what it is."

" – and a few syringes of sodium thiopental. Why don't I pull one out at random? If you're lucky, you'll get the sedative, and we'll have a nice, relaxed conversation where you tell me everything. If you're unlucky, you'll get the paralytic. You'll suffocate for four long minutes, and then you'll die." She dipped a hand into her coat pocket and pulled out a syringe. "Ready to roll the dice?"

Dave's shoulders slumped and he swore.

"That's better. It's good to know when you're screwed, isn't it? It focuses the mind. Now, Recombin was an engineered virophage. Who engineered it?"

"Chalys."

"When?"

"Sometime early last year. I don't know exactly when. I don't hang out in the Creation Labs. You oughta talk to Lev Chakra or Tommy Connors. They were the program managers. I'm just VP of Quality Assurance."

"I know that, boss."

"I'm not your boss anymore. I terminated your employment last week."

"I was planning to quit when Ada graduated high school, so I don't give a shit. That was the most depressing job ever."

"Hey, you said you loved it."

"That was just corporate happy talk. I detested it."

"Everybody thought you got a weird vibe outta testing drugs on terminal patients. Folks in the office called you 'Princess Die' behind your back, y'know, with an 'e'?"

"How witty."

"Hey, I thought it was kinda funny –"

She pressed the knife into his skin. "I don't."

He nodded and tried to shrink away from the blade. Victoria pushed a little harder, tempted to stick the thing through his neck and into the door. She'd felt these impulses ever since her long nightmare on the Mapper, and they were becoming harder to control. However, a dead Dave would give her no answers, which she wanted more than anything else. "All right, back to work. Since Chalys engineered Recombin, they must have had a sample of Neovirus to work with. Did they?"

He nodded. "They couldn't have done it otherwise. You oughta know that."

"And who supplied the Neovirus samples?"

"The Army. It came from Fort Detrick," he said. "It's an enteric retrovirus, or RVE."

"I know what an RVE is. Tell me what I don't know."

"What you don't know is that Neovirus is actually called nRVE Entivirus Ellesmere, a novel RVE the Army found back in '36 in Canada. If you recall, that summer was really boiling."

"How could I forget the Flash Thaw? The permafrost melted and dumped a few billion tons of carbon into the atmosphere, and that melted off the glaciers. But that's irrelevant. Don't get off track, Dave."

"I'm not. Thing is, the Army didn't even care that the sea level rose like seven friggin feet that year. They were more interested in the exotic microbes they found in the old permafrost. So that summer up in Ellesmere, way past the Arctic Circle, it got above freezing for the first time ever. That's when something weird happened. Ninety percent of the town started puking, a real spewfest. Fort Detrick sent epidemiologists up there to investigate, and they found viable virus particles in the corpses of some Norwegian sailors that froze to death in the 1700's. They were buried in shallow ice graves, and they'd stayed ice cubes till that summer. So the Army being the Army, they sent the samples to the Windy Mount labs, which potentiated the virus and weaponized it into the Ellesmere A4 strain. They figured it'd be the ideal bioweapon during a ground war – a bug everybody gets that provokes an intense immune response. And nobody on the planet has immunity, not unless they're four-hundred-year-old Norwegian sailors. It'd have all our enemies on their knees barfing their guts out while the Army strolled in and took over."

"You make it sound like it's just a tummy bug, Dave."

"Well, that's what it is."

"No, it isn't. I saw a man in a full hemorrhagic bleed-out die from it. That was no tummy bug."

Dave nodded imperceptibly, trying to keep from cutting his throat. "That's because he was infected with a variant called Ellesmere A7. In warm weather, Ellesmere A4 mutates fast into a hemorrhagic monster that makes Ebola look like a case of the November sniffles. The Army realized that when they field-tested the weaponized A4 virus in Upper Minnesota. The virus didn't make the soldiers barf as they expected, but most of them came down with low-grade symptoms that barely warranted clinical treatment. Then on Day Seven, the hemorrhagic shit started. Patients began barfing up their stomachs or excreting their intestines. Out of a unit of a hundred and four soldiers and medical staff, sixty-eight died between Day Seven and Day Nine. Kinda like one of your Phase I drug trials."

Victoria pushed the knife point into his carotid artery. "You keep forgetting the default ending here, pal."

"Yeah, no sense of humor, got it. Anyway, all the survivors tested positive for the virus after, so A7 wasn't only deadly, it was wicked transmissible. Luckily for the Army, an Arctic front blew in from Canada and stopped the virus from breaking out into the general population, but they were so scared that they locked it in deep-freeze and melted down the key. They decided Ellesmere A4 was a useless weapon unless they vaccinated our troops first against the A7 variant, and that vaccine – which didn't exist – would need to have one hundred percent efficacy. It would be a unicorn vaccine, easy to imagine but impossible to develop."

"And yet seven years later, Chalys engineered Recombin, a viral antagonist with one hundred percent efficacy. Why'd they build it so long after the Ellesmere program was shitcanned?"

"Antagonist? Hell, Recombin snacks on retroviruses like they're potato chips."

"That's not the question I asked." She pursed her lips, momentarily lost in thought. "All right, whoever authorized the design and production of Recombin knew that this Ellesmere virus would be released into the population. Who greenlighted this?"

"Nobody ever told me. The order to engineer the virophage came down from Simon Rance himself. We do plenty of biodefense work for the Army, so it wasn't unusual."

"But didn't it raise your suspicions when someone ordered mass production of Recombin?" she asked.

"I just figured the Army was deploying a vaccine for Ellesmere A7 in case the Soviet Bloc used it against us. The Reds have been developing their permafrost biologicals too. It made sense."

"All right, I'll buy that," she said. "Now, who told Simon to order the Recombin production? He didn't do this on his own."

"I have no idea. That's not my end of the business, Dr. Lang. Maybe you weren't listening, but you should try Chakra or Connors. I only manage the outgoing product."

"Still, you're a VP, and you had to know. You were privy to everything."

"Not as much as you believe. You middle managers think we're all rainmakers on the Executive Floor, but we're scrambling to save our hides like everyone else. We don't know all that much more."

"Spare me the wage-slave pretense. Look at this house, Dave. You're a prince in a land of serfs, and your common-man act doesn't play."

He shook his head and winced when he felt the blade press against his neck again. "Believe what you want. You have the knife."

"Excellent response, Dave. You might live to see the sunset if you keep this up. Okay, how much Recombin was requisitioned? You should know that."

Good Morning, Dave

"Of course I do. We shipped 302 million doses."

"There are four hundred million people in this country, Dave. You didn't wonder why Chalys wasn't making enough to vaccinate the entire population?"

"No, because I didn't think they'd have to. I didn't know it would go pandemic. I thought it was just a biodefense contract."

"But once it went pandemic, you knew it wasn't biodefense, right? You had to know that the Army released it, but you didn't say anything because you're the good corporate stooge who doesn't rock the boat, right?"

"Look, I'm not stupid, but what was I gonna do then? This Ellesmere thing had too much juice behind it, so I acted clueless. I wasn't gonna earn my do-gooder merit badge and tell the whole damn world and make myself a target. I mean, look what happened to you."

"Clueless didn't help you, Dave. You notice that you're on the pointy end of the knife and I'm not?"

"Yeah, right, you're in such a great spot right now. Y'know, every cop in the country is looking for you? You'll be dead in a week."

"And you'll be dead in a minute if you don't stay on track. Now, one last question, and this is the big one. This is where you can really make me angry if you don't cooperate, and I have serious anger issues." She drew a deep breath and tried to still the shaking in her hands. "Where's my daughter?"

He snorted. "How would I know?"

"Where's my daughter, Dave?"

"I don't know. Maybe she ran away from home. Hell, I would if I was your kid."

The shaking in her hands worsened, and she pressed the tip of the knife deeper into his skin so he wouldn't notice it. With another ounce of pressure, he'd be dead. "Answer the damn question! Where's my daughter?"

"I told you…"

Victoria's pulse pounded through her veins and adrenaline hit her brain, and she felt powerful and wild. She grabbed his hair and jerked his head back. "Pay attention, douchebag. I asked you where she was, not if you knew. Now answer the goddamn question, or your life isn't worth jack shit to me."

"Why are you getting so worked up about this? You oughta take that sedative –"

"Worked up? You think I'm worked up? You haven't seen me get worked up yet!"

"It's just a kid! Just go make another one! Go fuck Tommy Talbott a few more times!"

She pointed the shaking knife at his eye. "Enough! I'm giving you one last chance. You tell me where my baby is, or by God I will destroy you –"

"The fuck do I care about her?" He spat on her blouse and his mouth twisted into a sneer. "Your little bitch is even crazier'n you. Everybody knows the Feds nailed her for something big. Best thing for humanity is if Ellesmere ate her –"

Her arm rose high above her shoulder and swung the knife in a powerful backstroke, ripping through his throat to the spine. His eyes bulged and he clutched his neck, but blood ran through his fingers and down his sport coat in a pulsing red curtain. Then, with a gurgle, his head sagged forward onto his chest. He jerked once and sat still.

She saw her hand holding the black knife high in the air and watched droplets of his blood drip from the blade. For a moment, she didn't understand what she was seeing, but then she gasped and backed up until her foot found the stairs. When she reached the bottom, she turned and ran to the truck.

She couldn't conceal this. Her DNA probably covered the porch and the victim, and the police would know she killed him within minutes. She swore and paced around the pickup, twirling hair in her fingers as she thought about what to do.

Drag him inside and burn the house down?

Tie a rope to his feet and drag the body somewhere else?

Do nothing and run away?

None of those would work. Only one course made any sense: If she couldn't conceal what she'd done, the murder had to appear deliberate.

She walked back onto the porch and severed his ear with one deft knife stroke. It dropped onto his lap. She rifled through his pockets, found his keys, and then looked at the corpse leaning against the door.

Something was all wrong about this. Pursing her lips, she frowned at the bloody tableau, and then the problem became clear. It only took seconds to fix it.

Good Morning, Dave

As she unlocked the truck door, she glanced back at the porch once again. Dave sat slumped against the door, holding out the bloody ear on his palm as if offering it to the world.

A crooked smile came to her lips. *Yes, that looks simply perfect now.*

DISPATCHES

Molle's Hill
NewsHub Political Affairs Channel
Broadcast Transcript of September 22, 2043

Molle: And here we are again with Surgeon General Mae Esteban. It's a pleasure to see you back so soon, General.

Esteban: Thanks, Arista, but I'm afraid this is my last appearance. I'm retiring from public service at five o'clock this afternoon. After my disastrous meeting with President Gibbon yesterday, I've concluded that I can't serve the public health as Surgeon General.

Molle: I'm saddened to hear our country is losing a distinguished leader such as you. Your troops must also be dispirited to find themselves leaderless.

Esteban: Yes, my troops. Well, they'll have a new leader soon, Arista. Here, take my stars. Lead them with courage and vision.

Molle: This is an honor, General, a real honor.

Esteban: And one you deserve.

Molle: What follows, then, for the great Mae Esteban? Perhaps a lucrative speaking tour? Memoirs? I have a title for you: *Woman of Medicine, Woman of War*.

Esteban: I'm not ready to write my memoirs yet. I still plan to help this world where I can, so I've offered my services as an internist to St. Elizabeth's Hospital, which is like coming home for me because I was raised in Anacostia. If I can't serve the health of the public as a whole, then I'll serve each individual. Man by man, woman by woman, child by child. Fighting the war in the trenches, as it were, and I begin the fight this evening at ten o'clock.

Molle: Such courage! You're an example to us all. If you ever need your troops, General, you know who to call. We stand ready for you.

Esteban: Thanks, Arista. That's comforting to know.

ANARCHISTA

Krista leaned against a tree and gazed across a small lake with a swaybacked farmhouse on its far shore. The house was tucked against the hills of a remote valley where they were safe from prying eyes, and even the eagle-eyed airship cameras couldn't find them – she'd driven the Hugo through a hole in the farmhouse wall last night and parked inside the living room.

Ada had found cushions from an old sofa and immediately fell asleep on the floor beside the car, but the shakes kept Krista awake. Every time she tried to rest, some gruesome memory would return, adrenaline would flow, and all hopes of sleep would vanish. She took a walk instead and found a soft bed of leaves under an immense oak tree near the water, where she sat and looked across the lake.

She licked her little finger, dipped it into the instant coffee, and decided that she'd try to sleep after she finished writing. She needed the rest. They'd gone in the wrong direction last night and ended up in Indiana, and it would take a night of hard driving to get back into the South.

Her stomach rumbled. They'd found two glass jars of canned corn in the farmhouse's root cellar, which was their first real meal in two days. They ate all the corn, drank the liquid from the jars, and even swallowed the wax seals, but the meal wasn't enough.

Without food, they wouldn't survive more than a few days. She and Ada were already having difficulty concentrating on the simplest tasks, and they'd had trouble opening the jars.

The only food she'd found foraging in the woods was a few handfuls of blueberries the deer hadn't eaten. She'd eaten only half and pocketed the rest for Ada.

She rubbed her stomach and gazed across the lake again. On the opposite shore, the oak leaves were turning color, and a few floated in the light breeze and drifted aimlessly to the ground. A doe sauntered between the trees, sometimes looking up as if it knew she was watching.

Sighing, she felt the tension leave her bones. The Black Dog would never find this place, and she could rebuild the sagging farmhouse beside the lake and feed the fawns. The peace in her little valley would flow like the coffee in her fountain.

Miss Kellen, you must not –

"Can I have a minute to relax without you stompin in? Did I invite you into my private fantasies?"

This is a crucial time, and weakness will –

"Turn the key off on that mouth, or I'll have your natterin arse out on the curb so fast your head will spin, boyo! You're only rentin a room up there, y'know!" She listened inside her mind, but the blast had driven Figment off. "Why couldn't I get a voice in my head that says 'You're doing a grand job in a tough time. Sit back and take a load off?' Right, I get a bloody Marine drill sergeant who always pushes me around. Just my feckin luck."

Her eyelids drooped, and her head began to feel woozy, but she shook it off. Despite the hunger, weariness, and mind noise, she needed to put together a post today, one that would stand out from all she'd ever written.

On the long drive from Kentucky, she'd thought about revolution, and how much Americans needed to stand up and force radical changes. While she believed an uprising was next to impossible – and she wasn't the rebel to lead one, despite the pack of lies she'd told Downs – pretending she was the fearsome Anarchista might rouse a few dozing Americans and upset the nation's suffocating status quo. At the same time, it would confound and confuse the Federals, maybe even long enough for her and Ada to reach the safety of California.

ANARCHISTA
At long last, I'm ending this charade and taking off my mask

I'm sorry I haven't posted much about my road trip, but I've been doing so many exciting things that I just couldn't tear myself away and write. I'm having a marvelous time – I spent a comfortable night at a picturesque lakeside inn and just finished a farmhouse breakfast. Everything they say about them is true: scrambled eggs by the platter, sizzling rashers of crispy bacon, bowls of golden hash browns, and mounds of buttermilk pancakes smothered in fresh maple syrup. I'm stuffed! Later today, I may wedge myself back into the car and continue my tour of America.

Toying with our National Security Forces the past few days has been such a delight! They've been running around madly trying to find me, and it's a wicked pleasure watching them. It's like shining a laser pointer on the ground and watching a gaggle of retards try to catch the little red dot – they stumble around and bump into each other, and they make the silliest noises.

Was that politically incorrect? Oh, that's right! I'm the embodiment of political incorrectness now. I can do whatever I want. Ahh, it's so good to be free!

Now that I am, I'll admit something I've kept secret for so long: I've been a commander in a vast and secret rebel army for more than three years.

And I've been given the honor of revealing The Activity's existence to America. Remember the name, because we're about to rock your world.

I commanded the Capital Cell, a group of dissidents embedded in the machinery of Washington's government and industry, and I've been directing intelligence operations whose goal was to expose the crimes of the Gibbon/Cheyn Administration and bring about its downfall. The damning videos I carry in my tablet were captured by one of my agents.

Our operatives have infiltrated every Federal organization in Washington, including the Big Three intelligence agencies. That's how I knew that the Federals were coming for me last week in my apartment. I was warned by a dissident in an intelligence organization, giving me the time to execute my escape plan.

Yes, we're everywhere.

We not only have our spies and whistleblowers. We also have commandos, cyberwarriors, bombmakers, and armorers, as well as an elaborate support network to supply this unstoppable machine of revolution.

I know what you're thinking: Is this for real? Nobody has ever heard of this so-called Activity. Well, there's a good reason why you haven't.

Our organization grew in a time when every movement and every communication was tracked, but we're quiet and determined rebels, not flashy, fist-waving *libertad* barricade stormers. To protect our movement, we had to become diffuse and decentralized, leaving our fingerprints on nothing. And that's why the government fears us so. Its awesome surveillance network can't find us no matter what it does.

But just because you can't see us doesn't mean we aren't there – we're in your office and we're on your block. We're experts at blending in and seeming to be what we're not – after all, you thought the commander of the Capital Cell was just a frivolous gossip columnist. Didn't I fool everyone?

Join me in this cause. Join us and change this miserable world. Take it from me – it's exciting to be free, to shed the yoke of the ordinary, to be more than I ever thought I could be. Live and fight and stand for something greater than you, and you will become greater.

If you rise to resist, to obstruct, to confound and thwart evil, the Activists will have your back. If you speak out, you will not speak alone. You have my word on it.

Don't fear the NSF. They'd like you to believe they're listening to your thoughts and will stomp you to a pulp if you get out of line, but they're nothing to fear. They're the idiots of the Civil Service, the bloody stool of the body politic's digestion, and they're easy to fool and easy to defeat.

I've killed three of them single-handedly so far and outsmarted thousands of their "fearsome" agents. I've evaded their dragnets and their drones and their helicopters.

If I can do all this, think what you could do.

-KLW

A soft *crump* shook Krista out of her sleep just after dusk. She looked around groggily and saw a fountain of water in the middle of the lake, with Ada standing on the shore behind it holding a rake. She jumped to her feet and ran to the farmhouse.

"What happened?" she asked when she was in earshot. "Are you okay?"

"I'm fine," Ada said as she dragged the tines of the rusted leaf rake through the water. "I'm just fishing."

"I heard an explosion!"

"Right. I don't have any fishing gear, so I figured I'd bomb the fish and pluck them out with the rake."

"Where'd you find a bomb?"

"Under the kitchen sink."

"There was a bomb under the…oh, right, it's that mad scientist thing again."

She pulled the rake from the water and examined the tines. "Not even a minnow. I'm starving to death, Krista. I can't go on much longer like this or I'll pass out."

"Well, I found these in the woods," Krista said, holding out a handful of blueberries.

She snatched the berries from her hand and stuffed them into her mouth. "Are there any more?" she asked as she chewed.

Krista shook her head. "They're up in the woods, and I don't know the way back. I got the last of them, and we can't survive on blueberries anyway. We've got to break into someplace and get real food tonight. I'm not waiting till we get into the South. I'm starving too."

Ada downed the last berry and licked the juice from her fingers. "You weren't here when I woke up."

"I was across the lake, writing," Krista said. "You know, making crap up is a lot easier than writing facts? I wasn't blocked for a second."

"I thought the Federals got you." She threw the rake into the weeds and looked across the lake. "Don't do that to me again, okay? Let's stick together from now on."

"Sorry, I just nodded off." Krista took her hand and felt it tremble. "Hey, are you okay?"

"But now that it's dark," Ada said quickly, "we oughta get going. We'll need to get some miles under our wheels to reach the Deep South tonight. I was looking at the atlas while you were gone, and we can't head back the way we came. We'll end up in that maze of farm roads that screwed us up last night. I wouldn't have minded that if they hadn't harvested all the food. At least we coulda eaten something."

"Right, next time you and me head out to overthrow the government, we'll do it before the harvest," Krista said. "Which way do we go tonight?"

"We'll head west for a few hours and then take Interstate 57 south in Illinois. From there, we can get into Missouri or even Arkansas before sunrise. We oughta be safe on the Interstates. Nobody's looking for this car, certainly not the last owner."

DISPATCHES

Midnight Sun
News Post of September 22, 2043

NEW YORK CITY NOW DARK; CORDONS ANNOUNCED IN NEW YORK STATE AND ILLINOIS

Conditions in the Eastern and Midwestern United States remain difficult to assess. Official MRC news sources continue to broadcast that the spread of Neovirus has slowed and conditions in the region are improving. The Media Regulatory Corporation is well known for dispensing only Administration truths, though, so we regard their reporting as suspect.

Evidence from numerous other sources sketches a different picture. In fact, conditions in the region may be worsening, and the crisis may be deepening.

First, we go to the epicenter of the virus disaster, New York City. Of the forty-plus Witnesses we had in the area, none have reported since September 15. Furthermore, our sources in Québec haven't received television or radio broadcasts from any transmitter there for the last two days. The media-intensive city has gone dark.

Second, a cordon has been placed north of New York City along Interstate 84, which circles Albany and ends at the Long Island Sound. It is being patrolled and enforced by state troopers. If conditions were improving, this extraordinary step would be unnecessary. New York State government officials are unavailable for comment on this cordon.

Third, we turn to the battlefront of the epidemic: Ohio, Kentucky, Tennessee, Georgia, and Indiana. One week ago, *Midnight Sun* had almost fifty Witnesses in these states. Now three remain. The Witnesses who escaped noted a dramatic and lethal change in the virus, which is now killing its victims in one or two days.

Fourth, Illinois has imposed an absolute cordon along its eastern border to prevent the virus from spreading into that state, effective 7:00 PM local time tonight. No individuals, vaccinated or non-vaccinated, will be allowed to cross the border. Deadly force is authorized to prevent any breaches of the cordon.

THE BODY ELECTRIC

Day 35
Tuesday night, September 22, 2043
Twelve miles east of Vincennes, Indiana

"I'm not blaming you for it," Krista said. "It's not your fault –"

"It's *not* my fault!" Ada said.

"It's not your fault you were born blonde. Blondes do that kinda thing."

"Don't start with me, Warner. I have an IQ of 194. I do multivariate calculus in my head to relax. You can't pull that dumb-blonde crap on me."

"I'm not saying you're dumb. That's obviously not true. It's just that the blonde brain sometimes misses things."

"The blonde brain? Do you hear yourself?" Ada crossed her arms and glared through the windshield. "So why do clowns have red hair? Huh? You think that's a coincidence?"

"It's because watching smart people trip and fall over things is funny. People expect blondes to do that, so it wouldn't be funny. Actually, it's kinda sad."

Ada huffed and slapped her hands on her legs. "For chrissakes, the board was loose, and it was dark on that porch! I just didn't see it and that's the only reason I tripped and made all that noise!" She crossed her arms again. "Or maybe my blonde eyes didn't see the board sticking up."

"Look, I'm not blaming you for anything."

"It woulda been nice if you'd looked in the cabin windows first to see if anybody was inside – *before* I got on the porch!"

"My seatbelt got stuck. I told you to wait," Krista said.

"It woulda been nice if you told me a guy was inside the cabin with a shotgun. It woulda been nice if you warned me that I might get my ass blown off if I stepped on the porch."

"But you didn't. He missed us both. I think he just wanted to scare us," Krista said.

"It worked," Ada said. "I bet he had tons of food too. God, I'm so hungry now. I've eaten a chocolate bar and a jar of corn in the last two days. And a handful of blueberries."

"And don't forget that half a bun."

"Don't be cruel." Ada doubled over and groaned. "I'm so hungry that I've stopped feeling hungry."

"It won't be long now. I was thinking that if we can get into Arkansas tonight, we might find food there. Most of the Arkies got the vaccine, so the virus shouldn't be hitting down there as bad. Maybe they're not hoarding." Krista looked at the clock, and it was almost eleven at night. "We're making good time. We could get into Arkansas by sunrise, right?"

Ada opened the atlas. "If we drive right through and don't make any stops. We can travel during the day now too. Nobody knows about this car."

Krista smiled. "We're almost out of the woods. Things are finally looking up."

"We'll find a restaurant and order everything on page two," Ada said. "For an appetizer. Maybe we can find an all-you-can-eat restaurant, and I'll just pull up a seat in the kitchen and tell them to keep it coming."

"Stop, you're torturing me! Let's get there before we start talking about menus."

Ada aimed her flashlight at the atlas again and squinted. "We just passed Gordonville, so keep going west on Route 50. We'll cross over the Wabash River into Illinois in twelve minutes. After that, it's only another hour till we turn south on I-57."

THE TRAFFIC APPROACHING VINCENNES wasn't just bumper-to-bumper; it was fender-to-fender. The westbound road was so jammed that vehicles were even driving on the shoulders, and the two lanes had split into four ragged and narrow bands.

"What's up with this? We don't see a car for two hours, and now the entire state is on the road," Krista said. "Can you see what's going on?"

Ada lowered her window and looked out, and the blaring of car horns grew louder. "I see a sign up ahead. I'll go take a walk up there and see what it says. You stay here."

Krista snorted. "We've moved a mile in an hour. I'll be here."

Ada opened the door a few inches and heard swearing. "Well, look, Bonzo, if you stayed in your lane, I could open my freakin door without bumping yours!" Ada took a deep breath and prepared to fire another salvo, but Krista grabbed her by the shoulder and pulled her back in.

"That's a good way to get killed. These folks are ready to turn into a lynch mob. Just climb out the window and try not to make yourself a target, okay?"

"Yeah, yeah. It's just that I'm ready to bite some heads off myself. It's two in the morning, and the way it's going, I won't see that all-you-can-eat restaurant anytime soon." She wriggled through the window and slipped between the cars to the side of the road.

Krista wiggled in the narrow seat and tried to make herself comfortable, but her hips wouldn't fit no matter how she contorted her body. Giving up on comfort, she sprinkled a little water on a napkin and tried to clean the greasy film off the windshield again, but it only smeared the glass even more; the Hugo didn't have scrubbers, and the residue from the fug would take industrial-strength cleaners to remove. She rubbed harder and harder until the little car started to bounce, but the window never came clean. The impulse to take a walk hit her, but she saw the door of a pickup inches away blocking her in.

She settled into her seat, hoping to summon a peaceful fantasy that would make the traffic jam bearable, but then something thumped on the roof and a beer can rolled down the windshield. She lowered her window and looked up just as a hand let go of a sandwich wrapper, which fluttered toward her face. She batted it away and yelled to be heard over the engine's rumble. "Hey, could I trouble you to not go throwing your trash all over my car?"

Men's laughter echoed inside the cavernous vehicle, and then a porcine face with beady eyes appeared at the window. "Hey, babe, why doncha come on up here and give us a BJ? We got time for a quickie."

"If I come up there, boyo, I'll be hollowing you out and using you for a human trash can, that's what I'll be doing!"

"You got a big mouth. Show us whatcha can do with it."

"Right, I'll be showin you what I can do, gobshite." She reached behind Ada's seat, and just as she'd pulled out the shotgun, Ada wiggled back through the window. She looked from Krista to the gun and back.

"Keeping a low profile? Being non-violent?"

"Guy's pushing my buttons," Krista mumbled.

"Calm down. We have bigger problems. The sign says the Illinois border crossings are closed. That's a wonderful place to put it, right? Ten miles back would be better." She pulled out the atlas. "There's an exit a mile ahead, and we oughta be there in about fifty-two minutes at this rate. We have to take it anyway. The road's closed past it."

"Splendid. Just splendid," Krista said. Another can thumped on the roof and rolled down the windshield.

AFTER ANOTHER HOUR, they were roaring onto the exit ramp at one mile an hour and merging with another highway. Ada pulled the skin back on her cheeks. "Slow down! The G-forces are tearing me apart!"

"Funny. Look, after we get off, what do we do?" Krista asked. "Please tell me there's open road somewhere."

"Well, if Illinois is closed, then all we can do is go around the south of it." She leaned outside again and peered down the road. "Unfortunately, everybody else has the same idea. I see nothing but taillights heading south on Route 41. But if we go into Vincennes, there's a small local road that goes south."

"Good. That's what we'll do. At least we have a plan."

AN HOUR LATER, they were still creeping along the highway, this time heading south. Ada spotted an exit for Old Town Vincennes, and when they reached it a half hour later, the road was open. Krista gunned the car off the ramp and sped into the middle of the darkened town.

"Okay, next block, make a left and then we'll be on Old Route 41," Ada said.

Krista made the turn and found even more red taillights on the road south.

"We oughta get out and walk," Ada said.

"I can't take any more. Can we go north? Maybe we can find open road and cross into Illinois up there."

"Maybe," Ada said. "It looks like the river is the border only in this part of the state. Up north, the border cuts across land, so we don't have to cross bridges there. On the other hand, the sun will be up in three hours. Do you want to try an illegal border crossing in daylight?"

Krista shook her head. "We need to find a place to crash. Maybe we can try that tomorrow night. The road south might be open later on, too, once this traffic clears out, but I've got to get sleep."

"Funny you should mention it. I see a Brasser's way up ahead."

"Really? Perfect!" Krista reached into a pocket and pulled out a wrinkled handful of bills. "Here, go rent us a room for twelve hours. Rent some sheets and towels too. I'll meet you in about, oh, an hour or so."

Ada climbed out and walked up the street. Twenty minutes later, Krista pulled into the parking lot of an old Brasser's, a yellowed, cracked, and cobwebbed version of the ones they'd seen in Ohio. She parked near the road, and Ada walked over a minute later.

"You get us something?" Krista asked.

"Well, yeah, but this place is off-planet. The woman behind the counter was wearing a gas mask and these ginormous yellow gloves, like all the way up her arms. She looked at me like I was from Mars."

"You're not wearing a mask. That'd attract attention around here."

"But she seemed a little *too* suspicious."

"Probably because you weren't wearing a mask, Ada. Don't worry – the Federals aren't looking for you, they're looking for me, so she doesn't know your face. You got a room?"

"They just had one left, but it's a dump, even worse than the ones we stayed in before. Everything's falling apart in it."

"We won't be here long. Did you see any food?" Krista asked, but Ada shook her head.

They pulled their bags from the car and walked to a room at the end of the row. As they fumbled with the door key, a woman with yellow gloves walked out of the lobby and stopped short when she saw them. Ada smiled and waved, but the woman scurried back into the office.

The room was everything Ada said and less: The mattress lay on the floor, ragged holes dotted the wall where a headboard had once been attached, and the carpet was torn away in front of the bathroom sink, revealing a patch of scratched and dirty concrete.

Krista dropped her backpack on the bed. "I'm going to wash my panties, and then I want to shower. You can go first if you want."

"Yeah, might as well." Ada pulled off her jeans and panties, laid them on the counter next to the sink, and then pulled her shampoo and cigarettes from her pack.

Krista plugged her tablet into an outlet behind the door and laid it on a chair, and then she took off her clothes and threw them over it. She reached up to hook the door chain, but it fell off the wall when she touched it.

ADA DROPPED HER CIGARETTES and shampoo on the tiny windowsill over the toilet and started the bath water. She let it run until it got warm – not hot, because she was getting the virus sweats – and then yanked up on the lever to start the shower. It pulled out of the faucet, and she glared at it, hands on hips. She found a cracked rubber stopper, jammed it into the drain, and then stomped to the toilet.

The vibration of her steps shook a grille in the wall loose, which clattered to the floor and revealed an old wall heater. It still seemed to work: Three thick wires were connected loosely to the side of the heater, which had CAUTION 4800 WATTS printed on the face. She placed it back on the heater and propped the trash can against it.

She lit a cigarette and blew a plume through the window, letting her mind drift.

KRISTA LAID HER TOOTHBRUSH, shampoo, and panties on the counter. She yawned and walked back to the bed with an armful of sheets, and she'd just laid them on the mattress when a cool breeze tickled her naked back.

She turned to see if the door had blown open, but then a hand grabbed her mouth and yanked her head to one side. She tried to scream, but it clamped her mouth and nose so tight that she couldn't breathe. More hands pulled her arms behind her back. They threw her on the bed, and she tried to roll away but felt a weight on her legs. Something smelly was shoved into her mouth and a black sheet covered her face, making the dark room even darker.

ADA GAZED THROUGH THE BATHROOM WINDOW and watched a flock of birds winging westward without a care, far above the desperation below. She watched until the fug swallowed them, soothed by the white noise of water rushing into the tub, and then she heard a thump from the room. It sounded as if Krista had dropped something, or more likely, something else had fallen off the wall.

THE HOOD SMELLED LIKE OLD UNDERWEAR and the rubber bit jammed in her mouth tasted like armpits. She lay naked on the mattress with her hands cuffed behind her back.

She heard a man laugh. Another man said something she couldn't make out, but the tone of his voice was curt and sharp like he was issuing commands. The cruel laugh started again for no reason, and then the mattress sagged as someone sat on it.

"Got forty-five minutes, ma'am, and you're the loveliest thing I seen in a long time. Oh, yeah, darlin." A hand touched her groin. "You a natural redhead?" The hands were cold, and she flinched from the touch and squeezed her legs together. Her heart pounded, and she wriggled against the weight on her legs.

"Back off, Pete," a sharp voice said at her feet. "We have procedures, and we're going by the book on this. Our orders are to secure her and the tablet and wait for the rest of the team, and we haven't found the tablet yet. Stay with the program, man."

"Pat, the orders just say dead or alive. All we need is to bring back her head and the tablet, and we're heroes. And what I want to do with this lovely lady has got nothin to do with her head."

"We're not taking any chances," Pat said. "This is the highest priority, and I'm not gonna mess up. You wanna explain to Dickhead Downs that we had her and lost her? Not me, man, no way. This is unprofessional."

"So's working double shifts like we been doing. We deserve a little fun, the way we been runnin around the state for the last week." The voice came closer to her ear. "Yeah, the lady oughta pay a little handlin fee, that's what I think. Sounds fair."

Pat was quiet for a few moments. "You're gonna bust my chops for weeks if I don't let you do this, aren't you?"

"Here's my chance to beast the Rebel Commander, man. Look at those hooters, my friend, and tell me they don't give you some blue steel. How many chances we gonna get to do this? And hey, you get a crack at her after I'm done. I'll hold the gun while you're at it."

Pat laughed. "Like I want your sloppy seconds."

"I'll wear a rubber. You know I took the safe-sex pledge." The cruel laugh burst out again and Krista shivered.

"But the Dickhead will find out somehow, Pete, and then bad shit happens. That dude's brutal. I'm not taking the chance."

"We just need the head, man. When we're done, we'll kill her and cut the head off. Say she resisted arrest or something. We'll dump the body in the river. Nobody's gonna know."

Pat was silent for a long time; to Krista, it seemed like hours. "You'll use a new rubber? Not that ten-year-old donut you've got in your wallet? I'm not dipping my wick in your jizz." She tried to scream, but the rubber bit in her mouth absorbed the sound.

"You got it."

She twisted her torso and tried to wrest her legs free from the weight again; her head and shoulders slid off the bed, but the cold hands grabbed them and forced her into the mattress.

"Okay, fine," Pat said. "But take your boots off, man. You're an Executive, not an animal."

"Ya-a-h, baby!" She heard two thumps as the man dropped his boots on the floor.

ADA SAT ON THE TOILET LID and examined her leg wounds. They'd scabbed over already, and a few were an angry red, but they were healing fast.

The tub was almost full, and she was getting ready to climb in when she heard an unfamiliar voice from the room – a man's voice. She crept to the door and listened to the deep voices of two men talking to each other.

As she strained to hear more, one man laughed – an ugly sound filled with hate, not humor.

Krista was in trouble, and she needed to get help. She jumped onto the toilet and began to squeeze through the narrow window, but then she stopped – nobody out there would help her and Krista.

Pulling back through the window quietly, she thought about the few advantages she held. The men didn't know she was in the bathroom, so she could surprise them, but her only weapons were a half-empty shampoo bottle and a pack of Kamelles. The Commander could take down a man with only those, but not her.

She sat on the toilet again, wondering how to do the impossible, and then she heard water splash over the rim of the tub. She watched it trickle past the loose heater grille toward the door, and her lips rose in a small but wicked smile.

THE MAN LAY ON TOP OF HER, and she felt his ugly heat on her bare skin. Krista screamed into the rubber bit and struggled even harder to shake him off, but he was too strong.

She had just chewed off a piece of the bit when Ada called from the bathroom, "Krista! The tub's overflowing! Come help me! It's a real mess!"

The men stopped moving and whispered to each other, and then the mattress jiggled as they jumped off. Krista rolled off the bed and fell to the floor, but this time the men didn't stop her.

She tried to get to her feet but lost her balance and stumbled forward into a wall. Leaning against it, she pushed herself upright. She tried to find Ada by the sound of her voice, but her ears were ringing and her pulse thumped so loudly that she couldn't hear.

ADA PUSHED MORE WATER UNDER THE DOOR with the grille, and then she wrapped a towel around her hand. The wires were dirty, but she wiped them clean, found the white one, and laid it in the pool of water. With her hand still wrapped in the towel, she pried the black and red wires out of the heater and then climbed onto the porcelain toilet. "Krista!" she yelled. "I need help!" She moved the two wires to within an inch of the brass knob.

The Body Electric

A faint shuffling, scratching sound filtered under the door, and she sensed a presence on the other side. Once the knob began turning, she touched the wires to it. A blue spark flashed, and the smell of burning plastic filled the air.

KRISTA BANGED HER HEAD on something hard and fell back against the bed, but the men ignored her. She heard them whispering somewhere near the bathroom, and she tried to climb to her feet.

They wouldn't touch Ada if she could stop it. She crouched, and as she prepared to spring, the men began to moan as if they were auditioning for a zombie movie. A crackling sound filled the room, and then an overpowering odor hit her – a sharp smell of ozone mixed with grilled chicken.

THE DOOR WAS BURNING. The insulation on the wires smoldered, filling the room with choking blue smoke, and Ada blinked back tears as she struggled to hold on.

The knob jiggled and smoked, and she heard the moaning growl of pissed-off zombies beyond the door. A sharp pain lanced through her hand, and gray smoke rose from the towel.

Suddenly, the knob turned and the door burst open, and then something big and gray dropped onto the wet floor with a hiss. She screamed and leaped on the windowsill as another blur passed her and landed on the first.

The wires snaked in the air as the towel floated down to the floor. They fell on the top man and flashed a brilliant blue spark, and then the towel landed on the sparking wires and caught fire. A circuit breaker in the wall popped, throwing the room into darkness, and the sprinklers burst.

She jumped out of the bathroom and looked for Krista, but she only saw a naked zombie with a black head groaning and staggering toward her. She screamed and jumped onto the bed, reaching for a lamp on the nightstand. The zombie stumbled forward, but just as she was ready to clobber the apparition, she spotted a curl of red hair from under a black hood. "Krista! What happened?" She yanked it off her head.

Krista's eyes were wild and frightened, and she answered by shaking her head. Ada pulled a mangled black rubber baton out of her mouth, and Krista gulped a chestful of air. "Where…are they?" she gasped.

"In the bathroom. We're okay."

"Keys." Krista turned around and showed her the cuffs, and Ada ran back to the bathroom. The two men lay twitching on the floor, but they were still enough that Ada could take their keys. She ran back and unlocked Krista's cuffs.

"Gotta get out of here before they get up," Krista said as she stumbled to the chair holding her clothes. "More coming. Get dressed. Gotta get away."

Ada jumped into her jeans and slipped on her boots, stuffing her panties in a pocket. Krista was dressed when she turned around, and they picked up their bags and staggered through the door. "Wait!" Krista ducked back into the room and grabbed her tablet.

They ran across the lot to the car. As Ada opened her door, she saw the woman from the reception desk, still in her mask and gloves, pointing a huge silver pistol at them from across the lot.

She ducked just as the gun cracked and a bullet pinged off the Hugo's roof. Ada grabbed Micky Maussner, whirled around, and blasted away the windshields of a few cars with a three-shot salvo. The woman peeked over the hood of one and then sprinted for the safety of the lobby. Ada blew the windows out, showering her with glass as she scurried inside.

She checked the area through her gun sight, and after finding nobody else in the lot, she climbed back into the car. Krista floored the gas pedal, spun the wheel hard, and screeched onto the road heading north. Drivers in masks opened their car doors to gawk as they passed, but they ducked when gunfire cracked from the motel parking lot again.

"Son of a *bitch!*" Ada picked up the shotgun and began to climb through the window.

"The hell – ?" Krista skidded around a corner, and Ada tumbled back into the car. She landed in Krista's lap and tried to grab the gun's stock, but her fingers found the trigger instead. With a boom so loud neither could hear it, Mickey Maussner blew a foot-wide hole in the roof.

"Jaysus!" Krista yelled, waving the gun smoke away from her face. She swerved to avoid a parked car, throwing Ada against the passenger's door.

"You're all over the road!" Ada pushed the safety button on the gun and buckled her seatbelt, and then she pointed through the window. "Watch out!"

Two deer ran across the street, spooked by the gunfire. Krista veered around them and saw open road ahead. Seconds later, they passed under the highway they'd left a few hours before.

Ada raised her hand through the hole and wiggled her fingers. "I made a sunroof!"

"That's so bloody funny – oh, fuck!" She spotted flashing lights coming toward them a few hundred yards ahead. Seeing a side street, she yanked the wheel hard right. The car slid around the corner, its rear wheels juddering and squealing across the pavement as the front wheels dragged the car forward. She punched the gas again, and the Hugo sped down a residential street. As they approached a bridge, the flashing lights turned the corner and followed them.

Ada looked through the rear window. "He's coming. Go faster, come on."

The road turned sharp to the right and then left. The car leaned around each turn and threatened to tip, but they stayed upright and drove onto a narrow concrete bridge. "Fast as I can go," Krista muttered through clenched teeth. They raced over the bridge and squealed around a sharp corner at the bottom.

The road ahead was blocked by chain-link gates, and Krista slammed on the brakes.

"Oh, shit!" they wailed at the same time. The car crashed through the gates at full speed and threw them against parked school buses, and then it rammed into another bus's bumper. Krista tried to pull the shifter into reverse, but a white police cruiser screeched to a stop behind them.

Ada reached for her shotgun, but Krista laid her hand over it. "But he doesn't know I have Mickey," Ada said. "I'll shoot our way out."

Krista looked at the officer's face in the side mirror. "He isn't pulling a gun on us, though, and he doesn't look mad. I've got a hunch this'll be okay. These aren't the bad guys. Trust me."

"I hate handcuffs," Ada said. She had to lift her head off the patrol car roof to talk.

"I'm no fan of them myself," Krista mumbled, her hair dripping water on the roof. "I can't believe this is happening. This is the worst night ever."

"Hellacious hunch there, some throwing-the-toaster-into-the-bathtub kinda thing. Let's fill up the *Hindenburg* with hydrogen, *mein Führer!* What can go wrong? It's like –"

"Shut up, already. You made your point." Krista tried to turn her head to see what the patrolman was doing, but he was standing behind her. It sounded like he was talking on a radio. "I still think he's one of the good guys."

"At least I'm a minor. I'll just get a prison term. Or they'll send me to Los Alamos and chain me to a table and I'll make itty-bitty little bombs the rest of my damn –"

"Shhh. He stopped talking. Something's up." Krista craned her head and tried to see to each side. The fug glowed up on the bridge, and then another police car pulled up next to the patrolman.

A door slammed, and two men talked in low voices for a minute. One of them walked over to Krista and whispered in her ear, "You really Krista Warner?"

She tried to turn and see him, but he stood behind her with his hand on her cuffs. Sighing, she rested her head on the roof. "That I am. Officer, I can explain all this."

"Sheriff, if you don't mind."

"This isn't what you think." Krista's hands jiggled as the man pulled on her cuffs. "We were just trying to get away from –" The cuffs snapped open and her hands were free; she turned and saw a police officer with brush-cut white hair and the ramrod-straight posture of a career military man, a small paunch rolling over his leather gun belt. He unlocked Ada's cuffs as the other man stood by the trunk of the sheriff's cruiser.

The older officer looked at her up and down, an eyebrow arched. "Beggin your pardon, but you sure don't look like some shit-fahr rebel."

"Have you ever seen a real shit-fire rebel, Sheriff?"

He shrugged. "Fair 'nuff. Well, y'all follow me 'n I'll getcha somewhere safe. There's a bulletin out on this vehicle already, and the Federals will be on-scene in about ten minutes. We got a half an hour of drivin ahead of us, so we got no time to jabber on."

"What's this?" Krista asked. "You're letting us go?"

"You don't focus real good, do ya?" He threw the handcuffs to the other officer, a tall, broad-shouldered man with a chiseled face from a fantasy calendar. "Deputy Galahan's gonna run a diversion down south while we go north and get clear. After that, y'all are on your own. That's all we can do."

Krista nodded and rubbed her wrists. "Thanks. Do you have any food you could share? We're starving."

"Sorry, no. There might be food where I'm takin y'all, though."

Krista looked around and found Ada watching Deputy Galahan, who was leaning into the trunk of his patrol car. Ada's cheeks were flushed, and she watched the muscles ripple under his shirt.

"Ada," Krista said. "Ada! Are you ready to go?"

"No," Ada said in a husky voice, and her eyes turned to Galahan's rear. "Gimme another hour." She wiped a bead of sweat from her forehead.

Krista turned back to the older man. "Thank you, Sheriff," Krista said.

"You can thank us both by taking these bastards down. Hurt those sons-a-bitches as much as you can."

"I'll do my best." She held out her hand and he shook it. "Really, thanks. I wish I could...oh, hell." She leaned over and gave him a quick peck on the cheek.

The sheriff blushed, and behind her, the deputy cleared his throat. "Actually, it was my idea," he said. Krista smiled at him but stepped back.

"He deserves more than just a smile." Ada reached up on her tiptoes and kissed his cheek, brushing her fingers across his shirt. "Thank you *ever so much*, Deputy Galahan," she said, wrapping her arms around him and leaning her head against his chest. He smiled and rubbed his hands up her back.

"C'mon, people, we gotta go!" the sheriff called. Krista peeled Ada off the deputy and dragged her to the Hugo, and the officers walked back to their cars.

"You're too young for him, kiddo," Krista said, opening the Hugo's door.

"I don't care. He's a hunk," Ada said. "And I'm hornier than all hell. I'd do him in the dirt, right here, right now."

"He's a cop and you're a minor. Forget it." Krista sneaked a glance at him. "You're right, though. I've got to admit he's gorgeous. Magnificent."

"Is that ever an understatement," Ada croaked. "It should be a crime to walk around with an ass like that, right where everybody can see it."

"He should arrest himself."

"I'd pay big bucks to see the lineup they put *him* in."

The deputy bent over to put something in the backseat. "I'll bet he gets those pants tailored," Krista said, her voice cracking.

"I wanna be a tailor when I grow up."

"I wanna be a tailor *right now.*"

"That's the world's cutest butt," Ada said. "It hurts to look at it."

"It was sculpted by the gods. I could write a poem about that ass."

Deputy Galahan bent over further to pick up something from the ground. Hissing, Ada opened the door and stomped over to him, and then she jumped into his arms and kissed him so hard that his hat flew off. She rubbed her hands through his hair, and after a second, he wrapped his arms around her. They kissed and groped, stumbling back to the trunk of his car.

The sheriff whistled at them. "Hey, I gotta turn the fire extinguisher on y'all?" he said. "We gotta roll!"

Galahan let her go. She smiled at him and walked back to the car, the deputy's eyes tracking her every step.

Krista held out her fist, and Ada bumped it and sighed. "I'm in love," she said. "He tastes like wild cherries. I'm never brushing my teeth again so I can remember how he tastes."

Krista smiled and held up her little finger, and Ada laughed and wrapped her finger around it. "You got *that* right. Mom doesn't even let me date. She'd kill me if she knew I just jumped a cop." Deputy Galahan waved and then climbed into his patrol car. "I am *so* done with virginity. One kiss isn't enough."

He started his cruiser, flicked on his emergency lights, and roared away. The sheriff stopped his car at the gate and waved for Krista to follow.

KRISTA DROVE THROUGH STUBBLED FIELDS as they rumbled north on a rutted farm road. "Well, we've got a drive ahead of us. So tell me – just what the hell happened back there?"

"I heard men in the room, and I figured that something bad was going down."

"It *was* bad. They were Federals, and they were going to…to do the bad thing and cut my head off."

"Wow. That's about as bad as it gets." Ada took her hand. "Will you be okay? I mean, that's –"

"I'm alive," Krista said, rubbing her neck. "I really don't want to think about that, or I'll have a nervous breakdown on the spot. So what happened? They were already to, y'know, do the deed, and then they were standing by the bathroom making weird noises."

"I, umm, showed them the door."

"You just said 'umm.' I don't like it when you say 'umm.' It means you're covering up something bad, doesn't it?"

Ada lit a cigarette and looked through the side window. "I'll bet this place is pretty when the crops are growing."

"Ada, what happened?"

"Umm…"

"This is gonna be bad. Just tell me, and I promise I won't get mad. I just want to know what happened."

Ada sighed and looked down at the floor. "I electrocuted them."

"What!"

"Look, they were going to cut your head off and do the bad thing!"

"It was the other way around."

"What difference does *that* make?"

"It's a lot sicker if they cut my head off first. That's like necrophilia or something." Krista ran her fingers through her hair and sighed. "You're right, that's a fine point. So did you, umm, kevork them?"

"I didn't have time to check their vital signs, I mean, the sprinklers were going off, and you were stumbling into stuff. It was a little crazy back there, but when I went back into the bathroom to get the keys, they were making sounds…"

"Oh, that's good."

"…like the sounds hot dogs make in the microwave, y'know, that whistling, sizzling sound?"

Krista covered her mouth with her hand and gagged.

"Hey, it gets organic real fast when you put five thousand watts through a human body," Ada said. "I'm betting they kicked the oxygen habit. If it'll make you feel any better, I wasn't trying to kevork them. I was just trying to stun them so we could get away, but they held onto that doorknob for like, forever. That's what cooked them."

"So it was their fault?"

"Yeah," Ada said. "That's the story I'm going with, anyway."

Krista puffed out her cheeks and tapped the steering wheel for a few seconds. "Right, now I feel better about it." She took Ada's hand and squeezed it. "Thanks. You saved my life. Again."

T HEY PASSED THROUGH THE OUTSKIRTS of Terre Haute, continued north to a gravel quarry, and then turned and drove a mile until the road ended in a cul-de-sac. From there, they climbed a long dirt road to a small, ranch-style house with a large carport. The sheriff motioned for Krista to park inside it. They pulled their bags from the car and walked through dry weeds to the front door, where the sheriff stood waiting for them.

"This is my brother Roger's place. He bugged out yesterday. Didn't have nuthin to stick around for, and he couldn't get the shot," he said. "Well, this is a tough time for ever'body, I guess. He won't be back anytime soon, so y'all are welcome to stay here long as you need to." He glanced into the house and looked away quickly. "I cleaned up 'n all, but…I don't wanna go back in there, I hope you understand. But ever'thin still works."

"I'll go check it out," Ada said.

"Thank you, Sheriff. I really appreciate all you've done for us," Krista said.

He nodded and walked down the stairs. "Just keep your head down and lock up when ya go," he said over his shoulder, and then he turned around. "This Activity of yours. You got a real chance? Y'all can lay the wood on Cheyn?"

"We can," she said. "We've been preparing for years."

He pulled off his cap and examined the brim, running his fingers along the edge. "I worked my ass off day and night to get elected. You know why? I just wanted to keep the fine people of Knox County safe, and for the last seven years, I done that. I take my duty dead serious, every damn day. We got the lowest murder rate in Indiana, but now…" He turned his face up and glared into the house, his eyes narrowed. "But now my people are

fallin over like hogs in the August sun, and I can't do jack squat to stop it."
He stood at attention for a few seconds, his gaze still locked on the house
and a muscle in his jaw twitching, and then he turned to Krista and leaned
forward. "This is murder, just flat-out murder. Y'all squash the sons-a-
bitches that done this like you're wearin God's own boots, y'hear? I done
you a solid by pullin your ass outta that Federal sling, and now y'all gotta
bring the mustard. You promise me."

"I promise."

"Doncha hold back or nuthin. Too much ain't enough. God's the
judge 'n jury on shit like this, not you, and he'll tell y'all when to stop if
he's got a mind to. And if anybody gives you shit about that, you tell 'em
you're actin on the authority of the duly elected sheriff of Knox County in
the great state of Indiana. If they don't believe you, you have 'em call me,
and I'll give 'em a holy what-for they won't soon forget, nossir. Doncha let
nobody get in your way. I gotcher back if they do."

"I'll do my best," Krista said.

"I may be the fat ole sheriff of a podunk county, yeah, but doncha
think I got no pull."

"I think nothing of the sort, Sheriff. In fact, you strike me as the kind of
man only a fool would cross."

He locked his gaze on her for a few uncomfortable moments, and then
he nodded. "Now I gotta lay down some smoke for y'all south of
Vincennes." He climbed into his patrol car and then flashed her a thumbs-
up. *Bingo's Happy Ending.* Great stuff." He gunned the gas and raced down
the driveway trailing a cloud of dust.

"Jaysus," she muttered. "And I was just starting to respect you."

She walked into the house, which only had a large living room with a
galley kitchen on one side and two bedrooms on the other. The smaller,
pink-painted bedroom was bare, while the larger one was piled with trash.
Some brown liquid had been splashed across the far wall, staining the
carpet, while the other walls looked as if somebody had rammed a fist
through them. Krista's arm hairs suddenly rose and she couldn't breathe;
she backed out of the room and closed the door, walking backward into the
living room until she bumped into a piece of furniture. It was a couch with
an overstuffed recliner beside it, and she decided they'd sleep out here.

Ada had dropped her bag, briefcase, and shotgun beside the couch and
was rummaging through the kitchen cabinets. She opened every door but

found no food. However, behind a louvered door next to the refrigerator, she discovered a small pantry empty of everything edible except seven large cans. "Krista, I found something!" She pulled down a can of powder and turned it over to read the label.

"I found something too! C'mere, you'll like this!"

Ada walked out of the pantry holding the container behind her back. Krista kept her hands behind her back too, and she wore a wide grin. "Ta-da!" She held up a frosted glass bottle.

"Grey Ghost vodka! Vitamin V! I'm getting *so* lit tonight!"

"I thought you'd like it," Krista said. "Okay, whatcha got?"

Ada showed her the can. "It's baby food. Nutramensa, supposed to make your baby smarter, but it's still food."

"Why did Roger take all the other food and leave this behind? It's easy to carry, and it doesn't look like it would ever go bad."

"Dunno," Ada said. "But if babies can eat it, so can we. Wanna try?"

"Absolutely," Krista said. They took the can to the sink, mixed a glass each, and took a sip.

"Not bad," Ada said. "Tastes like plastic bananas and chalk."

"Good enough for me," Krista said, smacking her lips. She mixed more of the powder and drank another.

KRISTA AWOKE JUST BEFORE SUNSET and showered in frigid water. The bathroom had no towels, so she walked around the house and air-dried. She shivered, but she wasn't sure whether it was from being cold and wet, or if it was from the memories of the nightmare in Vincennes. However much she tried to forget, she still smelled that foul room and those foul men, and the taste of the rubber bit wouldn't leave her mouth even though she'd brushed her teeth twice already.

The place was empty of every memento and scrap of food, but Roger had left behind a woodshop in the garage filled with tools of every kind. She made a mental note to remind Ada about it.

Back in the living room, Ada was still face-planted into the couch, and she decided to let the girl rest. They didn't need to move on yet; they were safe and had food and running water. More than that, they needed to rest.

Besides, with an alert out on the car, she'd have to travel at night again, and trying to cross the Illinois border at night meant they needed a

The Body Electric

plan. That was something to discuss when Ada awoke, but they weren't likely to move on tonight.

She opened her tablet and checked the news. *Midnight Sun* was suffering from the loss of their Witnesses, and as a result, she couldn't learn the epidemic's extent in Indiana. However, she'd felt hot the previous night in Vincennes, so the virus was probably at the Illinois border already.

Aaron had also mailed her begging for another post. His site traffic had gone through the ceiling – literally, as he'd rented more space on the floor above to house a new bank of Spinnaker servers. While that meant more money for Aaron, it also meant her readership had grown. They deserved an update.

○─▭─▭─▭─○

The Rake
September 23, 2043

THE BODY ELECTRIC
Finally, a post with sizzle and spark!

I made a few mistakes last night. I'll admit that up front.

I pulled over in the lovely town of Vincennes, Indiana, and rented a room. That's where I made my first mistake – I offered to stay there while my beefy Activist bodyguards (oh, ladies, those tight butts! It's great to be a rebel!) went to forage for a midnight snack. It's a big problem around here since half the population fled and took their food with them. All who remain are the vaccinated and the diehards, both of whom will kill to protect their groceries.

While they were gone, two fine young Federals burst into my room and politely offered to rape and behead me. Now, I'm always up for a good party, but I felt entitled to a last request. I wanted to dance first. Dance with me, I said! Dance the dance of life till we drop!

Oddly, they refused. Maybe they don't teach their killers to dance at ~~Nazi Community College~~ MMU, which is strange because James Bond could really cut a rug. Maybe they realized at last that white guys will never be able to dance.

Whatever the excuse, they denied my last wish. As a woman scorned, I became even more determined that the night would end with our moneymakers a-shakin'. And so, like any righteous woman would do in my situation, I pulled out my handy alligator clips and hooked those boys right up to the house power.

How they danced then! How their eyes sparkled! How they lit up the night!

You may shake your heads at my folly, but in my defense, I've never been the sciency type – after all, I went to the science fair expecting pony rides and clowns. I honestly thought five thousand watts was safe, but when I turned off the power, my two hardy boys fell to the floor like spent condoms. Two more flaccid, empty Federal Friends.

Imagine my shock! (Oh, I slay myself!)

There's nothing sadder than a party that ends too soon. Worse than that, the corpses stank up the room, and we had to retire to an Activist safe house for the night so we could breathe. On the bright side, though, my stats are climbing: Activity 5, Federals 0.

-KLW

Ada lay on the couch, kicked her feet in the air behind her, and alternately blew smoke rings and sipped her drink.

"So I checked your Soapbox homepage while you were sleeping," Krista said.

"What's Soapbox?"

"You poor child. You didn't know? Soapbox is *the* social presence nexus on the Internet. If you don't post your life happenings there, you don't exist."

"Like I said, Blue Ball keeps me siloed," Ada said. "So am I an asshole?"

"Hey, I'd even beat you up if I saw you in the hallway."

"You? Krista Gandhi? You know how to fight?"

"I went to Catholic school in Manhattan, kiddo. I was a dirty fighter by the third grade."

"Huh. It's hard to picture you actually punching somebody."

"I just try to avoid it. It gets ugly."

The Body Electric

"I'll believe it when I see it," Ada said. "Anyway, what do I say on this Soapbox thingie?"

"Long story short, you hate everybody. Everybody hates you."

Ada snorted and raised her glass. "To my bestest best friend Blue Ball – may you suck my stinking ass berries for eternity." She took a swallow and sighed. "Like I needed help becoming a pariah. Well, whatever. I don't care anymore."

"Just as well. It's a colossal waste of time. I've got ninety thousand Soapbox Soulmates, and not one of them was there to frizzle a Federal when I needed it. That took a flesh-and-blood human." Krista tapped a few more crystals of coffee into her drink. "You should try this. It's like a coffee smoothie."

"That's just sick."

"It's delicious." Krista took a deep swig of the brew. "It's the perfect food – caffeine, calories, vitamins, and minerals. It's the nectar of the gods. The only problem is that it never fills me up."

Ada swirled her drink and watched lumps of baby food float by; no matter how much she stirred, the powder wouldn't dissolve in vodka. "Speaking of sick, I read your post. Wow, you made it sound like the whole night barely ruffled your feathers."

"I can still feel that creep's hands. It scared the crap right outta me, but I'm not telling the whole world that I'm not a hardass rebel." She emptied her glass and rested it on the side table with a sigh. "Krista the writer, Krista the rebel. I'll be surprised if I don't end up with multiple personalities by the time this is over. I've never figured out who I really am, to be honest."

"It's not such a problem having a bad-ass personality. You can use one right now. Besides, I like Kick-Ass Krista."

"Yeah?" Krista smiled and stretched in the recliner. "I like Bad-Ass Ada, and I'm glad she's on my side. You're dangerous, girl."

Ada looked up with twinkling eyes and blew more smoke rings into the air.

"You like being dangerous, don't you?" Krista asked. Ada's eyes twinkled even more, and Krista laughed. "Ada Lang – the littlest *femme fatale!*"

Ada lowered her voice. "*She has a Licence to Kill!* Did you hear that? I said 'License' with a 'c' just the way the Brits do." She raised her glass with her pinky extended. "Cuz I'm sophisticated and all, doncha know."

Krista snickered. "I like you when you're drunk."

"I do too."

"Sorry to burst your bubble, but you've got to be eighteen to get that license."

"No prob," Ada said. *"She has a Learner's Permit to Kill!"*

"Speaking of learner's permits," Krista said, "I'll be teaching you how to drive tonight."

Ada's eyes opened wide, and she shook her head. "No. Nuh-uh. Not happening."

"What's wrong? We've got the time, and besides, it'd be great if you helped out with the driving."

"I told you. Disasters happen when I get behind the wheel."

"It's easy. Don't worry about it," Krista said. "That car's nothing but a roller skate with a lawnmower engine." She sat back and smiled. "Really now, what can go wrong?"

AN INFINITE NUMBER OF MONKEYS

Day 36
Wednesday night, September 23, 2043
National Tranquility Center, Fort Belvoir, Virginia

Downs sat in a large chair at an oval conference table and watched Raphael through the window. Cochon, standing next to a wall monitor, fiddled with a handheld device and groused about connectivity.

Raphael stepped off the podium and left Ari watching the Wall. He sauntered into the conference room, closed the door, and dialed the glass down to opaque white. "I just needed to get Ari up to speed," he said. "The witness from Vincennes identified Ada Lang. That Science Camp was just an elaborate cover story. I've got to say that threw me, I mean, the implications of this…"

"…are what we're here to discuss. Cochon's been trying to make sense of this mess today." Downs nodded to him.

Cochon stood to attention. "Sir, I tasked the Syllogic Engine to perform a Level 3 analysis of the available data and arrived at definitive conclusions today. I've prepared a presentation of the results." He pointed his tablet at a wall-length monitor, which flicked to life.

Raphael rested his feet on the table. "Phil, the King hasn't knighted me yet. Don't call me sir." Cochon glowered at the soles of Raphael's shoes, and he dropped his feet to the floor. "Fine. Let's get on with this."

Cochon cleared his throat and clicked his remote, and a graph with mathematical equations appeared on the screen. "Seven cross-reinforcing pattern states emerged that suggest actionable conclusions. This analysis considered the following events: One, Lang prepared an escape plan from St. Elizabeth's, implying that she possessed accurate intelligence identifying the risks of meeting Tommy Talbott. Two, Warner had a similar escape plan from her apartment. Three, Lang secured her daughter in a safe location that was also known to Warner. Four, Warner was probably running the spy Paparazzo for several years. Five, Warner was able to contact dissidents in Maryville who not only had a bomb-making facility but also an experienced chemist, implying that technical resources were available to her on demand. Six, a false identity was created for said chemist, one so airtight that the FBI still can't determine if Amy Lichtblau exists or not. Seven, DNA analysis shows that Warner and Lichtblau were present in Mike Miller's car, but we only retrieved DNA tissue samples from the remains of Miller and an unknown male. This unsub male possibly overpowered Miller and then sacrificed his life by driving a tracked Silverback to draw us away from Warner.

"And such a committed operative was available when she needed him. In a matter of minutes. In rural Kentucky. In the dead of night.

"Individually, these conclusions are subject to significant error as we have insufficient data to determine exactly what occurred or why. But when considered together as cross-reinforcing pattern states, the Syllogic Engine offers only one interpretation: We are confronting a well-organized and widely distributed resistance providing intelligence and logistical support to its operatives. The Linked-Event Coherence is ninety-seven percent."

Raphael sat straight up in his seat, and Downs stood and paced in a small circle. After a moment, he turned to Raphael. "What do you think?"

"Guys, sometimes we rely on this probability juju too much. There's a non-zero probability that if you put an infinite number of monkeys in front of keyboards, one of them will type out the Bible. But realistically, will it ever happen? Is that actionable?"

"Raf, this is a ninety-seven percent probability," Downs said. "By our guidelines, this is actionable."

Raphael sat back in his seat and looked at the graphs. "Yeah, you're right. And my gut says this makes too much sense. There are too many coincidences surrounding Lang and Warner, and I don't believe in coincidences."

"I agree," said Downs. "A resistance would put all these disparate events into context, and I've been wondering if we have a shadow organization behind it all."

"I think we do," said Raphael. "Hey, at least now we have someone to crush! I'm actually relieved to hear this."

An Infinite Number of Monkeys

Cochon laughed, and even Downs allowed himself a grin. "I know what you mean. Unorganized individuals acting randomly are hard to suppress, but we can decapitate an organization with one stroke if we can find the head." Downs leaned back against the wall and looked at the ceiling. "I'll admit I never saw this coming. I had no clue a resistance was growing in the shadows. How did the Engine miss it? It's supposed to pinpoint dissent before it begins. How could this Activist movement grow and not pull any of our strings?"

"They're clever," said Raphael. "They adapted to changed circumstances while we continued to surveille the world like we did ten years ago. While we were reading email and listening to phone calls, they were probably meeting in person or using a new communication technology that doesn't leave a digital trail."

"It's a new paradigm, sir," said Cochon. "No one can anticipate quantum evolution."

"And now we have to catch up with a machine of unknown power and reach," said Downs. "We need to learn fast before they act. We can't end up behind the curve."

"Sir, we already are. The Syllogic Engine suggests that the Activists may be ready to strike," said Cochon. "There's a sixty-five percent consequence probability that they'll attack in the next two to four weeks."

"Two to four weeks?" Downs and Raphael said simultaneously, and Cochon nodded.

"There's a pattern in their behavior, sir. Lang's ritualistic slaughter of a Chalys executive yesterday and Warner's similarly bizarre execution of two officers last night, along with the tone of her phone conversation with you, suggest a movement with high confidence and readiness. Almost to the point of cockiness."

"Cockiness?" Downs asked. "Warner walked right into our house and got in my face, Cochon. That's way past cocky."

"Yes, sir. Consider also the remarkable chain of successes they've enjoyed in the last two weeks. Consider that they have an advanced bomb-making capacity as well. Consider that they've accomplished these things without attracting any notice. All these factors point to a well-prepared and capable organization. In addition, they've demonstrated that they can reach into secure government files and do what they wish."

"What!" Downs said. "We had a file breach? When?"

"It wasn't our file. It was an FBI file on Ada Lang. It's being blackwalled, sir," Cochon said. "I'm certain of it. The file's packed with falsified information."

"Blackwalling is reserved for Intelligence and National Security personnel – covert operatives, nuclear weapons gurus, people like that. *We* can't even blackwall a file. How could they pull it off?"

"I don't know, but they did," Cochon said. "Also, in the past two weeks, she sent a hundred text messages as if she was home, and we know she wasn't. And a new post appeared on her Soapbox page at the same time the real Ada Lang was shooting out the windows of an Indiana motel." He clicked his tablet, and an Internet page flickered on the screen.

Downs leaned forward and read it. "I didn't know children could harbor such malicious thoughts."

"Wow, that is one mean girl," Raf said.

"It's fake, and we have to assume that the rest of the data we have on her is similarly fabricated. It's probable that the Activists blackwalled her digital presence to protect her."

"I'll have Mochyn track down this blackwall's origin. Maybe we can catch someone in the act and unravel that operation," Downs said. "They're definitely a cocky crowd. They're not even concealing their ability to strike in cyberspace with impunity for use at a strategic time – they're flaunting it. They're daring us, Cochon."

"It seems they are, but I caution against rushing to a conclusion. We can't assess their capabilities yet. It's also possible that this blackwall was an overreach on their part, or even that the Activists aren't responsible, sir. A ninety-seven percent probability means the Syllogic Engine is completely wrong three times out of every hundred. This could be one of those times."

"I don't think this is a statistical fluke. It feels right to me, and we'd be neglecting our duty if we didn't take this threat seriously." Downs rubbed his face and looked at Raphael blearily. "Two to four weeks, though. That's all the time we have to bring down an opponent that can do all this. We'll be working around the clock." He stood away from the wall and began to pace again. "But there's a bright side. We know where Victoria Lang's package is now – her daughter has it. Lang must have known she was being tracked and relayed the girl and the package to Warner. Warner's videos –

An Infinite Number of Monkeys

and the vaccine Lang stole – are in the same location now. Concealing our role in the RVE Initiative has become much easier."

"Okay," Raphael said. "Let's cancel everyone's leave and get the crews working double shifts. If we roll up our sleeves and get to work, we'll make progress."

"Right. We'll bring in some cots and take over the cafeteria," Downs said. "First, we need to inform Noah about these Activists. There's a strategic and political dimension to them he needs to consider."

"I'll talk to him before the Elder's Synod on Sunday," Raphael said.

"Excellent. As for us, this is a straightforward tactical operation to decapitate this resistance," Downs said. "We'll start by finding the safe house where the Lang girl was, which is between the West Virginia border and that rest stop, and bring in those people. Then we'll bring in every known contact of Lang and Warner in the past four years, put them on the Mapper, and crank the dial up to eleven. If we use all our personnel –"

"Excuse me, but there's something else to consider before we involve the entire staff," Cochon said. He clicked another frame of equations, and both men turned to see the screen. "The Syllogic Engine also indicates a ninety-four percent consequence probability that the Watch Room has a mole."

Downs and Raphael looked at him sharply, and Cochon turned back to the wall monitor. "Lang escaped from the Mapping Suites and passed eleven cameras without being seen. We've ruled out solar flares for the system malfunction, so there's no other explanation except that an Activist mole in the Watch Room assisted her. Another reason they're so cocky."

"A mole," Downs said in a hollow voice. "Do you know who?"

Cochon shook his head. "I've been looking for personnel record anomalies, and I can only point to two possible suspects right now."

"One has to be Sara Hogue," Downs said. "She's been pretending to be an Archangelist. She might be pretending to be loyal too."

"Yes, sir, she's one of the suspects," said Cochon. "The other is Ryan Beckmann."

Raphael bolted from his seat. "Are you nuts? I've worked with Ryan for six years! He's never been anything less than loyal!"

"Yet he's the Night Chief for Acquisition, and he was on duty the night Lang escaped. He was in a position to suppress the surveillance camera input, and Lang couldn't have escaped unseen otherwise," Cochon said. "In addition, he was in the Navy and served with Admiral Adam Harris. There's a strong relationship between Beckmann and Harris, as there is between Harris and Lang. That's merely two degrees of separation between Ryan Beckmann and Victoria Lang, and it's enough to suspect he knew her well enough to facilitate her escape."

"A lot of people were in the Navy, for chrissakes!" Raphael paced the room from one corner to the other. "We're getting seriously paranoid here. Let's try to keep some semblance of reality about this. No way is Ryan a mole, and coincidences won't make him one."

"Coincidences, sir? Do you believe in them now?" Cochon asked.

"Raf, we have to investigate further," Downs said. "We can't allow a mole into the Watch Room, and Warner *did* say she had dissidents in the Intelligence community."

"This is gonna be a witch hunt. You two need to –" Raphael stopped and grasped the top of his chair until his fingers turned white. "All right, let's look at this another way. The Activists might be playing a psy-ops game. Maybe they know we'll get paranoid, and the Watch will self-destruct trying to find a mole and save them the trouble."

"But the Engine says there's a mole, Raf, and that's something we can't ignore," Downs said. "We should begin a full investigation of the Watch Room staff, with special attention paid to Beckmann and Hogue, and I won't take any disciplinary action without clearing it with you. The investigative team will be the three of us and Ari Stein. We're the only ones that can be trusted. And we have to find this mole if just to protect ourselves. The four of us are the only operatives in the Watch Room that know the details of the RVE Initiative and the Transition, and we'd be a valuable catch for the Activists. What do you say?"

Raphael grumbled and nodded. Downs walked to the monitor and tapped until a deployment status map appeared on the screen. "We have a few problems, but they're surmountable. There's a resistance, and we have to find it and break it. But if we can't, we have to counter it," he said. "We can't have our Executives and Special Activity Groups running around and reacting to every sighting."

"Exactly, sir. The Syllogic Engine also suggests this is an intentional strategy to divide our resources prior to the initiation of Activist hostilities in the coming weeks," Cochon said. "Warner is drawing our resources west and Lang is drawing them east, thus increasing our response time and reducing force projection."

"Excellent work, Cochon. You've clarified the challenge," Downs said. "We'll deny them that advantage, and this is how. Raf, get all our Blackwings in the air to watch the Illinois border. We'll make three ready-response teams, each with two helicopters, an Executive team, and a Special Activity Group. We'll recall the rest of our personnel to base. Bring in all reserves, quarter all our forces on the bases, and keep them on standby. If the Activists make a move, we'll be ready to respond with overwhelming force."

"Then how do we continue the pursuit of Warner, sir?" Cochon asked.

"We'll use the hammer and anvil, Cochon." Downs displayed a map of the Midwest. "We have our hammer – the virus. It's moving west and leaving the dead and the desperate behind. The area is unsafe, and food is in short supply, so Warner will continue to move west. And when she does, she'll hit our anvil." He pointed to the Illinois border. "We'll build an impenetrable line here."

"If we're pulling everybody back, how do we do that?" Raphael asked.

Downs turned away from the screen. "The Collateral Tactics Unit. We have an entire brigade sitting in North Carolina doing nothing. If we send them in without body armor, nobody will know who they are."

Cochon looked at his feet, and Raphael coughed into his hand. After a few moments of silence, Cochon said, "The Collaterals haven't been deployed for eighteen years, sir. Ever since the Second Detroit Riots."

"Are you sure about this, Bob?" Raphael asked. "The Ironshirts are crude, and they tend to break things. Like cities."

"And they break resistance and dissent as they do, which we need now more than ever," Downs said. He turned to the deployment status map. "Warner will find herself face to face with armed Ironshirts. Let's see how cocky she is then."

TERMS COMMONLY USED IN 2043

Aluminati: Pejorative slang for members of the Second Creation movement, an extremist group within the Archangelists. The term implies that they wore tin-foil hats, although there is no evidence this actually occurred.

Archangelist: a member of the Archangelic Church of the Son of Christ.

Arkie: Popular term for an Archangelist.

Base-M: A hallucinogenic street drug that was growing in popularity in the early 2040's. Due to eradication efforts, the drug disappeared by mid-century and is unknown today..

BoHo: Bohemian Homeless, itinerant urban artists of the working class.

Collateral Tactics Unit: The military arm of the National Security Forces, known popularly as the Ironshirts.

Corporate-Americans: Corporations. The 31st Amendment provided them all the rights and protections of human citizens, as well as exemption from taxation.

Elders: Leaders of the Second Creation movement. See *Aluminati*.

Ellesmere A4: An enteric retrovirus weaponized by the US Army to incapacitate enemy forces. It readily mutated into the deadly Ellesmere A7 variant and was deemed too unstable for combat use. See *Neovirus*.

Executives: Elite operatives of the National Security Forces, often used for assassinations and surveillance.

Federals: Popular term for the National Security Forces.

Fug: A mixture of acidic coal smoke and ground fog, primarily affecting the eastern two-thirds of the country. The word is believed to be a contraction of the F-word and Fog.

Great Correction, The: A prolonged recession that eliminated the American middle class and placed all economic power in the hands of corporations.

Joe Slick: Navy term for the Lancet Missile.

MRC: The Media Regulatory Corporation, a public monopoly formed to control the dissemination of news and information on the Internet and other electronic media.

Neovirus: Civilian term for the RVE viruses Ellesmere A4 and A7.

NSF: National Security Forces, whose primary mission is to uncover and suppress domestic dissent. See *Federals*.

Patriot Class Boat: A guided-missile submarine originally designed to carry Warhammer cruise missiles. The submarines were retrofitted in 2041 to carry the Lancet missile with the new W104 nuclear warhead. The Pacific Fleet boats in 2043 were:

SSGN 807 – USS *Patrick Henry*	SSGN 814 – USS *Ethan Allen*
SSGN 808 – USS *Paul Revere*	SSGN 815 – USS *Nathaniel Greene*
SSGN 809 – USS *Thomas Paine*	SSGN 816 – USS *John Paul Jones*
SSGN 811 – USS *Nathan Hale*	SSGN 817 – USS *Seth Warner*
SSGN 812 – USS *John Adams*	SSGN 818 – USS *James Otis*
SSGN 813 – USS *John Hancock*	

PRC: The Persian Regional Conflict, a naval and aerial war in which the United States sought to prevent the unification of Persian and Arab populations into one nation. It ended in a stalemate and an embargo on the shipment of Persian Gulf oil to the United States.

Ranks: The rank and file, or the lower class. This group once comprised skilled laborers but after the Great Correction came to include most of the surviving middle class as well. Also known as Breeders, Naggers, Mullets, or Working Class.

Recombin: A virophage engineered to attack Neovirus.

SAG (Special Activity Group): Action squads of the National Security Forces, often used for pursuit, capture, and localized suppression efforts.

Soviet Bloc: Also known as the Group of Sixteen, those nations allied with Russia to achieve nuclear parity with the United States.

Stiffer: A person who has died on the street from an untreated illness.

Tenpez: A coin containing ten grams of gold issued by the State of California in the 2020's. In 2043, its value was approximately one thousand dollars. The name is believed to be inspired by a candy popular in the mid-20's.

Transition, The: Archangelist euphemism for a hostile takeover of the United States government.

Transportation, The: The forced resettlement of the urban poor from Detroit and Cleveland after a period of rioting and urban warfare in those cities. See *The Troubles*.

Troubles, The: A period marked by the broad repeal of civil liberties and repression of public dissent, spanning from early 2024 to late 2027. See *The Transportation*.

www.ingramcontent.com/pod-product-compliance
Lightning Source LLC
Chambersburg PA
CBHW050936120626
46552CB00001B/229